Anthea

by

Christine Hunter

MOODY PRESS

CHICAGO

ISBN: 0-8024-0285-2

1

Rookery Nurseries was situated almost halfway between the villages of Bewdley and Melworth. As it was higher than either of them, on a clear day one could look down on the cluster of houses built in the days when there was no idea of town planning. Some stood sideways facing the one main street, some ran in rows like a line of little girls all pressed close together, but others of varying sizes, and with differently sloping roofs, seemed to gather their skirts closely around them as if wanting to keep a respectable distance from their neighbors.

Along that important street in each village were a butcher's shop, which also sold vegetables, a general store—which contained the post office—a cottage bakery, and the village pub. At one end there was the church and small school and at the other the chapel and the village hall.

In the distance in the daytime one could see the haze of smoke that denoted the market town of Newbridge, and at night there was the glow of the lights and the bright gleam from one or two tall buildings with floodlights.

For the most part the villagers went about their own business, but there was a deadly rivalry between the two villages, although they often joined together for functions like the Women's Institute and the church fete. They played cricket and football against each other, but secretly Bewdley looked down on Melworth, and Melworth folks had little

3

use for the poor specimens who grew up in Bewdley. Sometimes a girl from Melworth married a boy from Bewdley, but that was almost a disgrace to the families involved. Far better choose a lass from their own village or get fresh blood from Newbridge or further afield.

One Saturday morning Anthea Gordon looked up from the rock plants she was putting into small plastic pots to watch her father walk up the path with a well-dressed middle-aged man, followed by a fair-haired girl and her tall, dark companion.

"Nice place you've got here," she heard the older man say patronizingly. "I intended ordering the shrubs and plants we need from Newbridge, but my gardener suggested that I call here first as you have some rather unusual specimens."

Mr. Gordon smiled. "I suppose this is more like our own garden than a nursery business. Sometimes I find it hard to part with plants we have collected and nurtured. Do you live near?"

"Just moved into the district. Towers is the name. I have bought Tall Timbers and am anxious to get the place in order. The last owner let it go, but at least that brought the price down. Do you know the house I mean?"

"Yes, I knew the former owners, but since her husband died Mrs. Hewson lost interest, and her old gardener was too crippled to do much."

Mr. Towers nodded. "We fortunately have been able to get a young man who evidently knows his business, and with the help of a couple of boys we should be able to get the grounds knocked into shape. This is my daughter, Geraldine."

"Very pleased to meet you, Miss Towers. May I also introduce my daughter, Anthea, who is a great deal more businesslike than I am."

4

Mr. Towers nodded, while his daughter's eyes swept over her so casually that Anthea was suddenly conscious of her slightly grubby pants and well-washed blouse. Her hair was naturally curly and she kept it short, but beyond creaming her face at night and wearing rubber gloves most of the time, she never worried about her appearance.

Now she realized how she must appear to Geraldine Towers, who was dressed in a beautifully cut suit and expensive, high-heeled sandals. Her hair was very fair and glinted in the sunlight, her eyes dark brown with long lashes, and her face skillfully made up.

Their companion had wandered into one of the greenhouses, obviously bored with the whole business.

"We need some good roses, various flowering shrubs, and some fruit trees for the walled garden. We'll look around, then send Benson, the gardener, to get as many as he thinks necessary. We hope to get the hothouses repaired and then produce some of our own stock. In the meantime we need quick-growing plants to make the place look less like a wilderness."

Mr. Gordon led the way to the various sections, while Mr. Towers scribbled in a notebook, and Geraldine pointed out the colors she preferred. Anthea went on with her work but turned suddenly when a voice said, "Those are good specimens. They make me wish I had a rock garden myself. I always feel that they look like the most naturally growing plants—far more attractive than beds of roses, geraniums, or shrubs that look like regiments."

Anthea smiled. She too loved the variety of these small, hardy specimens.

"Must be an interesting business," the other went on.

"Plenty of hard work and not a lot of profit, but I'd rather do this than anything else," Anthea replied coolly.

"Some of those remind me of Switzerland and other remote European areas. Do you order from abroad?"

Anthea shook her head. "Sometimes Dad and I manage to get away for a few days and hunt up some of the less common ones. We have been to Switzerland, but Scotland and Ireland are good hunting grounds too. It is always interesting to see if we can grow plants that have been transplanted from their natural habitat."

"Max," came a voice from the other side of the wall, "come and help me choose these roses."

"Duty calls," Max said with a wry smile and sauntered in the direction the others had taken.

Anthea's thoughts were busy. Who were these people? Max did not look like either of the other two. He was tall, with dark hair and alert blue eyes. He wore casual clothes, but there was nothing sloppy about him. Was he a relation or a fiancé?

Several other customers wandered in, and Anthea went to serve them. Ron, their helper, gave her a list of orders that had been phoned in, and Anthea got out the old van while he collected them and gave her the addresses. Saturday morning was often like this if the weather was fine. Evidently people got a sudden urge to spend the afternoon gardening and wanted some plants or shrubs sent immediately while the mood was on them. Ron did not drive, preferring his old bicycle to anything more dangerous, so it usually fell to Anthea to deliver orders, and she enjoyed the break and the glimpses she got of other people's gardens.

Often she amused herself by guessing from the orders what sort of people she was going to visit. She usually guessed that old-fashioned plants like lobelia, delphiniums, marigolds, and dahlias would be for an elderly couple or spinster ladies. Expensive roses, azaleas, magnolias, and more exotic shrubs probably would be for the newly rich who wanted to be able to walk their visitors around a well-kept lawn and admire the display of color.

Many of her customers were men or women living alone, whose garden was their dearest hobby. Often they were anxious to show Anthea some prize plant they had reared from a small cutting, or they wanted her advice on some plant that was not as healthy as it ought to be. Anthea knew she often spent far longer with those lonely people than she ought, and the visits brought in very little profit, but it was good to know that those people were friends, not merely customers.

She drove in as her mother was ringing the bell that called them to meals, and she washed her hands quickly in the small outside kitchen.

Ron already had eaten the sandwiches he brought with him, as many people came in during their lunch break.

Her father was seated at the kitchen table when she arrived. The dining room was used only when they had guests, because Mrs. Gordon objected to Anthea and her father's using it when dressed in their everyday clothes. She was a tall, slim woman who never looked untidy, no matter what she was doing. She took no interest in the nursery and never had plants or cut flowers in the house.

Anthea often wondered why her mother and father had married each other; they were so different in temperament and interests.

Her father was gentle, dreamy, affectionate, and a great reader, but her mother was withdrawn, had very little to say to her husband or daughter, and seemed to live a life of her own. She never accompanied them on their brief vacations, never asked Anthea to go shopping with her, but made it obvious that she preferred to go alone.

7

She kept the house in an immaculate condition, always dressed smartly, saw that meals were on time, and did not expect Anthea to help in the house, but she was cold and kept her family at arm's length. Anthea loved her father dearly, but her mother always stood outside their little world; it was impossible to break through the barrier she had erected.

She knew that her parents had met during the war, and that her father had been a teacher in biology for several years until trouble with his voice and throat had made him give up teaching. He had moved from the town, and, with the money left to him by his grandmother, had bought an old house with several acres of land and started a nursery business. She knew too that she had been born twelve years after her parents' marriage, and as her father had often told her, she had come like a miracle when he had given up all hope of having children. Therefore, she was extraspecial to him.

Even as a small child Anthea had felt that her father loved her more than her mother did. It was her father she turned to if she was hurt or upset. Her mother saw that she was well-dressed, well-fed, and well-mannered, but she never remembered her showing her any affection; Anthea was conscious that even her father loved her more openly when her mother was absent. As she grew older she realized that her mother resented their way of life; the quiet, rather humdrum sort of existence she and her father loved did not satisfy her. To them, living in the country, working among growing things, and being able to read during the long, dark evenings was utterly satisfying. Her mother only really came alive when they had visitors or when she was going to some sort of entertainment in Newbridge with her sister or her friends.

8

As she slid into her seat, Anthea noticed that her mother was wearing a new dress she had not seen before, with a lace apron tied around her waist.

"How smart you look, Mother," Anthea said.

Her father looked up and blinked.

"She never looks anything else to me. Are you going into town, dear?"

"I arranged to go shopping with Kathleen, then have dinner with her and some of her friends. I have left your evening meal ready, so I hope that you will manage if I am not back until fairly late. There is a good show on, and Kathleen wants me to go with them."

"One of the car's taillights needs attention," Anthea said quietly. "Better have it checked if you are going to drive in the dark."

"That old car is hopeless. There is always something wrong. I am ashamed to be seen driving it."

Her husband laughed. "I know, dear, and maybe at the end of the season we'll manage to get a more up-to-date model for you. Why not stay with Kathleen overnight and come back in the daylight?"

"I might do that. I'll take a small case with me, so don't wait up. I have my key if I decide to come home."

"I'll do the dishes, Mother. You get off in good time and have that rear light checked just in case you need it."

"Very well. I'll probably see you tomorrow sometime."

She walked out of the room, and Anthea collected the plates and took them to the sink, her eyes moist. Why was her mother so distant and so polite? She might have been talking to boarders or strangers instead of her family.

She heard the car driving away as she hung out the dish towel and watched her father walk back to the office, his shoulders bent and his steps slow. Her mother was **never**

9

discussed between them. All her life her father had been absolutely loyal and had never criticized her mother, no matter what his private thoughts might have been.

She had noticed that lately his movements had become slower, and that sometimes his face looked drawn and gray, but he would never admit to any actual pain. She wished that her mother would insist that he have a medical checkup, but he laughed off any remark Anthea made, saying it was only old age coming on.

"Can't expect to have the energy I had forty years ago," he would say lightly.

"But, Dad, you aren't old."

"Over sixty, girl. I'm nearly ten years older than your mother. I was past forty when you were born."

"Then you have got to do less and leave the harder work to Ron and me. Or we can hire another man."

"You know we can't afford another wage."

"Why not think about selling this as a going concern, moving to a smaller house, and me taking a job?" Anthea had suggested several times.

"What would I do with myself all day?" her father returned. "I'm not ready for the chimney corner yet."

"You could have a smaller garden to keep you occupied but without pressure of customers."

"Well, maybe I'll have to come to that. Your mother would like to move back to town, but I like it here, though often I think I am not being fair to you. You are too young to be stuck in an isolated spot."

"Rubbish! You know I'd hate being in a busy, noisy town. I love this place, and if we could afford another man, you could be head adviser and let us do the heavier work."

There was a rush of customers all afternoon, and it was almost dark when Anthea had time to think about preparing a meal.

Her father came in, kicking off his boots at the back door and pushing his feet into his slippers. He sat down heavily in the old armchair at the side of the stove.

"A few more days like this, and maybe we'll get that car for your mother," he said, but Anthea noticed how exhausted he looked. She poured out some coffee and took it to him saying, "Drink this, Dad. You can listen to the news while the vegetables cook. I ought to have come in before. Good thing Mother left everything prepared."

"She is a marvelous organizer," her father replied between sips of coffee. "You and I would get into very slipshod habits if she did not keep us up to scratch."

"I'll go up and change my clothes before we eat, but don't you bother."

When Anthea returned, her father had his head back and was fast asleep. She tiptoed around, looking at him lovingly. What a wonderful father he had been, but she could see him aging almost before her eyes these last few months. Somehow he must be persuaded to take things more easily. She determined that at the first opportunity she would talk to her mother.

She turned down the heat under the pans and waited until her father awakened.

"Bless me, why didn't you wake me up?" he said, rubbing his eyes.

"You've only had a catnap," Anthea said. "You'll feel more rested and able to enjoy your meal, and I guess you could do with an early night after such a busy day."

"Mark calling in tonight?" he asked as they began to eat.

"I'm not sure."

"Seems a long time since he was here. Not long ago he was always under our feet."

Anthea colored, then laughed. "He's very busy these

11

days. Now that he has passed his exams he is hunting up clients and learning the practical side of the business, I imagine.''

''Must be a queer job, an attorney,'' her father said thoughtfully. ''Have to get mixed up in all sorts of messy situations. I prefer flowers and plants to people who are all mixed up and claiming what isn't theirs.''

''You and I were never cut out for big business and lots of social activities, Dad.''

''If you marry Mark, you'll have plenty of that.''

''Who said I was going to marry him? You know we have been like brother and sister for years. We aren't engaged— just good friends who enjoy the same sort of activities.''

''If Mark married someone else you wouldn't be heartbroken?''

Anthea hesitated. ''If Mark finds the right girl for him, I'll wish him happiness,'' she said slowly, and not even her father, who knew her so well, guessed at the effort that it took to say that calmly and unemotionally.

Mark and she had never been what might be termed passionately involved. They had been close friends over the years, had gone hiking, cycling, swimming, played tennis and golf together ever since they had been in the same class at school, and always sat together on the school bus. It had been taken for granted that Anthea was Mark's girl, and it was a foregone conclusion that someday they would marry.

They had lived near each other until Mark had moved with his mother to Newbridge and had started his training as an attorney. Anthea had studied horticulture, taken a commercial course, and settled down to help her father, believing in her heart that when Mark had finished his training and could afford a wife, they would be married.

He had acquired a secondhand car and used to come on

12

Saturday afternoons to lend a hand or on Sundays, when they would go off on long, rambling walks.

But this last year his visits had been less frequent, and Anthea had sensed a change in him. He was less easy to talk to, did not offer to help, and his visits were usually very short. She realized that he had a lot of studying to do, and sometimes had to visit clients who lived at a distance, but without putting it into words she knew that Mark was drifting away. He still put his arm around her and kissed her lightly when he arrived or departed, but it was as a brother, not a lover.

To change the subject Anthea said hurriedly, "Did Mr. Towers give you a big order, Dad?"

"Not yet. They chose what they wanted and said that the gardener would come to collect what they needed."

"Let's hope they don't change their minds. What sort of business is Mr. Towers in?"

"He said he was trying to retire, but he did not mention how he had made his money. His daughter keeps house for him and is very keen on horseriding and show jumping."

"Does the stepson live with them?"

"Evidently not. Mr. Towers said he was only visiting for the weekend."

"Why don't you take a long rest tomorrow morning, Dad? I can open the greenhouses and do anything necessary before I go to church."

Her father smiled at her affectionately. "Stop babying me, girl. You'll be suggesting breakfast in bed next, and you know how I hate that. I'd rather get up for a quiet walk as usual. That does me more good than lying in bed."

"OK," she replied, patting his shoulder. "Have it your own way."

Anthea had just finished clearing up when there was a

13

knock at the back door, and Mark pushed his head in.

"Hello, folks, Thought I'd pop in to see if you are still alive and to ask if Anthea feels like being energetic tomorrow afternoon."

"Come in, boy," Mr. Gordon said, holding out his hand. "We were just saying that we hadn't seen much of you lately. Sit down if you don't mind being in the kitchen. Anthea and I are having a quiet evening after a rather hectic day."

"Business good?" Mark inquired and, pushing Anthea into the chair opposite her father, sat down on the arm.

"We can't complain. We get spells when it is quiet; then everything happens at once. How about you?"

"Run off my feet. The boss hardly gives me time to breathe. Even tonight I'm off to a sort of working dinner. A client of ours has moved into the district and needs some papers and some information that couldn't be given over the phone. He's bought Tall Timbers. You remember how we used to think what a lovely house it was when we passed by it on the bus, Anthea. I used to dream that someday I might have a place like that, but I guess my sights are a bit lower now."

"Mr. Towers was here with his daughter and stepson this morning choosing plants," Mr. Gordon said. "You should enjoy your dinner. I don't imagine they'll eat in the kitchen like the Gordons."

Mark looked around the familiar room and put his hand on Anthea's shoulder: "I've had some mighty fine meals in this old place. Their food won't be any better than Mrs. Gordon's; she is a first class cook."

"We'll pass on the compliment," Anthea said lightly. "Or you can tell her yourself tomorrow afternoon."

"Well, I'd better get moving, or I'll be late. Never does

14

to keep the big tycoons waiting. Half past two tomorrow, Anthea. We'll drive up to the beacon and walk from there if the weather is fine.''

"I'll be ready."

Anthea waved as Mark drove off and returned to the kitchen with a lighter heart. Maybe she had only fancied the change in him. Probably he had been extra busy and occupied with the complexities of such a demanding occupation. He hadn't forgotten her anyway, and a long tramp tomorrow would be like old times.

They watched a wildlife film, the nine o'clock news, and after a hot drink made their way to bed. They were always up before six on Saturdays, and that made a long, tiring day.

The nursery was not open on Sundays, and that was one of Mrs. Gordon's special grievances. She believed that Sunday could be the most profitable day of the week, but her husband had never given in to this. He insisted that everyone needed a day of relaxation, and if business could not be done in six days, then they ought to reorganize.

Ron did not come on Sunday either so there were still a few chores to do, but they were kept to a minimum.

Anthea sang in the Bewdley Church choir, and Mr. Gordon liked to attend the morning service, but his wife never accompanied him. In the afternoon he loved to wander on his own, enjoying the peace and beauty of the countryside. Sometimes Anthea went with him, but he saw more when alone because he would take his binoculars and watch birds and animals for hours. When he found a rare plant he came home as excited as if he had found a precious jewel, and on Sunday evening his favorite occupation was writing up his nature diary, illustrating it with small, beautifully executed illustrations. Only Anthea had ever seen this notebook, and she had begged him to offer it for publication, but her father

15

had never thought there was anything outstanding in what he had drawn or written.

"There are thousands of books far better than anything I have done," he said firmly. "I only do it for my own enjoyment."

Anthea was awake early the next morning, her heart light, and she sang happily as she cooked breakfast and prepared what was needed for lunch. The thought of meeting with Mark made her bubble with excitement. Surely if she did not mean something special to him he would not have tried to take up their old relationship.

"Ready, Dad?" she called upstairs. "We've got to practice one or two pieces before the service starts. Will you lock the door while I get the van out?"

Mr. Gordon climbed in beside her. "Not a very elegant vehicle to take you to church," he said whimsically.

"It runs, so that is all that matters," Anthea replied. "That horse looks lively," she exclaimed, pulling as far over to the side of the road as she could and reducing her speed.

The horse was a magnificent animal and the rider beautifully dressed in a dark green riding habit with a hard, peaked black hat. She was obviously having to make an effort to restrain the horse, which was prancing sideways.

Anthea breathed a sigh of relief when they had passed.

"That was Geraldine Towers, wasn't it? She ought to keep that animal off the road until it is easier to control."

"It looks too big for a girl," her father replied. "I hope she doesn't intend riding through Melworth where children may be playing on the street."

"Perhaps she'll turn along Croft's Lane or another side road, although she may not know the neighborhood yet. I am surprised that her stepbrother is not with her."

The Gordons had attended Bewdley Church ever since they came into the district. Mr. Gordon had once taught the man who was vicar at that time. Since then he had moved on to a bigger church, but by then both Anthea and her father loved the simple country church and had made friends with the parishioners.

Mark's family had attended there also before they moved to Newbridge, and Mark and she had both sung in the choir and joined in the young people's activities.

This morning as Anthea took her place in the choir loft she looked over the well-known faces and started as she saw Max Sinclair sitting alone at the end of a pew near the back. There was no mistaking his dark hair and deep blue eyes.

So, he is more interested in attending church than going riding with his stepsister, Anthea thought as she dropped her eyes to her music. She was singing the solo part of the anthem this morning, and she needed to concentrate on the service, not let her mind stray to thoughts of the family that had come to live at Tall Timbers. She would probably hear more about them from Mark this afternoon.

Anthea's voice was not powerful, but it was sweet and true, and she sang as if she meant every word. Some years ago she had taken Jesus Christ as her personal Savior, and for a long time had longed to become a missionary. However, she believed she was needed at home and that her duty was to her parents, especially to her father who worked too hard.

Religion was not a subject easily discussed in her home, because her mother had no use for what she termed sanctimoniousness, but Anthea believed that her father was very close to God, and in his quiet way he lived out his faith without a lot of talk.

Max Sinclair was striding down the road as they passed

him in the rattletrap van. He lifted his hand in a salute, and Anthea felt her color rise. There was something about this stranger that aroused her curiosity. He was striking to look at, but it was more than his appearance that disturbed her.

"That young man does not fit in with the rest of the family, I imagine," Mr. Gordon observed thoughtfully.

"I wonder if Mother has returned," Anthea said after a few moments' silence. For some unknown reason she felt threatened by the Towers family and did not want to discuss them.

"Probably she will stay with Kathleen for the afternoon. It is a good day for you and Mark."

Anthea's heart lifted at the thought. "You won't mind being on your own, Dad?"

"Bless me, Anthea, haven't you learned yet that I enjoy being alone? Anyone who doesn't enjoy his own company when he can get out into the woods or along the river must be a poor specimen."

"I know," Anthea replied, patting his knee. "People just clutter up your world, don't they?"

Her father laughed. "Only some people. I never think of you as clutter. I'd like to see you married before I die, but life will be very cold for me when I have to hand you over to someone else."

"Not much sign of that yet," Anthea replied lightly. "I haven't got a string of suitors lined up to claim my hand. Now let's stop talking nonsense and enjoy our lunch. The car is not back, so we'll have to feed ourselves."

Anthea was lifting the casserole from the oven when the phone rang.

"I'll get it," her father said. After listening he called, "It's Mark, Anthea. He wants to talk to you."

Anthea pushed the dish back, hurried to the hall, and took the phone from her father's hand.

18

"Anthea here," she said gaily. She heard Mark say, "I'm sorry to have to cancel our date, Thea. Some new business has cropped up, and this afternoon is the only time I can meet this particular client."

"Even on Sunday, Mark? That sounds tough."

Mark gave a little laugh. "Some people do most of their best business deals on Sundays. I wish I needn't disappoint you, love, but maybe your father will accompany you. We'll plan another date soon, I hope. I can't lose my oldest girl friend, you know, but at present I'm only at the bottom of the ladder, the general errand boy, so I have to do as I am told. I would come this evening, but my mother and I are invited out for dinner. No hard feelings, Thea?"

"Of course not," Anthea replied, trying to speak gaily. "But Mark, don't let business get too important in your life."

"Aw, honey, don't get preachy. I haven't any choice at present. If I want to get anywhere I've got to oblige our clients."

"See you soon, Mark. I must get Dad's lunch as Mother is not back yet."

Her father looked at her closely as she came back into the kitchen and picked up the potholders.

"Mark isn't free this afternoon after all, so he had to call off our outing."

"Rather short notice, isn't it?"

"He says that he has to see another important client, and his mother and he have a dinner engagement."

"Poor Mark. He'll have to struggle hard if he does not want to get bogged down with business and that very ambitious mother of his."

"Oh, well, he must make his own decisions," Anthea said, placing the casserole and baked potatoes on the table.

"That smells good. I always enjoy Sunday's lunch better than any meal of the week."

"I hope you aren't disappointed today. I know I can't compete with Mother's cooking."

"Suppose we drive up to the beacon, and I'll try to fill in for Mark," her father suggested after a few mouthfuls. "I feel that I'd like some good fresh air in my lungs. We'll certainly get it up there."

"Wouldn't you rather wander on your own?"

"Only if you don't want to go with me."

"That's fine. I'll hurry up and change, but I'd better leave the kitchen in apple-pie order, or Mother will be on the warpath. We'll leave a note to tell her where we've gone. Let's take some sandwiches and a thermos of coffee in case we don't get back until late. Why don't you have a short nap, Dad, while I get ready? I'll be about half an hour."

"Can't I help?"

"No. I'll work more quickly by myself."

Guessing that Anthea wanted some time alone, her father wandered into the little used lounge and flopped into an armchair.

Why on earth had Mark upset Anthea again if he did not mean anything? For his own part he would be glad if the long, drawn-out friendship became nothing more serious. He had never considered Mark good enough, or stable enough, for Anthea, but he hated to see that disappointed look in her eyes. If only she could meet more young men she would be able to get over her girlish first love more easily, but there were few opportunities of meeting suitable friends in their kind of life. He wondered again, as he had done so often lately, if he ought to put his own preferences aside and move into town as his wife wished. Then Anthea could join in more social activities.

2

Later as they climbed into the van Anthea said, "I've put in a blanket and our raincoats. One never knows when we might get caught in a shower up there."

They said little as they drove steadily higher, parked the van in a rough patch among some trees, and started off. Neither of them ever chattered unnecessarily. Their eyes were busy as they looked at the distant view or darted here and there noticing the small plants and birds that fluttered among the bushes. They halted as a rabbit hopped across the path and disappeared. A few steps further they found a bird with its leg caught in some fine wire.

"Hold it while I cut it free," Mr. Gordon said. He watched as the terrified creature flew away.

Sometimes one of them would stop to examine something unusual, but they had learned long ago that the quieter they were, the more they saw. Occasionally Mr. Gordon lifted a small plant with his trowel and placed it carefully in a tin he took from the knapsack that he carried on his back.

Both he and Anthea were particular about what they collected. They loved their wild flower garden, and if there was an abundance of the same species, they thought there was no harm in transplanting a specimen that they had not already collected. Up here on the downs there were hundreds of varieties of all colors, sizes, and designs.

They found several nests, but they never disturbed the eggs or the fledglings. Often Mr. Gordon took out his notebook and made a quick sketch.

After about two hours Anthea said, "Time we returned. I'm ready for a cup of coffee, aren't you?"

They turned back, but as they neared the place where they had left the van Anthea said, "Sit down on that rock, Dad. I'll bring the basket here where we can sit in the sun."

Her father sat down on the flat stone, feeling more tired than he would admit, while Anthea hurried between the bushes and came out on the path. Suddenly she darted back. A vehicle was standing beside the beacon, and it took only a quick glance to recognize Mark's car with the top down. Sitting beside him was Geraldine Towers with a scarf over her golden hair.

Anthea bit her lip as she stood clutching a tough branch. What should she do? How long would Mark sit there with his "important client?" What would he say if she suddenly confronted him?

She could not let her father guess at Mark's duplicity, but somehow she had to get the sandwiches and coffee. If she went the longer way around and walked carefully she could perhaps reach the van without being seen.

She was trying to pick her way through the bushes without snapping twigs as she walked, when she heard a car start and drive away. Obviously Geraldine had seen all she wanted. Probably walking was not her favorite exercise.

Anthea breathed a sigh of relief; nevertheless she went back to the path very carefully, but the patch by the beacon was empty and the car already out of sight. She shook her head angrily as she felt her eyes fill with tears. This was obviously the farewell to her dreams. Mark would probably cook up a good story, but she would never again believe what he said.

She collected the basket of food. By the time she reached her father, she had got herself under control and could manage a smile.

"Did you think I was never coming back? It was further that I thought. I tried to take a shortcut, but it turned out to be longer than if I had kept to the path. I hope you didn't get cold."

"Not a bit. The sun is still quite warm. I've seen a hare, a field mouse, a toad, a small grass snake, a sparrow hawk, and a skylark's nest since you left."

Anthea smiled affectionately at his kind, satisfied expression.

"You know, Dad, all my life I'll be grateful to you for teaching me to enjoy the simple beauties of nature, which cost nothing. You are never bored, are you?"

Her father sighed. "In a way I suppose it is a kind of selfishness. Maybe I ought to have done more with my life, not just settled in a remote place like Bewdley. I haven't done much for other people."

Anthea bent down and kissed his bald patch as she handed him his cup of coffee. "Drink this and stop fishing for compliments. You know no one could have been a better father or husband, and it wasn't your fault you had to give up teaching."

"But I've made your mother and you live a very restricted life with very little social activity."

"Mother goes out whenever she wishes, and as far as I am concerned, I'd hate to live anywhere else or any other sort of life."

"I wish I could have seen you married before I die."

"Goodness, Dad, why do you keep on talking about dying? You'll live for years yet."

"Maybe, but Anthea, if I do go suddenly, don't grieve for

me. I've had a good life, and I would hate to be dependent on anyone."

"You haven't felt ill recently, have you?"

"No, but I get tired quickly, and, after all, no one lives forever."

"Stop talking like that. It's time we got back. You can have an early night. We ought not have walked so far."

"It has been a lovely afternoon. We may not have the opportunity for many more like it."

Anthea glanced at him sharply. It was seldom she had heard him in this sort of mood. Usually he was so cheerful and optimistic.

They walked back to the car rather slowly, she helped him into the passenger seat of the van, and put the blanket around his legs because the van was certainly not draft-proof. Now that the sun had gone down the temperature had dropped quickly.

Her mother was at home when they reached the house, and Anthea sighed with relief.

"Just go in, and I'll bring your slippers," she said, putting her hand through her father's arm and pushing him gently toward the kitchen.

Her mother looked up from the stove where she was stirring a pan of soup.

"Hello, dear. It's good to see you back," Mr. Gordon said with a smile. "I hope you had a good time."

"Thank you, yes. The show wasn't all that it was cracked up to be, but we had a good group for dinner. I'll have the meal ready as soon as you wash up."

Anthea turned away. Her mother showed no interest in what they had done or where they had been.

"I think we walked too far," she said flatly. "Just wash at the back sink, Dad. There's no need to go upstairs. I'll be down in a few minutes."

24

She saw her mother's lips set in a straight line, but she said nothing when Anthea, after a hasty wash, sat down at the table.

"Are you not eating, Eleanor?" Mr. Gordon asked as he noticed that there were only two place settings.

"No, thank you. I am not hungry. I'd like to watch TV while you eat."

Mr. Gordon dropped his eyes, then sipped slowly at the bowl of soup before him.

"It tastes delicious," he said as she removed the soup bowls. After bringing in some sandwiches, Mrs. Gordon walked into the next room. Anthea could hear the announcer's voice on television.

Her father took several bites from a toasted cheese sandwich but left the rest on his plate.

"I really don't want any more," he said, pushing his chair back. "I'll go in and keep Mother company before I go to bed."

"I'll walk around to see that everything is OK," Anthea replied. "We left the top window of the big greenhouse open slightly, and it feels almost like a touch of frost tonight. I'll feed Beau and take him for a run."

"Bless you, my dear. I don't know how I'd manage without you."

Anthea washed the few dishes they had used, pulled on an old coat, and picked up a flashlight.

Beau was a Doberman pinscher and strictly a guard dog. He was never allowed in the house but was kept on a long chain during the night and on the weekends to scare off anyone who might be tempted to steal valuable plants or do willful damage. During the Christmas season he was especially necessary, as people often tried to steal Christmas trees or some of the special chrysanthemums, poinsettias, or expensive bulbs.

Neither Anthea or her father ever took Beau on their long wanderings as he would scare away every small animal. Besides, when the place was left unattended, Beau was "on duty."

Anthea had had him since he was a puppy, and he was definitely her dog, but she had been strict with him, knowing that too much petting or overfeeding would make him useless as a watchdog. Her mother never fed him or attempted to pet him; he would obey Mr. Gordon, but he made it perfectly clear that Anthea was the only person who really mattered to him. He was a one-owner dog.

Anthea gave a peculiar whistle, and immediately there was the rattle of his long chain.

"Hi, boy," she said softly, as she slipped the lock from his collar. He held up his leg, solemnly they shook "paws," and he looked at her questioningly until she said, "This way." Together they set off. Beau never jumped up, but his whole body showed his delight as he bounded off on his long legs, then ran back to see that she was not far behind. She took the field path so that he could race over the grass without any traffic to bother him. He had been tied up for hours so he deserved to be free. It was almost dark, but as the moon rose above the clouds the scene around her became clearer. She could see the lights of Bewdley and Melworth and farther away the bigger lights of Newbridge.

She loved these evening rambles, even after a tiring day. It was so peaceful, and she was never afraid with Beau as her protector.

Mark had often said laughingly that he pitied the person who ever tangled with Beau.

She could let her thoughts wander now that no one could see her face. Had Mark deliberately lied to her, or had he really had an appointment with Mr. Towers and had taken

26

Geraldine out on the spur of the moment? Part of her mind tried to believe that, but the other part told her to face the truth. Mark had been a wonderful friend, but since his move to Newbridge their meetings had been spasmodic and erratic. It was a long time since he had mentioned their future. Once she had taken for granted that when he had finished his training they would join forces; they had never been sentimental or emotional. Now with more mature vision, she admitted that she had been more dependent on Mark's friendship than he had been on hers.

She had no brothers or sisters and few close friends, but Mark was the youngest of a family of four. His father had died while he was at school, but his mother was left comfortably off, and she had great plans for her family. She had always been the dominating factor in the house and had driven the children to study in whatever profession they chose.

The eldest son, James, was a doctor; the second, Philip, a computer expert; and the only daughter, Esther, a pharmacist. Mark's father had worked so hard to keep up with his wife's ambitions and his family's needs that he had burned himself out and died suddenly when he was only fifty. By that time James, Philip, and Esther were independent, and only Mark had to be prodded along.

As Mark had often said to Anthea, none of them were brilliant. Without their mother's drive behind them, they would have settled down to humdrum, ordinary jobs, but Mrs. Latham never relaxed herself and certainly had no intention of letting her family slacken either.

She was always smartly dressed and involved in all kinds of social activites. No one knew that Mary Latham had been brought up in a very poor home, had won a scholarship, and had gone to high school where she had suffered because her clothes were wrong and she could not afford proper equipment or other extras. But it had given her the opportunity to watch how other girls lived, and she had determined to get away from her home and her slovenly family as soon as possible.

She had left school at sixteen to start in an insignificant office job, had taken night classes, and moved quickly to a better position. As soon as possible she had transferred to another town, spoke with no trace of her parents' accent, lived in one small room until she could afford a better apartment, and severed all connections with her family.

One or two young men had been attracted to her, but they were soon repelled by her cold, calculating manner until she met David Latham. She had seen in him the possibilities of a promising future. He was madly in love with her, was the managing director of the family business started by his grandfather, and was reported to be very wealthy. Obviously when his father died, David would inherit everything, as he was an only son.

They had married after a short courtship, had a beautiful home, and had their children in quick succession, as Mary decided that if she had to have a family she would get it over as quickly as possible since they could afford plenty of domestic help. Soon after Mark was born it was discovered that the business was on the verge of bankruptcy, and all her dreams of wealth came crashing down.

The big house had to be sold, and the family moved into a very modest house in Bewdley, which had belonged to an aunt who had died suddenly. Mary Latham never forgave David and his father for what had happened, and she became even more hardened and determined that her family would make names for themselves, no matter what sacrifices she or they had to make.

By the time David Latham died, the business was once more a successful concern, but since neither James nor Philip had any desire to be involved, it was sold. Mrs. Latham proceeded to live as a fairly wealthy widow. Only Mark was still at home, and in many ways he was like his father. He had a simple, kindly disposition but could not stand against his mother's forcible character. For her sake he had worked hard, struggled through his exams, and for the sake of peace gave in to her social aspirations.

His mother had never liked Anthea and was delighted when they moved to Newbridge and Mark began to meet other girls who interested him. Mary Latham was clever enough to know that Mark would not have deliberately hurt Anthea, who had been his friend for almost all his growing up years, but she believed that once he got into town and moved among more exciting, more glamorous girls, he would forget her, and their friendship would gradually fade away.

Mark did not realize that he was being manipulated. He admired his mother and the way she had struggled to restore the family's position. He believed they owed her a great deal, and he was proud to take her with him to business dinners or other social functions.

He had met Alan Towers when dealing with a corporation lawsuit. He had been designated to do the groundwork for a senior partner and had been invited to Tall Timbers. There he had been attracted to Gerry, and evidently Gerry had found him interesting, for he and his mother were invited for dinner.

Mrs. Latham made up her mind immediately that here was the sort of girl who would make Mark a suitable wife. She was strong-minded, well-groomed, obviously the joy of her father's life, and lacked nothing.

29

She did not like the idea of losing Mark, but the break had to come someday, and she believed that Mark was too fond of Anthea Gordon for his own good. She was determined that such a marriage would not help him socially, so if she could encourage an early engagement with Geraldine Towers, she would give Mark her blessing. Alan Towers was rolling in money and would deny Gerry nothing. Mark had very little himself as yet, and she couldn't afford to help him substantially, but she was certain that Alan Towers would buy Gerry a house like Tall Timbers and probably make her a good settlement or allowance.

She hugged herself with quiet delight as she watched Mark get more deeply involved. She was sure that the affair with Anthea was dying a natural death. She encouraged Gerry to call when she drove into Newbridge, invited her and her father for dinner before a show, encouraged Mark to take Gerry out on weekends, and was thrilled when Mark was invited to accompany Gerry and her father on a short vacation to Scotland where Alan Towers was going on business.

Mrs. Latham did not believe in prayer, but she certainly believed that by forcible, but subtle, means she could make what she wanted to happen. She was sure that her hopes for Mark were going the way she planned.

Anthea watched her father carefully the week following their Sunday outing and had a chat with Ron, suggesting that they should arrange that Mr. Gordon do as little heavy work as possible.

She waited for an opportunity to mention his health to her mother, but it did not come until one afternoon when her mother was addressing the Women's Institute in Bewdley, demonstrating some of the beautiful needlepoint pictures and chair seats she had made. The old van was in the village garage having the brake linings renewed, so Anthea arranged to drive in with her mother and return in the van.

Her mother looked as neat and calm as usual, her hair beautifully set, and her face so subtly made up that she looked years younger than her actual age.

Anthea smiled at her as she finished depositing the box of finished or half-finished articles in the back seat of the car.

"You look more like my older sister than my mother," Anthea said.

"You never do yourself justice," her mother returned sharply. "You could be much more attractive if you spent more time on your face and hair and clothes."

"But I like to feel comfortable when I am working," Anthea said calmly. Her mother's criticism was one she had heard dozens of times during the years.

After a short silence she broke out, "Mother, I'm worried about Dad."

"Why?" her mother asked. "He appears perfectly normal to me."

"He gets tired so quickly. Last weekend he kept on talking as if he felt his time was limited."

Her mother did not take her eyes from the road or show any sign of distress.

"I am not surprised. What can anyone do when he is so stubborn? I have wanted him to give up this strenuous life and move into town, allowing both you and me to have some social contacts, but nothing will move him. I never imagined when I gave up my freedom that I'd be stuck out in the country with no neighbors worth cultivating and married to what amounts to an ordinary gardener. With his education he should be in a profession. Oh, I know he had to give up teaching, but there were other openings in education such as an adviser or inspector."

31

"But Dad would have hated being tied to a desk or bossing people around."

Her mother flushed angrily. "It always comes back to what *he* wants. I hate the life we live, but *I* have never been considered."

"I am sorry. I did not know you felt like this," Anthea said quietly, though inwardly appalled at her mother's bitterness.

"Often I have felt like leaving," Mrs. Gordon went on, as though talking to herself. "But I have done my duty to both of you, although I realize how little you have appreciated it. I had thought that if you married Mark, your father would be forced to give up the business. With the money we would get for the business and house we could buy an apartment, and I wouldn't mind taking a light job myself. I have had one or two offers that are quite attractive. But Mark seems to have changed his mind and has found someone who obviously meets with his mother's approval."

Anthea clenched her hands and turned her face away. Was her mother being deliberately cruel or just taking her bitterness out on her? She had known that her mother did not like the quietness of the country, but she had never guessed at the hatred that seethed beneath her cold exterior. Her mother knew that Mark and she had always been close friends, but she would not give her the satisfaction of knowing how her remarks hurt.

"There was never anything serious between Mark and me," she said as calmly as she could. "He is meeting new friends and moving in different circles now, and, of course, things have to change."

"Not for us," her mother snapped. "What chance have you got to meet any suitable young men?"

"Here we are," Anthea said, with a sigh of relief. "I'll collect the van if it is ready and go straight back. I hope the women enjoy your demonstration because your work is beautiful."

"Thank you. I'll be back before the evening meal. Good-bye."

Anthea turned away quickly. She ought to have offered to carry in the boxes, but she felt that if she had to be with her mother any longer she might say something for which she would be sorry later.

She waved to several of the women from Melworth who had come in a bus, and some of the Bewdley members who walked up the street by ones or twos. This was one of the days when the two institutes joined forces—by invitation, of course—and the Bewdley group were putting on a good show. They were determined that their program and refreshments would outdo the poor affair Melworth had given them a few months ago. Mrs. Gordon was smart and a good speaker, even if she was a bit stuck-up. She had sent flowers for the decorations, and everybody knew about the beautiful needlepoint she had done and often displayed in exhibitions. There was a good soloist, and the vicar's wife gave really funny recitations.

Today was the tenth birthday celebration of the Bewdley Institute so Mrs. Pierce, who managed the baker's shop, had made a beautiful birthday cake. There was a booth of things the members had made—homemade jam, pickles, and a raffle for a patchwork quilt old Mrs. Barnes had spent weeks on for which everybody had contributed her most attractive scraps.

The money that they made was to give some of the old-age pensioners a day out, so everybody had done her best, and they would show the Melworth folks that Bewdley women were not coarse, anyway.

Anthea passed the garage and hurried on, not stopping to speak to anyone. She did not notice where she was going until she found herself on the outskirts of the village and then drove into a small wood and sat down on a log. She put her head in her hands and for a few minutes sat there, her thoughts churning inside her. How awful to realize how little love that her mother had for her father or for her. He had worked so hard to make the business pay and had always been so kind, thoughtful, and undemanding, but her mother appreciated none of that. Even as a child she had sensed vaguely that her mother never demonstrated tenderness like other mothers, but she had grown up with it and thought that it was only her natural behavior. Now she realized for the first time something of the strain that her father must have lived under all these years. His was such a sensitive nature. How he must have suffered to know that his wife regarded him as a failure.

She tried to blot out her mother's unkind remarks about Mark. For the last few weeks she had attempted to reconcile herself to the fact that Mark was not for her. She had waited, hoping that he would explain why he had canceled their arrangements or that he would repeat his invitation as he had promised. It was three weeks since he had called her, longer than he had ever gone before without either a short visit or a phone call.

She wiped a few tears away hastily. What had she to cry about anyway? It was her own fault if she had read more into Mark's friendship than he had intended.

"Oh, Lord, help me to face up to this disappointment," she prayed silently. "Mark has changed, I know, but he has been special to me for so long. Please don't let anyone, least of all Mark himself, guess how much I cared for him."

She stood up, pulling her shoulders back, and hurried to

34

the garage. The van was ready, and as she joked with Mike, the mechanic, she thought, *Thank You, Lord, for plenty of work to do, and the fact that Dad needs me.*

That evening and in the following days she worked so hard and late that she was exhausted when she went to bed and fell asleep almost immediately. She awakened after a few hours but was determined not to lie in bed letting her thoughts tie her in knots, so she was up and back in the nursery as soon as it was light.

Her father tried to reason with her, but Anthea simply said, "I would rather keep busy, Dad. Please let me work out my own problems my own way."

Her father looked at her sharply, then dropped his eyes. Anthea knew that he understood that she did not want to talk about it.

On Saturday afternoon Mark appeared in the office where Anthea was going through some accounts. "Hi, Thea," he said gaily. "You look very busy."

Anthea smiled and stood up, trying to hide her apprehension. "We can always find work to do in this job," she said lightly.

"You and I are about even then," he replied. "I've never been so rushed in my life. I thought when I'd got through my exams that I could slacken off and have some sort of life of my own, but I'm like a spinning top that can't stop."

"But at least it is exciting, isn't it?"

"I suppose so, but a lot of it is routine and working out little details. Of course, when I become a big boss I'll have subordinates to do the footwork for me. It is Mother's birthday tomorrow, and she is having a little dinner party. I thought since I was out this way I'd see if you had any special flowers that I could get her for decorations."

"What about some chrysanthemums or poinsettias? They

35

are just coming into their prime. Or freesias? I think your mother used to be fond of them, didn't she?"

"I knew you'd know what was best," Mark said brightly. "Come with me to choose."

Anthea walked out, her back very straight, and led the way to the different hothouses. They chose two pots of beautiful white chrysanthemums, a poinsettia that was a mass of huge red flowers, and a bunch of delicately scented freesia mixed with some maidenhair fern.

Are Gerry Towers and her father the guests who are going to the birthday party? she wondered.

Mark paid the price Anthea stated. Then she helped him carry the plants to his car.

"Give your mother my best wishes," she said as they stood by the door. "I hope she'll like what you have chosen. Don't tell her I helped you. She'll like them better if she thinks that you chose them for her yourself."

Mark gave her a quick glance, then nodded. "Probably you are right as usual. Sorry we haven't had that day out, Thea, but it will have to wait a bit. We have this party tomorrow, and next week I am going to Scotland on business."

"That's all right, Mark. I find I haven't much free time these days. Dad isn't too well, and I am trying to make him ease off. I find I have to spend most Sunday afternoons working on accounts and records."

"No wonder you look tired," Mark said bluntly. "Can't you sell this place and take an easier job?"

Anthea shook her head. "Maybe it will have to come to that, but Dad would be like a wild bird in a cage if he were stuck in an apartment as Mother would like. If we can get another man before the spring, we'll be able to carry on. Business has been good these last few months, so I hope we'll be able to afford extra help."

36

"Stubborn little creature, aren't you?" Mark said, suddenly ruffling her hair as he used to do years ago. "Your father has always been the most important person in your life, hasn't he?"

"He's very special," Anthea said firmly. "I don't care what I do if it helps him."

Mark grinned. "Good old Thea, you don't change. But remember, it doesn't always pay to be so unselfish. Folks have to look out for themselves if they don't want to be taken for granted."

"I'm happy as I am, Mark, and I'll leave the future to take care of itself."

"OK, chum, we'll continue our argument when we have that long postponed ramble. I'd better get going, or I'll be in trouble. Good-bye, Anthea. See you again before long."

"Good-bye, Mark. Nice to see you," she said bravely and lifted her hand in salute as he drove off.

She walked back to the office, dropped the money in the cash drawer, and with her lips set firmly, forced herself to carry on with her work. A few minutes later her father wandered in.

"Was that Mark I saw just now?"

"Yes. He wanted some flowers for his mother. It is her birthday tomorrow, and she is giving a little dinner party."

"Nice of him to drive so far, when he could have bought them in Newbridge."

"But not as fresh as ours," Anthea said, trying to speak gaily. "He said he was out this way anyway," she added. Her father glanced at her quickly and then turned away.

"How about a cup of tea? Shall I bring one out here?"

Anthea looked out the window and saw Mr. Towers drive into the parking space.

"Seems we have special customers this afternoon," she

said. "Let's hope Mr. Towers needs another large order."

"Not likely, after all the stuff his gardener took last time. Shall I serve him?"

"Yes, please. I want to finish these."

Anthea watched, nevertheless, as her father greeted the other man, then walked with him to the biggest greenhouse. Some time later she saw him walking out with a large pot of white chrysanthemums. She pretended to be extra busy when both men came into the office.

"Just add that to my account. We'll probably need a good many more during the winter months. Gerry likes a lot of flowers about the place. Afternoon, Miss Gordon."

Anthea pulled out a large plastic bag, fitted it neatly around the pot and over the flowers, and handed it to Mr. Towers.

"I always feel a fool carrying flowers, but Gerry insisted I come for them. She's out with the hunt this morning. Just crazy on anything to do with horses, that girl."

Mr. Gordon returned, saying whimsically, "I hope Mrs. Latham doesn't feel she is swamped with white chrysanthemums. Towers said they were for a friend who is giving a birthday dinner party tomorrow, so he thought chocolates and flowers were in order as he doesn't know her very well. I don't imagine there are two birthday dinners on the same night, do you?"

Anthea laughed. "Well, we gain by the sales, so we won't worry. Mr. Towers may feel his gift is a bit superfluous. Mark insisted on white, so we aren't to blame. Let's go into the kitchen for our tea," she said, putting her arm through her father's. "Mother is out, so we'll have to help ourselves anyway. Perhaps you could snooze for half an hour. I'll attend to any more customers."

"You are doing too much, girl, but you are stubborn. I guess there is no use arguing."

Anthea smiled wryly. "That makes two people who have told me that I'm stubborn this afternoon."

"Mark being the other, I imagine. Someday he'll realize that being stubborn when it means being loyal and unselfish is a very precious trait. Mark has a lot of growing up to do yet. He is callow and inexperienced."

"How dare you say that about someone who has got his law degree? I guess Mark would say that you and I are the innocents abroad and don't live in this world. He thinks that I might as well live in a cloister."

"Just as I said, he needs to grow up and think straight."

"I guess you are prejudiced, Dad. I was dying for that tea. Rats. There's the bell, and Beau is barking. Keep the pot hot until I get back."

She hurried out, glad for the diversion. Her father's eyes were too sharp, and he was suffering for her. Maybe he was right about Mark. Someday she too might be able to think about him without this awful ache of rejection.

The following Saturday morning Anthea was busy putting hyacinth bulbs into pots when she turned to see Max Sinclair walking down the path, then stopping to speak to Ron, who was tidying up one of the beds.

What was it that disturbed her so much about him? He was one of the Towers family; and the less she had to do with any of them, the better.

"Miss Anthea, this gentleman wants some rock plants," Ron said, putting his head around the door. "He'd like you to attend to him."

Anthea put down the trowel she was holding, shook earth from her gloves, and walked toward the man who stood looking over the gardens. *Must be a great advantage to be so tall and be able to see so far,* Anthea thought quickly.

"Good morning, Miss Gordon," he said as he turned.

"Great place, even in the winter. Hope I haven't disturbed you, but I want your help in choosing some plants for a rock garden. You looked as if they were very special to you that first morning when we called here."

"It is not the best time to move them," Anthea replied, "but we have plenty in little plastic containers that you can lift without damaging the roots. I thought that you said you hadn't a garden."

"I haven't. I live in a small apartment, but I'm horse-sitting at present. My stepfather and sister are in Scotland, and Gerry was bothered about leaving Captain, the horse she is so crazy about. Since I had a couple of days off I decided to come to Tall Timbers, get some studying done, exercise Captain, and have some peace at the same time."

Max had been watching Anthea's face closely and had noticed the flicker of what looked like pain in her eyes when he mentioned Scotland. Was it true what Mrs. Latham had hinted, that at one time Mark and Anthea Gordon had been inseparable? Had they been more than just old school friends?

"Then you decided to do some gardening as well?"

"I was up early, gave Captain a good gallop, and decided it was too beautiful to sit indoors. I left Bill, the gardener, clearing out the old rock garden, as I decided I'd have a go at making it more worth looking at. You have some sturdy heathers there, or I suppose I ought to show I know something about it by saying ericas."

"They are about all that are in bloom at present, but there are other hardy specimens that will bloom early in the year."

They chose a good selection, and Anthea called Ron to bring some boxes.

"I guess you'd be glad if the boxes are returned," Max

40

said, walking toward the office. "I'll drop them in on my way back on Monday."

"Thank you," Anthea replied primly. "Will I put these on Mr. Towers's account?"

"No, I'll pay cash. They will make up for all the meals Sarah, the cook, has fed me this weekend. I'll come back in a few weeks' time to tell you how they have taken and get some other specimens."

"If they die, we guarantee to replace them," she said in a businesslike voice.

"Well, we can't have anything fairer than that," he said, walking behind Ron to his car, which Anthea noticed was neither new nor as expensive-looking as the ones Mr. Towers and Gerry drove.

Anthea went on with her bulb planting automatically. So that was why Mark was in Scotland—business evidently covered quite a wide range of activities. Why hadn't he been honest? Why go on pretending he wanted a day out with her, when obviously Geraldine Towers was a much more exciting proposition?

3

The following Wednesday evening Anthea answered the phone and heard Mark's voice say, "Hi, Thea, how're things?"

"This is a surprise, Mark. I thought that you were in Scotland."

"Came back last night after a wonderful week. Anthea, hold onto your hat. Yours truly has just got engaged. I still can't believe it, but I wanted you to be the first to know— after Mother, of course. Even the rest of the family haven't been informed yet."

"Congratulations, Mark," Anthea heard herself say and was glad that her voice did not tremble. "But you haven't told me who the lucky girl is yet."

"Told you I didn't know if I'm on my head or my heels. It's Gerry, of course. I thought you would have guessed by now."

"I hope you'll be very happy."

"I want you two to become bosom pals. You don't live far from each other, and I've told Gerry that you'll always be my best friend. She said that you must come to dinner and to the engagement party she and her father are planning. Wow, I never thought a girl like Gerry would want an ordinary guy like me."

"You were never ordinary," Anthea said, managing to laugh but gripping the receiver like a lifeline. "You were always full of surprises. Does your mother approve?"

"You bet! She's as proud as punch. You'd think she'd arranged it all herself. It means her last chick will be leaving the nest and she'll be on her own."

"Probably you won't be far away."

"I hope not, but houses are mighty expensive, and I'm not in the landed gentry bracket yet."

"But Mr. Towers is, so that should help," Anthea said, and then could have bitten her tongue for letting that remark slip out.

"Listen, honey, you aren't suggesting that I'm interested in Gerry because she's got a rich father, are you?"

"Of course not," Anthea said hurriedly. "But he is sure to help when it comes to buying a house since Gerry is his only child."

"Well, maybe, but a man likes to feel that he is able to provide for his wife himself. Anyway, that's jumping too far ahead. I'll bring Gerry to introduce you properly the next time I am out your way."

"Do that," Anthea said brightly. "And again, the best of everything, Mark."

"Bye, Thea. See you soon."

Anthea leaned against the wall for a few moments after she had replaced the receiver, feeling as if she had aged ten years. She moved stiffly, took a coat from the hall closet, pulled on some gloves, then put her head around the kitchen door.

"I'm taking Beau for his run," she said, and without giving her parents time to reply, turned and hurried out of the front door, shutting it with a slam behind her. Afraid to face anyone until she had calmed down, she stood still on the steps until her eyes were accustomed to the dark. She could find her way around blindfolded, so she whistled for Beau and put her hand on his collar.

"Easy, boy," she said, rubbing her face against his head. She held onto him until they reached the fields, then let him go while she wandered on, being able to see the dark outline of the fence or hedge and not caring where she went.

She had to face up to the fact that her friendship with Mark was finished. No good trying to excuse him any longer. Had he deliberately closed his mind to how much they had meant to each other, the plans they used to make for the future? Or had the past only been a game to him? She would have to tell her father, and she knew that he would be upset for her sake. She would wait for a convenient time when they were on their own.

Beau kept rushing back and forth. He could not understand why Anthea was dawdling like this instead of walking briskly or even running as she usually did.

"Time to get back," she called, then gave her own peculiar whistle. He ran to her, then peered up into her face and whined.

"Good dog," she said, pulling his head against her body and patting it. She was the only one allowed to do this, but Beau wriggled with delight and pushed against her for more of the same treatment.

"It's good to have one faithful friend even if it is a dog," she muttered. "Stop being sorry for yourself, Anthea. This isn't the end of the world. If Geraldine Towers can be the kind of wife Mark wants, then evidently I wouldn't have filled the bill. It is a good thing that we found out before it was too late."

She gave Beau an extra hug as she fastened his chain and walked briskly through the kitchen into the lounge where her parents were watching the news.

"Who was the phone call from?" her mother asked, turning her head.

"Mark, saying he was back home," she gulped and added, "and to tell me that he is engaged to Geraldine Towers. They have all been in Scotland on a business trip."

Her mother stared at her while her father, after a startled glance, kept his eyes on the fire.

"Well, they aren't wasting much time. They hardly know each other, but then Mr. Towers is wealthy so his daughter is a good catch. She will be much more to his mother's taste than you were."

Anthea shrugged. "We have grown up now and changed our ideas. Anything special on the news?"

"Only the usual stories of strikes, bombings in Northern Ireland, and the rise in unemployment. I really don't know why we bother to watch what is so depressing. I think I'll go up to bed. Is it cold out?" her father said.

"Touch of frost, but dry," Anthea said. She continued, "Dad, I think we should drive over to visit Aunt Ellen on the weekend. We haven't seen her for weeks, and the last time I was there she looked very frail."

"She would have phoned if she were ill," Mrs. Gordon said sharply. "I saw her in town recently, and she was as cantankerous as ever."

"That's a good idea, Anthea. We'll go on Sunday afternoon, but we'll phone her first. The weeks slip by, and I forget that she is all on her own."

"Good night, Mother. Good night, Dad. I'm ready for bed too."

"Good night," her mother said, her eyes already on her needlework. "I am going to watch the movie tonight. I certainly couldn't sleep if I went to bed at this hour."

Anthea followed her father as he went slowly upstairs. He stopped and looked at her, his eyes full of sympathy.

"It's all right, Dad. Don't worry about me," Anthea said as bravely as she could. "I had got used to the idea that Mark was never more than a childhood friend."

"I know, and for my part, I'm glad. I did not want you to make a mistake like I did. Good night, my darling."

Anthea hurried to her room, turned the key in the lock, and throwing herself on the bed burst into tears. For a few moments she let down the barriers and stopped pretending.

Maybe she had only been dreaming of Mark because no one else had entered the picture. Suddenly into her mind came the picture of a tall, dark-haired man with blue eyes that seemed to look right inside her. She pulled herself off the bed and made for the bathroom. A hot bath would help her sleep, and tomorrow she would start a life in which Mark had no part. There would be no idle dreaming about Max Sinclair either. He meant nothing to her, and she had no desire to have anything more to do with anyone connected with the Towers family.

On Sunday afternoon Anthea drove her father into Newbridge to Great-Aunt Ellen's, leaving her mother at her sister's house. Mrs. Gordon detested the aunt, and Anthea knew that there was no love lost on the older woman's side either. She never accepted their invitations to visit the nursery, not even at Christmas. Anthea still tried to keep in touch and remind her father to pay regular visits. She knew that he had been brought up by his grandparents and Aunt Ellen after his own parents were killed, and he had told her often how good they had been to him. They had paid for his education, and when his grandmother had died, her money was divided equally between himself and his aunt, who had never married. It was this money that had made it possible for him to buy the house and land that he had turned into Rookery Nurseries.

Why her mother hated Aunt Ellen so much Anthea never understood, and she had never dared to inquire.

Ellen was watching for them from her front window. The house was run-down now and far too big for one elderly woman, but she had lived there all her life and intended to die there. She was over eighty but still able to look after herself. She was small and alert with snow-white hair and faded blue eyes, but her spirit was as indomitable as ever.

The front door opened almost before they were out of the car.

"So here you are. This a pleasant surprise," she said as Mr. Gordon bent to kiss her. Taking Anthea's hands she held her away for a moment, then pulled her to her.

"Come in to the fire. Tea is all ready."

They followed her into the parlor, as she still called it, where drawn up near the settee was a cart set with sandwiches, cakes, and the best china.

Anthea smiled at the sight. "Ever since I was a little girl a meal was always ready as soon as we got into the house. Are you still baking for yourself, Aunt Ellen?"

"Of course, though it's not worth doing much just for myself. One cake lasts me a week now. Take off your coat, Andrew. Anthea will hang it in the hall closet for you. The room is warm, but I enjoy a good fire; those electric new-fangled things aren't the same. Is Eleanor well?"

"She's as energetic as usual," Andrew replied, sitting down in the chair that used to be his grandfather's. "We left her at Kathleen's and will pick her up on our way back. You never seem to grow a day older, Aunt Ellen. How do you do it?"

"Early to bed and plain food is my recipe. The years are telling, but I've a lot to be thankful for. Now I'll just make the tea, as you are probably dying for a cup."

"Let me do it, Aunt Ellen," Anthea suggested.

"You can carry the pots if you like," she consented, and Mr. Gordon gave Anthea a sly wink.

This was a great concession. Usually no one was allowed in her kitchen.

As soon as she had put the kettle on the stove, she turned and put her hand on Anthea's arm.

"Lassie, was it a shock to you when Mark got engaged to somebody else? I always thought you and he were only waiting until he finished his training."

Anthea smiled into the anxious blue eyes. "How did you hear of it?" she asked.

"Saw it in the paper on Friday. I could hardly believe it."

"It wasn't really a shock, Aunt Ellen. There was never anything beyond friendship between Mark and me. We haven't seen much of each other since he moved to New-bridge."

"Then I'm glad, dearie. I may be old, but I hear odds and ends of gossip all the same. Folks told me Mark was going places with different girls, and Mary Latham always struck me as having big ideas. The Lord has someone far better for you, and there are worse things than not being married. I'd rather be lonely and have my independence than have to live like some folks with their bad-tempered, bossy husbands."

"The kettle is boiling," Anthea said, carrying the teapot over to the stove. "Aunt Ellen, I'm worried about Dad. Do you think he looks ill?"

"He hasn't looked well for months, but he just brushes me off when I tell him that he works too hard for his age. He's not young, child, and life hasn't been all that kind to

48

him. You make up for a lot of other disappointments. Now let's give him his tea and not let him think we are fussing over him."

"Come back soon," Aunt Ellen called as they walked down the path to the car. "Don't let your father work so hard, Anthea."

Anthea laughed. "I'll do my best, Aunt Ellen, but you know he doesn't think anyone else can do the job properly."

"Talk about being henpecked," her father exclaimed. "I'm bossed about all the time by you women. Can I drive, Anthea, or is even that beyond my aged ability?"

Anthea patted his shoulder. "We only fuss because we love you, Dad. Of course you can drive. I'll be glad to have a chauffeur for a change."

"Wonderful old dear, isn't she?" Mr. Gordon said as they drove away, and he could see Aunt Ellen waving as he looked into the rearview mirror. "She doesn't seem to change. I wish she lived nearer so that we could see her oftener or that she would come out to stay sometimes, but it is useless to invite her. I am glad that she has a telephone, although it was quite a time before she agreed to have it installed. Sometimes I wonder what she will do if she can't look after herself. She was so good to me when I was a boy that I hate to think of her being alone so much. I don't suppose she has many visitors, as most of her generation have already gone."

"I'll try to call more often," Anthea promised. "We aren't very well off for relations, so we need to look after those we have. I'm glad we went this afternoon. Perhaps I could go other Sundays because she was saying how she misses going to church in the evening, but the distance is getting too much for her, especially when it is dark or slippery."

"If only your mother and she could understand each other, but they have never got along. Aunt Ellen is too outspoken at times and inclined to criticize too openly. She has a heart of gold, but she's too honest to suit some people. Here we are. I hope we don't have to stay too long. I'd like to have a quiet evening."

"Wait in the car, Dad. I'll tell Mother we are here."

"Won't you come in?" Kathleen said as she opened the door. "We are watching an interesting program."

"Dad is tired, Aunt Kathleen. I think we should get back and let him rest."

"Your mother was saying that he seems to have lost all his energy. Why he doesn't give up that place and move into town, I can't figure out, but maybe he is really carrying on for your sake."

"I am hoping that we'll get more help so that he can do less, but he'd be very miserable if he had nothing to do all day." Anthea moved into the sitting room and said cheerfully, "Ready, Mother? Dad wants to get back as soon as he can."

Her mother got up and exchanged glances with Kathleen. "Then of course that is all that matters. I'll arrange for next weekend, Kathleen."

With her back and face registering resentment, Mrs. Gordon stalked out and sat in the passenger seat, staring in front of her.

"Had a good visit, dear?" her husband inquired after a long silence.

"You might have had the good manners to spend a few minutes with Kathleen," Mrs. Gordon snapped. "But obviously your Aunt Ellen is more important than my sister."

"I'm sorry, dear. I thought the plan was that we just pick you up. I did not realize that you wanted to stay longer."

"Oh, it doesn't matter. Next weekend Kathleen and I are going to spend a few days in London. I'd like to see the shops, and Kathleen wants to buy some new clothes."

"I'm glad," her husband replied. "The break will be good for you. This time of year can be depressing."

Anthea, sitting behind, marveled at her father's patience. Her mother had not even inquired about Aunt Ellen. She was never interested in anything that did not directly affect herself.

On the following Wednesday the worst storm of the year swept over the country. The wind blew with tornado force, and there were gale warnings interrupting every program on television and radio. During a slight lull, Anthea could hear Beau howling. Pulling on a coat and tying a scarf on her head she said, "It is too bad to leave Beau out. I'll put him in the toolshed."

"Be careful," her father warned. "There may be tiles blown off. I hope the greenhouses stand up to this. Get back in as soon as you can."

Anthea smiled. "I certainly will. No walk for Beau or me tonight." She whistled, put Beau in the toolshed, and could hardly get the door closed as the wind tried to tear it from her hand.

Another violent gust almost blew her backward, and she clung to the door handle until it passed. Then struggling with her head down and walking carefully, she managed to make her way to the back door. Again she had to lean against it to bolt it from the inside, and she was out of breath as she returned to the kitchen.

"What a wind," she exclaimed, pulling off her scarf and pushing her hair out of her eyes. "I am sorry for anyone on night duty."

At that moment there was a loud crash. "What was

that?'' her mother exclaimed, her face pale under her makeup. "Why do we have to live in such an open place?"

"I don't suppose it is any better in town tonight," Mr. Gordon said quietly. "There will be plenty of roofs damaged and trees and telegraph poles down. I am afraid that that crash was probably one of the greenhouses, but no one is going out in this, no matter what has happened. Good thing you managed to get Beau inside, Anthea."

The gale continued; they could hardly hear themselves speak. Television was so bad that they turned it off. Anthea and her father tried to read, but neither of them could concentrate, and Mrs. Gordon's hands trembled so that her needlework was set aside.

She moved about nervously, peering out of the window. As the smoke eddied back down the chimney and out into the room she screamed. "How can you sit there like that when the place is falling to pieces? Maybe this will help you make up your minds that I can't stand it any longer."

"Anthea, make some tea," Mr. Gordon suggested. "Would you like to go to bed, Eleanor? Take one of your strong sleeping tablets and try to forget it. There is nothing we can do, but at least we are safe inside."

"Go to bed! How could anyone sleep in this? Probably the roof will be gone by the morning. As for your precious plants, they'll be worthless."

"My dear, you will make yourself ill. Please go up and lie down. Anthea will bring you a tray. The worst will be over soon. As for our roof, I guess it has weathered many storms as bad as this, and the plants will grow again."

"Come on, Mother, let me switch on the electric blanket and pull your curtains," Anthea said patiently. "We might as well all go to bed. I guess there will be plenty of work when this is over."

52

Mrs. Gordon stomped upstairs. When Anthea took in a tray of tea and biscuits she was in bed with the blankets pulled over her head.

Anthea had to hide a smile. *Poor mother. She is terrified,* she thought. *She has no resources if things don't go her way.*

"Mother, drink your tea and take your pills," she said, putting the tray down on the bedside table.

"You and your father are so unimaginative," she said, throwing back the covers and sitting up. "You have no idea what sensitive people like me suffer. Your father infuriates me with his Pollyanna ideas. I'm so sick of this place that if I don't get away soon I'll go mad."

"Think of the time that you will have with Kathleen in London," Anthea said gently, as if talking to a child. "Go over all the activities you have planned."

"Not much excitement when I have so little money to spend, and I hate having to let Kathleen pay for me, even though I know she can afford it."

"Try to sleep. I'll persuade Dad to come upstairs too. I'll see that everywhere is locked up and the fire is put out. Good night, Mum."

"I am sure that I won't sleep. How I hate this house."

Guessing that her mother was working herself up into a hysterical tantrum, Anthea hurried out and closed the door firmly. She went next door, switched on the electric blanket on her father's small, single bed, and pulled the curtains.

It was pitch dark outside now, except for occasional flashes of lightning. She could hear the wind howling and heavy objects hitting the window and walls. What a mess the gardens would be when the storm abated!

She ran downstairs and put her hand on her father's shoulder.

"Come on, Dad, there is nothing you can do tonight. We'd better have as much rest as we can to be ready for the big cleanup tomorrow."

At that moment there was a tremendous crash, and her father sighed. "That is another of the greenhouses."

"But at least none of us is in danger, and we are insured."

"Bless you, dear. You always see the brightest side. Yes, I suppose I may as well go upstairs. Promise me that you won't try to go outside. Tiles and trees may be falling."

"No, I promise. I'll lie down even if I don't undress."

Largely to persuade her father to rest, Anthea went upstairs herself. Pulling the eiderdown over her she tried to close her ears to the thunder and roar of the wind. She prayed that the roof would hold and that the damage would not be too disastrous. Dawn was breaking when the wind dropped, and she fell into a light sleep. Two hours later she awakened and jumped up, wondering why she was fully dressed. Then as the memory of the awful night returned she hurried to the window and pulled the curtains aside.

What a mess the place looked. Leaves and branches were all over the lawn, and plants and bushes were smashed down. She pulled on her oldest clothes, hurried downstairs, and switched on the light, but nothing happened. Evidently the electric wires were down.

She went to the phone, but that too was dead. She raked out the kitchen stove and collected paper, wood, and coal. She hoped she would have the kettle boiling and the place warmed before her parents came down. She was determined that she would not awaken them, as they must have slept little during the night.

She set the breakfast table, then ran out to let Beau out of the shed, but she had to fight to hold back the tears as she saw the awful state of their carefully tended plots. She could see that many of the prize shrubs and fruit trees were broken, and glass was scattered all over the place from the broken panes from the greenhouses. She would have to tie Beau where he would not cut his paws. If only she could keep her father out of the way until the worst of the damage was cleaned up. That was impossible, and her mother would do nothing to help. All she would do would be to moan and grumble. How much easier life would be if she were behind them, but theirs was a house divided. Anthea knew in her heart that they could not go on much longer with the unpleasant tension that had destroyed the happy home life they could have had. Now her mother really did have something to grumble about, and she would only add to their problems. Her father came into the kitchen as Anthea returned.

"Why didn't you wait until I brought your tea?" Anthea said, putting her arm around his shoulders. "Sit down. The kettle is boiling. Is mother awake?"

"I hope not. Is it very bad outside?"

"Two greenhouses are damaged, but it could have been worse. It won't look so bad when we get the place tidied up. The electricity is off, and the phone is dead."

"The temperature inside must have gone down. We'll have to pray that it doesn't freeze before the electricity is on again. I wonder if Ron will be able to get through."

"I'm sure that he will. Now drink your tea while I see to the eggs and toast. I will just let Mother sleep, as I guess that she got very little rest last night."

They were finished when Ron knocked at the door and put his head in.

"I came as early as I could to see if you were OK."

"Bless you, Ron. I guess there'll be a lot of cleaning up to do. Has there been a lot of damage?"

Ron nodded. "A couple of big trees across the road. Cars can't get by yet, but I could climb over with my bike. Rogers' garage roof has gone, and Andrews' big window was blown in. Stannard, the policeman, told me that the electricity is off and the phones are down."

"What about your own cottage?"

"Our house is as solid as a rock, but one of the hen huts got smashed, and I had to prop up the wire netting. I left Billy to tidy up down there."

"The end of the big greenhouse is gone," Anthea said calmly. "A lot of the plants will need tying up. Have some tea and toast."

"Not yet, Miss Anthea. Mollie got me breakfast before I left. None of us slept much last night, so we got up as soon as it started getting light. I'll have a look around. I'll measure the glass and get it mended as soon as I can."

"When the road is clear I'll take the van to collect what you need," Anthea replied. "What a blessing that you can put in glass and do so many odd jobs, Ron."

Ron backed out hastily. He was always embarrassed when anyone complimented him, but secretly he adored Anthea and would do anything to make things easier for her and Mr. Gordon.

"Nobody ever had a kinder boss," he often told his wife when she grumbled because he worked longer hours than she considered necessary. "I can't bear high and mighty Mrs. Gordon, but I'd do anything to help Mr. Gordon and Miss Anthea. She works like a man and never grumbles. I'm thankful that I don't have a wife like Mrs. Gordon. I'd give in my notice tomorrow if I had to take my orders from her, miserable woman that she is!"

Mollie nodded. "Makes me sick when she comes to speak at the Institute. Always looks as if there was a bad smell under her nose. But don't you forget, Ron, that you can get a job anywhere. You could work less and get more money if you wanted."

"Maybe I could, but money isn't everything. I enjoy my work, Mr. Gordon treats me fair, so I'm stopping where I am."

Ron was thinking of this as he measured the frames where the glass was cracked or broken. He looked up at the roof of the house and could see that several tiles were missing or had slipped into the gutters.

"Better see what's needed up there," he muttered.

Mr. Gordon came out as he was climbing the ladder. "Trouble there too, Ron?" he asked.

"Just a few tiles, I reckon, but we'd best get them fixed or we'll have the rain coming in."

Anthea appeared with her coat on. "Think I can make it down to Dalton's, Ron?"

"Maybe, if the road is cleared. I guess the highway men will be moving the trees as soon as they can, but I don't know if Bob Dalton will have enough heavy glass. You may have to go to Newbridge. I'm going up to see how many tiles are missing. You might get them at the same time."

"OK. We'll start checking some of the young trees until I know what you want. I'll get some stakes, Dad, and some strapping. If Ron can repair the glass, maybe we won't lose so many plants after all."

Anthea knew that her father would feel better if he kept busy, but she was determined that he would not do anything that was too strenuous.

She collected some wooden stakes, put them in a wheelbarrow, and joined him in the fruit tree section. Some of these were valuable because it took so long to nurture them to strong, well-developed young trees.

Some branches were broken right off, but others were only bent or cracked. Mr. Gordon touched them gently as he tried to tie them up or to bind the ends together.

"Perhaps we can save some of them," he said hopefully, "but it's going to hold up our other work."

"Twenty-four tiles as far as I can guess," Ron said, holding a broken piece in his hand. "Take this bit to see if you can match it. They are Marley tiles, but rather an unusual size. I've written down the size of the glass you need cut, and the amount of putty we need."

"Better get thirty tiles," Mr. Gordon said. "Have we enough paint to touch up, Ron?"

"Aye, there's a tin in the shed."

"What about that grafting wax, you use, Dad?"

"Get another tin. We have some in storage, but we'll need more, I expect."

"Ron, the garage door is stuck. Will you help me to open it?" Anthea asked. Ron followed her and bent down to clear away the sticks, stones, and mud that jammed it.

Anthea pretended to help, but as she poked she said in a low voice, "Please keep your eye on Dad, Ron. Don't let him try to lift anything heavy or tackle anything too hard. I wish I didn't have to leave him, but we've got to get that glass back as soon as possible."

"I'll watch out for him, Miss. Don't you worry. Plenty of little jobs he can do. I'll do the lifting."

"Thanks, Ron. I don't know how we'd carry on if you weren't here to help."

"Watch how you drive, Miss Anthea," Ron said hurriedly. "There may be more broken branches to come down yet."

Anthea nodded. "I'll get back as soon as I can, but if I've got to go to Newbridge that will take all morning."

She drove the van out of the garage and called to her father. "I'll be back soon, Dad. Don't try to do too much."

"Don't worry about me," he replied, straightening his back to wave as she went down the drive.

Anthea drove very slowly, especially at corners, but fortunately the trees had been pulled to one side of the road, and men were busy chopping off the branches. The road was a mess with branches and wet leaves, which made driving dangerous. Already a truck had skidded into a hedge, and a tow truck was trying to pull it onto the road again.

Anthea headed for Daltons, the builders, but found that several people were there before her.

Jack Dalton shook his head when Anthea told him what she wanted. "I'm afraid I haven't got that much heavy glass, Miss Anthea, but I'll have a look. I've got some of those tiles, though. They're not made that size now, but I found a stack of them in a corner a bit ago.

Dalton's yard was a conglomeration of all sorts of building supplies that had been collected over two generations. Jack's father had been a jobbing builder all his life. Now Jack's son was also in the business.

There were stacks of bricks, corrugated iron, old bathtubs, and piles of wooden planks in various sizes. In the enormous old shed there were tins of screws, tools, door and window frames, ladders, and sheets of glass wrapped in sacking.

Probably only old Mr. Dalton knew what was in their possession, and Jack called to the old man who was poking around in a corner of the shed.

"Dad, have we got any glass for Gordon's greenhouse?"

His father pushed his old hat back on his head and rubbed his whiskered chin.

"Aye, there's a good bit, but we'll have to lift the other stuff out first. How much do you want?"

Anthea handed over the paper with Ron's measurements. The old man pulled out his wire frame spectacles and peered through them. He whistled.

"Seems like you caught it bad last night. Send Johnnie here, Jack, and we'll see what we can find. Suppose you'll want it cut. Johnnie loves doing that."

"I'll get the tiles and the putty and put it in the van, then see to some of the other folks who want us to do all their repairs at once. You're lucky to have Ron up at your place."

"I know," Anthea answered. "He's one of our blessings."

Jack nodded. "I've asked him a few times to come here, but he can't be tempted even with more money."

"Pity there aren't more like him," old Mr. Dalton said, pulling some sacking away from the dusty glass. "Most folks want big wages for doing nothing these days. Johnnie, give me a hand with this lump of glass. Be careful now. We'll need to measure up, but I doubt we'll have enough."

Johnnie was a hefty specimen of well over six feet; it was amusing to see him being ordered about by his small, wizened grandfather.

"Get your measure," the old man said and started reading out the sizes they wanted. "You can get busy cutting this, and remember that it's expensive stuff, so mind how you go."

After about a quarter of an hour Johnnie said, "We can't manage the two big frames, Granddad."

His grandfather nodded. "Just as I thought. We don't get much call for this heavy stuff, Miss Anthea. Mostly it's just window glass. Will you have what we've got and go on to Newbridge to get the rest? Johnnie could be cutting what we have and that will save time."

"That will be fine," Anthea answered. "I need more grafting wax anyway, so I'll collect this on my way back."

"I'll have it ready," Johnnie promised, and Anthea sighed as she drove off. This was what she had hoped to avoid. There was so much to do back at the nursery, and she could ill afford the time to drive to Newbridge and back. If only her mother had helped. She could have driven the van and collected the glass while they cleaned up. It would be late before Ron could get started repairing the greenhouse, and he wouldn't be able to finish before dark. If the electricity was restored they might be able to rig up outside lights, but without heating, the plants would probably die.

4

It was almost two o'clock when Anthea drove in through the nursery gate. She noticed a strange car at the front door and saw Ron standing, looking out over the battered gardens.

A sudden fear struck her. There was something about the way Ron was standing that frightened her.

He turned slowly when she stopped the van and walked toward her. She noticed how gray his face was.

"I've got everything, Ron, but I had to go to Newbridge."

"Miss Anthea, I've got bad news for you," he said, and she saw that there were tears in his eyes.

She backed against the van and groped to grip the handle. "Is it Dad?" she said in a low voice.

"I'm afraid so. I had him picking up the glass from the greenhouse beds and went into the shed to have my sandwiches. He must have started picking up the broken glass outside, because when I came around he was lying on the ground and a bucket of glass was beside him."

"Where is he now?" Anthea gasped.

"In the house. Thank the Lord that the phone was mended and your mother called the doctor. I got Billy Watson to help me carry him up to bed, but I don't know if it was a stroke or a heart attack."

"Is he dead?" she questioned.

"I don't think so. Maybe the doctor will want to take him to the hospital. I couldn't help it, Miss Anthea, honestly I couldn't. The doctor got here just five minutes ago."

"I know, Ron. I've been afraid of this for a long time."

She ran across the yard into the house and tiptoed upstairs.

Voices came from her mother's room, and she looked inside. She gasped as she caught sight of her father's face.

The doctor turned quickly.

"How is he?" she asked.

"I'm afraid it is too late," the doctor replied and guided Anthea to a chair. "He must have gone without any pain."

"If only I hadn't gone to Newbridge," Anthea said in a low voice.

"It probably would have happened just the same. Evidently he was bending down, and his heart gave out. My dear, he has been saved a lot of pain."

"What can I do, Mother?"

"There is nothing we can do," her mother said coldly. "I told both of you that this would happen, but neither of you would listen."

The doctor saw Anthea's face go even paler, and he said quietly, "Have you had lunch, Miss Gordon?"

Anthea shook her head. "I wanted to get right back. I can't eat anything."

"Make some tea and put in plenty of sugar," the doctor said to Mrs. Gordon. "I'll phone for the nurse. Maybe you can ask someone to stay with you. There will be many arrangements to make."

Mrs. Gordon walked out of the room, her back very straight. The young doctor, who had never visited the family before, wondered what sort of a wife and mother this cold, unemotional woman had been. He had never seen anyone accept death of a husband in this manner before.

Anthea stepped over to the bed and touched her father's face with her hand. She bent down and kissed him lovingly. Still the tears did not come.

Very gently the doctor pulled the sheet over Mr. Gordon's face, which looked so peaceful but remote.

"Nurse Somers will be here to help your mother," he said, leading Anthea away from the bed to downstairs. "You have had a bad shock, my dear, but don't blame yourself in any way."

Anthea felt like a robot as she drank the tea her mother had poured. Then she walked outside.

"He's gone," she said to Ron who hurried toward her. "The doctor says he died instantly."

"Oh, no. Why didn't I stay with him?"

"You aren't to blame. Neither of us could have made him rest. The nurse is coming. We'll get on with the work."

Pulling on old gloves Anthea helped Ron lift the glass from the van and stood it on end beside the greenhouse. Ron glanced at her several times. *Why doesn't she cry?* He knew how she loved her father. Maybe the shock had been too much for her.

Ron was puttying the first large frame when the district nurse drove up and walked into the house. Anthea continued trying to tie up the broken branches.

Mrs. Gordon appeared at the back door. "Ron, the nurse needs you."

Ron put down the putty, wiped his hands on his trousers, and went inside.

"Better kick off your boots and wash your hands before you go upstairs," she said flatly. "There are some slippers there."

Ron dropped his eyes. Those were Mr. Gordon's slippers. How could she offer them to someone else so soon? He followed her upstairs.

"Nurse wants you to help change my husband's clothes and lift the body into his own room. I have already changed the sheets, and I've phoned for Mr. Rawlings, the undertaker. I'll leave you to it. Call if you need anything."

She walked downstairs and Nurse Wilson shook her head. "Help me take his old clothes off and put on this suit Mrs. Gordon wants him to wear. We are to put him in the next room. Think we can manage it, or should we wait until Mr. Rawlings arrives?"

"We'll manage," Ron said gruffly. "I'd like to do all I can for him. He was the best boss any man every had. Since he had to die, it is a good thing he went quickly. He would have hated to be helpless or an invalid."

They worked quickly and soon carried him to his own small bed.

Ron wiped his eyes several times. "He was a fine man," he said huskily, following Nurse Wilson downstairs.

"Is there anything else I can do to help, Mrs. Gordon?" Nurse Wilson asked as they went into the kitchen.

"No, thank you. My sister will be here soon, and she will help me make the final arrangements. Would you like a drink or some tea, nurse?"

"A cup of tea would be lovely," Ron heard her say as he slipped his boots on again and hurried back to work.

He saw Mrs. Gordon's sister arrive some time later, then Rawlings, the undertaker, and later Mr. Andrews, the vicar of Bewdley Church. He had heard the news of Mr. Gordon's death from Nurse Wilson and had called mainly for Anthea's sake. He was in the house only a short time. He proceeded outside to where Ron was replacing the glass.

"Don't stop. I know it is vital to get those mended as soon as possible. I was shocked to hear what had happened. Mr. Gordon was my dear friend as well as a parishioner."

Ron nodded, his eyes on the putty he was softening. "Aye, he'll be sadly missed. Miss Anthea is in the fruit garden. I'm bothered about her."

"I'll find her, poor girl. Not many daughters are as close to their fathers."

He walked slowly down the path looking sadly at the havoc the storm had caused. He saw Anthea binding a thin tree to a stake she had driven in the ground and he called softly, "Anthea, let me help you with that."

Anthea turned, and he was shocked at the blank expression in her eyes, which were usually so alive.

She did not protest when he lifted a stake, saying, "Shall I deal with this one?"

"Please don't trouble yourself," Anthea said listlessly. "It will take weeks before we get this mess cleaned up, but maybe it doesn't really matter."

"My dear, let me express how grieved I am. I know that you are the one who has suffered the greatest loss."

Anthea made no answer.

"But let me tell you that the last time I had a long talk with your father he said, 'My time is running out, and it is only because of Anthea that I want to live longer. I'm ready to go, and I'm praying that I'll go quickly. Tell Anthea that if anything happens suddenly.'

"His prayer was answered, my dear, he is at peace, and he is with the Lord whom He served so quietly and faithfully. Don't grieve too much. Someday you will be able to thank God that he did not live to suffer."

Anthea's expression still did not change. "I must get on, but thank you for your visit, Mr. Andrews."

"I have a few spare hours. Let me give you a hand," he said quickly, and she did not refuse, so he went on hammering in stakes and binding the young trees to them.

"I'll leave the broken ones to you as they need expert treatment."

Without speaking they went on working until it was too dark to see.

"I'll come again tomorrow if I may," Mr. Andrews said as they picked up the tools and took them to the shed.

Beau started barking fiercely as they approached.

"All right, boy," Anthea said, going forward and putting her hand on his head.

Mr. Andrews kept his distance. He always thought that a Doberman was one of the meanest looking animals. Now he watched as the dog licked Anthea's hand, whined as if in sympathy, and pushed his head against her leg.

Does the dog sense what has happened? he wondered.

"Good night, Anthea. I'll see you tomorrow. Your mother will tell you what arrangements she has made."

"Good night, Mr. Andrews. Thank you for coming."

Anthea put the tools back in their place. Slipping on Beau's leash she set off with him down the path and over the fence into the fields where she let him run free, but Beau only moved off a few yards, then came back and licked Anthea's hand.

Suddenly her eyes filled with tears. Beau was showing more sympathy than her mother had done. She bent down and pulled his long head with the short, pointed ears close to her. He nuzzled in toward her neck and did what he had never done before—he licked her face.

She stood up suddenly and fought to hold back the sobs. She was determined that she would control her sorrow until she was in the privacy of her own room.

She walked on with Beau, but it was pitch dark by now, so she turned and let him lead her back. She wondered why Ron had not said good night but had gone off without telling her. She switched on the light in the greenhouse and sighed as she saw that many panes were still missing.

She headed back toward the house when Beau started barking fiercely, and she turned back.

"It's me, Miss Anthea," came Ron's voice, and she saw some figures coming up the path. "Jack and Johnnie Dalton and my Billie have come to help me finish."

"But you have worked all day," Anthea said blankly.

"Aye, well, this job needs doing," Ron muttered.

"Miss Anthea, we all can spare a few hours and will be glad to do what we can," Jack Dalton added.

"That's right," the other two agreed.

"We can put the light on and finish the glass," Ron said matter-of-factly. "Is Beau tied?"

"I'll put him in the shed and fetch his supper," Anthea said huskily, a lump in her throat.

The back door opened, and her mother's figure showed in the light.

"Who is there, Anthea?"

"Ron has brought some friends to finish the greenhouse," Anthea replied. "Quiet, Beau."

She put Beau in one of the sheds, then went back for his supper and took it to him.

Her mother was in the sitting room with Kathleen. "Your meal is in the oven," she said as Anthea pushed the door open. "Kathleen and I have had ours, but I knew you would not come in until it was dark."

"You sit still, Eleanor. You've had enough upset today. I'll see to Anthea."

Mrs. Gordon sighed heavily and took up her embroidery.

"You must be famished," Aunt Kathleen said as Anthea sat down wearily at the table.

"Only thirsty," she replied.

"Well, eat as much as you can. You'll need all your strength. I know you've both had a terrible shock. Eleanor is marvelous, so calm and resigned, but she'll crack up after it is all over. You'll need to stand by her. She never shows her feelings, but she suffers all the same. She hasn't been a happy woman for a long time. She was afraid that this was going to happen, but she couldn't persuade Andrew to give up the nursery. I guess you don't really understand how she felt. She never liked being away from town. I can't blame her, for I'd hate to be stuck out in a lonely place like this. It's so quiet that it gives me the creeps."

Anthea pushed her plate away after a few bites but poured out another cup of tea and drank thirstily.

"Will you stay with Mother for a few days?" she asked.

"Until after the funeral anyway, and then I'll see. I'd like her to come home with me, but she can't leave you on your own."

"Ron and Mollie would come here to sleep for a few nights. Then we'll have to make other arrangements, I expect. Maybe we could hire another girl so that she could stay with me if Mother wants to be away at times."

"Don't rush into things. Take one day at a time. It's too early to make decisions."

Anthea kept her eyes fixed on her empty cup. She felt a chill of fear that her mother and Kathleen had already been making decisions that would alter her life.

That night when Anthea was sure her mother and aunt were asleep, she crept into her father's room and knelt by the bed on which his body lay. How peaceful and finely drawn his face was. The lines had disappeared, and he looked years younger.

69

She put her hand on his hands and laid her face against his cold one, while a strange calm filled her heart. She kissed his lips, sat down beside the bed, and gazed upon his face, which might have been carved out of marble.

"Oh, Dad, what will I do without you?" she whispered. "You have been so good to me. All my life I have depended on you. I can never remember you being impatient or unfair with me. How can I go on alone? I am glad that you did not have to suffer, but I feel as if I have no one left. Why did I have to lose Mark and you?"

Suddenly the words that her father had spoken recently came into her mind. "Anthea, don't grieve for me if I go suddenly. I am ready to die. You have made life worth living for me, but I am tired."

Her eyes filled, and the tears that she had held back all day poured down her face. She pushed her handkerchief into her mouth to stop the sobs, as she realized that this was her real farewell to her father. It would be almost her last chance to spend time with him. After she had quieted down, she sat for over an hour, her eyes fixed on the one whom she loved so much. She was glad that she would have the picture of his unlined face in her mind, rather than that of the tired, strained man who had tried so hard to comfort her these last months.

"Goody-bye, Dad," she said softly, then crept back to her own room and slipped into bed.

She shivered, but it was as if a heavy weight had been lifted from her. Her tears had cracked the frozen blank that had possessed her all day. The future looked empty and lonely, but she would carry on for her father's sake and trust that God would help her, whatever the problems. If only her mother were more sympathetic. Then they could continue the business that her father had worked so hard to build. If they could get another helper, perhaps a girl just leaving horticultural college, they would be able to cope with all that was necessary.

The grounds were laid out, and in spite of the storm there was a lot of money invested in the plants and trees they had developed during the years and the greenhouses that had been built. Her father had taught her so much, and there was no other work that she would rather do. But would her mother give her a chance to prove that she was capable of running the place herself?

The alarm clock awakened her, and she jumped up in a daze, feeling that she had only just fallen asleep. Suddenly she remembered what had happened the day before, and she bit her lip to stop the tears from falling. There was too much to do to feel sorry for herself, and her mother would hate any great emotional outburst.

She pulled on her working clothes, including a thick sweater, for she could see that the window panes were frosted.

She knelt down at her bedside and said simply, "Lord, give me strength and quietness to face what is before me today. Thank You for helping us to get the glass mended and the heat on before the frost last night. Please make Mother understand how much I want to carry on the business Dad has built."

She tiptoed down the stairs, switched on the kettle, raked the kitchen stove and got it glowing, made herself a hot drink, and hurried outside into the dim light.

It was too early to awaken her mother or aunt, and she would need every moment to get the nursery, which was quite extensive, into decent order.

It was still too dark to continue with the damaged trees and shrubs, so she took Beau off his chain and let him run free over the fields at the back. Probably he would have to be kept in the toolshed or his kennel most of the day, as there would be a stream of visitors.

She fastened him on the slip chain again and started to sweep up the leaves that were piled against the walls and scattered all over the lawns, plots, and paths.

She was taking a wheelbarrow to the compost heap when Ron and his son Billie arrived on their bicycles, their breath like steam in the frosty air.

"Miss Anthea, we'll do that," Ron said after pushing his bicycle into a corner. "Billie has the day off, so he wants to help."

"Thank you, Billie. I appreciate that."

At that moment the small breakfast bell rang, and Anthea hurried inside, kicking off her rubber boots and washing her hands before she went into the kitchen.

"You must have been up early," Aunt Kathleen greeted her.

"I did not waken you, I hope. I thought you'd rather sleep than have early tea."

Her mother put a plate of scrambled eggs and toast in front of her. "Thank you for getting the stove going," she said. "Kathleen and I are going to drive into Newbridge this morning. I want some clothes and some other things. Is there anything you need? Would you like me to bring some clothes for you to try on, or will you go in yourself this afternoon? One of us ought to be here in case anyone calls."

"You get what you think I ought to have, Mother. I really haven't time to waste shopping."

"What a strange person you are, Anthea," Aunt Kathleen said with a smile. "Most girls your age would be glad for any excuse to buy new clothes. You really could dress attractively, but your mother and I will do our best. Shops sometimes send out clothes on consignment in these circumstances.''

Anthea kept her eyes on her plate and tried to swallow what was in her mouth. How could her mother and aunt be so casual about what to her was a tragedy? What did clothes matter? Her old winter coat and fur hat would have sufficed as far as she was concerned, but without putting the thought into actual words even in her own mind, she realized that she would have to humor her mother just as her father had done if she hoped to be allowed to continue the business.

''If we are not back for lunch, there is plenty of cold meat and some potatoes you can fry,'' her mother said as she was leaving the table. ''We'll bring extra supplies back with us. I'll bring some wine so that we can offer people something if they call. Your father was always so adamant against alcohol, but everybody expects a drink these days.''

Anthea kept her lips firmly set. She was determined that she would not argue with her mother. From now on what happened in the house would be her mother's affair; all she hoped was that she would be allowed to make the decisions concerning what happened outside.

She collected her tools and continued in the tree section. An hour later the vicar joined her saying, ''Good morning, Anthea. Shall I go on with the stakes?''

''Thank you,'' Anthea said, straightening up and staring over the low wall. There were at least six figures moving about the various plots sweeping, raking, and filling and emptying wheelbarrows.

''Did you bring men with you, Mr. Andrews?''

''No, I came in the car on my own.''

''Then what are all those men doing? I'd better see who they are.''

73

She saw Ron in the big greenhouse digging around the plants with a trowel where the soil had been walked on or disturbed.

"Ron," she said, slipping in the door and closing it quickly to keep in the heat. "Who are all those people working around the place? Did you arrange for them to come?"

Ron shook his head. "Billie is the only one I brought. The rest have come on their own. There are Jack and Johnnie Dalton, Jim Turner and Dick Smith from Melworth, Albert Jackson, and Wally Bell. I guess when word got around about what had happened they thought they could help sweep up if nothing else. Your father had a lot of good friends, Miss Anthea. Folks all admired him. He was never too busy to talk to a man, and he didn't put on airs, even if he was a lot cleverer than most of us. I expect a few others will likely come for an hour when they can."

Anthea's eyes filled with tears, and she said huskily, "How kind of them. But we can't pay them."

"They'd be insulted if you suggested it. Folks are glad to do their part to help at a time like this. That's one of the things I like about living in a village. People may gossip and know your business, but they always rally in time of trouble. I lived in a city once, but nobody even bothered about their next-door neighbor. You go on with your jobs, Miss Anthea. We'll do all the cleaning up."

Anthea felt too touched to speak to anyone, so she slipped into the house, put the kettle on to boil, put the teapot, cups, tea, sugar, and milk on the table, and found a large package of cookies.

Feeling a little more in control, she returned to Ron saying, "Take the men in and give them tea. I can't face them yet, but tell them how grateful I am."

74

"Right. I'll do that as soon as I've finished tidying up this place. Doesn't look as if we've lost many plants after all."

Anthea returned to her work, saying to Mr. Andrews, "Some of these men I hardly know, but they have come of their own accord to help because they loved my father."

The vicar nodded. "No man in the district was more respected. People were very proud to have a man as gifted as he was living among them and treating them as equals. You may not know it, but he helped a lot of people in trouble. He trusted men and lent them what he could when they needed it, and I don't think anyone ever betrayed that trust."

Anthea looked at him in surprise. "So that is why we were sometimes short of money, then at other times there would be sums I couldn't account for. Yet Dad never breathed of what he had done."

Mr. Andrews nodded. "He believed in not letting his left hand know what his right hand did. And you know when anyone in the village was ill or died that your father always sent flowers. He might have made more money if he had wished, but he preferred to make friends."

Anthea could hardly see what she was doing; she had to stop to blow her nose and wipe her eyes. With an effort she went on smoothing on the grafting wax and binding the cracked branches.

"I have to visit old Mrs. Peat in the hospital, Anthea, but I'll be back when I can," Mr. Andrews said and put his hand on her shoulder. "May God be very near you, my dear." Then he hurried off.

"Why are all these strangers poking about?" her mother demanded when she and Kathleen returned with the car piled with parcels. "And why are all these dirty cups in the sink?"

"They have come of their own accord to help with cleaning the place up."

"I suppose they expect payment. Did you give them tea?"

"I left it ready, and Ron made it."

"Well, I certainly don't want a crowd of strange people tramping into my house and poking about. Please thank them, but tell them that you and Ron can manage."

"Eleanor, that is rather foolish," Kathleen said before Anthea could reply. "Why not get the place put in order before the funeral if you can. It will help for the future and cost you nothing."

"Have it your own way then," Mrs. Gordon said angrily, and Anthea slipped out. She was putting on her boots when she heard her aunt's high-pitched voice say, "I'd go slowly, Eleanor, if I were you. You'll have to handle Anthea carefully. She is like her father. She appears quiet and good-natured, but there is a stubborn streak also. You haven't seen the will yet, so maybe you'll need Anthea's help. Don't antagonize her until you know how things stand."

Anthea hurried outside and almost ran to the toolshed, where she fought to keep herself from giving way to the bitterness that overwhelmed her. What was her mother planning? Had she already decided without even consulting her that the house and the business had to be sold? Where would they go, and what would she do?

That was the first time that she had thought of a will. Had her father ever made one? If so, he had never mentioned it, but then he probably never thought he would die so suddenly that there would be no time to do any planning or to make arrangements.

Looking back afterward, Anthea remembered that week as a jumble of very mixed emotions—the quietness and kindness of the villagers; the exhaustion; the ache for her father's comfort and counsel; the cold, businesslike attitude of her mother and aunt; the funeral itself, when the church was packed; the cold reality of the graveside.

Later back at the house where her mother had invited a chosen few acquaintances, Mark had managed to get Anthea alone for a few moments. He took her hand, saying, "I tried to phone several times, but I could never reach you. Thea, I am so sorry. Your father was a very special person, and I know how much you will miss him. If there is anything I can do for you, perhaps in legal matters, will you let me know? Gerry and her father asked me to give you their deep sympathy."

"Thank you, Mark," Anthea said quietly. "I have no idea what is before me. It will all depend on Mother."

"But you promise you'll let me help if I can?"

"I don't think I'll have much choice in my decisions," Anthea replied. "But I appreciate your thoughtfulness. Now I must speak to some of the other visitors before they leave."

"Your mother is marvelous," Mark said as she moved away. "She is so calm and impressive. It is so much easier for other people if there is no violent outburst of emotion in public."

Anthea nodded, her face set, then hurried over to Great-Aunt Ellen who was sitting in a corner by herself. Anthea had driven to Newbridge to bring her for the service and would drive her back as soon as the visitors departed.

5

"Anthea, Mr. Joslin would like to see you and me in the study," Mrs. Gordon said, after speaking to a tall gray-haired man Anthea had not recognized. "Please excuse us. My sister will pour out fresh coffee and drinks if you would like some."

"I'll take you back as soon as I can, Aunt Ellen," Anthea whispered, before she followed her mother into the small study-office that her father had used.

"This will not take long," Mr. Joslin said, opening his case. "I suppose you knew that Mr. Gordon had left his will and legal papers in our possession."

"He never mentioned business matters to me," Mrs. Gordon said, a bitter note in her voice.

"Well, he wasn't particularly businesslike, although he was a very clever man. This will was made immediately after your marriage. It is very clear and simply leaves everything that he possessed to his wife. Later on he used our firm to deal with the legal details of the money his grandmother left him and with which be bought this house and land, but evidently he did not think about changing his will. Of course, I understand Miss Anthea was not born until you had been married for several years."

"May I see the will?" Mrs. Gordon said, holding out her

78

hand. Mr. Joslin handed it to her and looked at Anthea, who had not spoken.

He noticed that her hands were clenched, her face very white, and her lips clamped together. He knew Andrew Gordon had loved his daughter devotedly; from various sources he had gathered that Mrs. Gordon was not in sympathy with the life her husband had chosen. He had seen Mrs. Gordon at different functions but never with her husband or daughter. Why had Andrew Gordon not made another will and left something for this girl who looked so utterly stricken?

The mother appeared to him to be a hard, unemotional type of woman who would consider her own interests first. As Mrs. Gordon read over the terms of the will, his mind wandered to many other occasions when a will had shattered the happiness of the family or there had been fierce recriminations and objections. This business of reading the will to relatives after a person died was one of the parts of his job that he disliked. He had never been intimate with Mr. Gordon, but now he wished that he had mentioned to him that his will was a very ancient one. It had been made before he had had a child, and when he possessed very little beyond a modest house and a small insurance. Since then he had acquired a daughter who had worked hard to help him, a house and property that had greatly increased in value, and had built up a flourishing business.

"This means that I have complete control over the business?" Mrs. Gordon said calmly, handing back the document.

"Yes, you are the sole beneficiary. There will be one or two papers to sign, you will be required to inform the bank, and of course we must have the house, land, and business appraised because there may be death duties. Would you

79

care to leave that in our hands at present? We have the title deeds to the property in our possession.''

''Will it take long before the settlement is complete?''

''A few weeks at most, but in the meantime we will help over the transition period. Will you let us know when it is convenient for you to visit the Newbridge office? I will wish you good afternoon and say again how greatly I sympathize with you on your sudden bereavement. I know that you wish to return to your visitors. I will let myself out.''

''Good afternoon, Mr. Joslin,'' Mrs. Gordon said, opening the door. After he had departed she turned to Anthea, who still sat without moving. ''Pompous creature,'' she exclaimed. ''Anthea, don't stare at me like that. Your father left everything to me, naturally, but you will not suffer.''

''Will you please let me continue with the nursery?'' Anthea begged.

Her mother looked away. ''I am deciding nothing in a hurry. We must find out how we stand financially, but in the meantime we must go on as we are. Believe me, I will do what I feel is best for both of us. It is time we went back, although I expect most people have left by now.''

''Ready, Aunt Ellen?'' Anthea said to the old woman, who sat upright in a straight-backed chair, her face gray but her eyes as penetrating as ever.

''I am sorry that you have this long drive. I could have gone on the bus.''

''Or you could have stayed the night,'' Mrs. Gordon said dryly.

''No, I like my own bed best,'' Aunt Ellen replied. ''At my age strange beds don't make easy resting. Good-bye, Kathleen. Good-bye, Eleanor. You have buried one of God's gentlemen today. He'll be sadly missed.''

She took Anthea's arm, walked slowly down the front

steps, and was helped into the old car. Anthea slipped into the driver's seat, and for a time they drove in silence.

"What are you and your mother going to do, lassie?" Aunt Ellen asked at length.

Anthea shook her head. "I just don't know. I would like to try to continue with the nurseries. If I got another girl to help we'd manage, but Mother hates the place and I am sure that she will sell it and move into town."

"Did Andrew leave a will?"

"Only the one he made soon after he married, leaving everything to Mother. That was long before I was born."

"You mean that he never changed it?"

"No. You know that Dad wasn't really a businessman. I don't suppose it ever occurred to him."

"And I was never bright enough to think of mentioning it to him. Well, dearie, remember that as long as I am alive there will always be a home for you, and I'd be glad for your company. What little I have will be yours when I go, and that may not be far off now. I never thought Andrew would go before me. You are all I've got left in the way of family now."

Anthea managed to summon a smile. "Perhaps I'll need that home sooner than we think. I guess I can get some sort of a job in Newbridge, but I'd hate to be tied to an office or shop all day."

"Best take a day at a time, dearie. When the Lord closes one door, He always opens another. Your mother made no end of fuss when Andrew had to give up teaching, but it meant that he had a life he loved in the open air among growing things. He was never really cut out for the strain of dealing with unruly youngsters. I believe that he was happier these last years since you were able to join in the business than he'd been since he was a young man."

"Why did he marry someone like Mother, Aunt Ellen?"

The older woman glanced at Anthea's strained face and said with a sigh, "It was all a mistake. Andrew was studying for the ministry when the war came and he was called up for service as he had been in the Officer Training Corps when he was at school. He was friendly with a girl called Grace Struthers, although there was nothing definite—no engagement or such—but Mother and I always thought they were just right for each other. However, Grace, who was a nurse, was sent overseas, and so was Andrew after a time; so they were separated.

"Andrew met your mother who was in the Women's Army Corps, and I've got to admit she was a smart and very attractive girl. Andrew fell violently in love, and Eleanor, I suppose, thought Andrew a good prospect and the kind of man any girl would be proud to be seen with. After a very brief engagement they were married when on leave. You have got to realize that life in those days was very uncertain. I guess lots of people were irrational and grabbed at whatever happiness they could get.

"Well, Eleanor certainly wasn't the type to be a curate's wife on a small salary in some inconvenient house. She insisted that your father take up teaching. He went back to the university and took extra biology and zoology courses and had no trouble getting a job. He loved nature, but his heart was never in teaching. Your mother always wanted a busy social life, which he hated.

"It was twelve years before you came, and he could hardly believe it. The night you were born he was more excited than if he had been left a million pounds. He wanted more children, but your mother refused—said she was too old and they looked ridiculous anyway. I guess Andrew turned all his affection on you; in her queer, perverted way

Eleanor was jealous of the closeness between you. She couldn't give the love Andrew needed herself, but she hated anyone else to have his affection. She tried to keep him from visiting Mother and me and hated us to have you for more than the briefest of visits. Andrew never forgot what your grandmother had done for him, and he used to bring you whenever he could, even if it caused trouble. I guess that he gave in to her over most things, but he could be stubborn too.

"He had to give up teaching because of trouble with his voice and throat. Personally, I think it was caused by all the tension and unhappiness at home. This was just after your grandmother died. She left me the old house, and her money was divided between Andrew and me. With his share and what little he had managed to save, Andrew got a mortgage on the house and land where he started the nursery business. You know how hard he has worked to make it the place it is now. I don't know if it still has a mortgage on it or if he has paid it off, but I guess the place is worth twice what he paid for it. Your mother hated going to what she called "the back of beyond," but Andrew just went ahead, and she had to make the best of it. Poor soul, I've often felt so angry at her I could scream, but I'm sorry for her too. She's always been dissatisfied and bitter.

"I guess with both of them it was a case of marry in haste and repent at leisure. They were never suited for each other, and Eleanor always had the feeling of being cheated. Selfish people are always frustrated and unhappy. You'll need to have patience with her like your father had, Anthea. Many a time I have wondered how he put up with the life he had, but after you came he had somebody who made life worth living. If it wasn't that you will miss him so much I could almost feel glad that he is at peace. If he had been an invalid he would have hated to feel that he was a burden, and Eleanor would have had no patience.

"Someday you'll be able to thank God that he went quickly, Anthea. Death is a happy release for many of us, especially when we don't fear what is afterward. Andrew did not talk about it a lot, but his faith was very real. Now he is with the Lord whom he served so quietly."

"Thank you, Aunt Ellen. I understand things better. I've had twenty-two years of happiness with a wonderful father, and, whatever the future holds, no one can take those memories from me. Now here we are. I'll see you in, and we'll have a cup of tea before I drive back. I am sure that you'll be glad to get to bed early."

"Try to believe that God knows what is best for you, dearie," Aunt Ellen said as Anthea was leaving. "Pray for strength to face an upheaval if it has to be. You are too young to be tied down with so much responsibility."

Anthea nodded, then bent down to kiss her wrinkled cheek but could not manage to speak. She ran down the steps, started the car, and bit her lip hard to stop the tears. As she drove home, almost without seeing the road before her, her thoughts were busy as she pondered over what Aunt Ellen had told her. It explained so much she had never understood before. If only her mother would let her go on managing the nursery. Mrs. Gordon could move into town, live near Aunt Kathleen, and lead the kind of life she had always wanted. With another girl they could do the work, and her mother could have the biggest share of the profits. She would work every hour of the day if only she could carry on with the business her father had built. If her mother was determined to sell the house and nursery, perhaps she herself could be kept on by the new owner, even if she had to live in the village. To have to face losing the home and work she loved, as well as her father, was almost more than she could bear.

Aunt Kathleen and her mother were sitting in front of the television set when she went in, but her mother turned it off almost immediately.

"Do you want a meal?" she inquired.

"No, thank you. I had some tea with Aunt Ellen. I'll take Beau out, as he has been tied in all day."

"Maybe we could talk first," her mother said firmly. "Sit down for a few minutes. There is a lot to discuss."

Anthea took off her coat, draped it over the arm of the chair, and sat down with her gaze on the fire, her hands clenched, and her lips set in a straight line.

"We feel that your mother needs a break after the shock she has had," Aunt Kathleen began. "We plan to go away for a couple of weeks if you can arrange for someone to sleep in the house and look after you."

"Ron's Mollie offered to come for a time if I needed her," Anthea replied. "But what about after your vacation, Mother? Will you let me try to carry on the nurseries with Ron and perhaps a girl to help? Dad taught me a lot about the business."

Her mother shrugged impatiently. "Probably you could do it quite as well or better than he did, because he was the most unbusinesslike man I know, but I've served my prison sentence long enough. I don't intend to stay here a day longer than I can help. As soon as I get back we'll put the place on the market, and then as soon as it is sold we'll move into Newbridge."

"Mother, please let me try for a time at least. You need not stay here. You can take the profits, and I'll work harder than I've ever done. Please let me try. I can't bear to think that all Dad's work will go for nothing."

"It won't go for nothing, Anthea. I'll see that we get a good price for it. Maybe you'll have to run it for many months until we find the right buyer, but get it into your head that I am going to sell. I need the money to buy another house and have enough to live on. There is no use arguing. I have always had my mind made up that if anything happened to your father, I'd be out of this place the next day if I could."

"You will be free to live your own life too, Anthea. We both feel that you are too young and attractive to be stuck in a place like this. What sort of life would you have with no opportunity to meet other young people or to find a suitable husband? Believe me, we want what is best for you as well as for your mother," Kathleen added.

"But I love the life I have here. I've been perfectly happy. I don't mind how hard I work if I can stay in the country."

"*You* may have been happy, but I certainly haven't. Your father and you were wrapped up in your plants and in each other, but my wishes never counted. I was just part of the furniture, someone to keep the house clean and have your meals ready on time, but you never seemed to realize that I was bored to death; in fact if I had had to go on much longer I would have had a breakdown."

Aunt Kathleen nodded. "I could see that Eleanor was heading for trouble, and I got her to consult my doctor. He told her only a month ago that she was full of tensions which would lead to serious ulcers, and that she must change her way of life."

"I tried to tell your father this, but all he said was that I could go away with Kathleen or have a vacation whenever I wished, but that you and he loved this place too much to give it up. Maybe you will be shocked, but I had already considered a divorce. I felt that I had fulfilled my obligations. You are old enough to lead your own life, and if your father insisted, you and he could go on without me. Now all that is changed. We can sell the house and the business as a profitable concern. I'll get a smaller, more modern house in Newbridge, and you can find a job there. In the meantime I'll expect you and Ron to get the place put into good shape so that it will attract someone willing to pay a good price. As soon as Kathleen and I return we'll have it appraised and put on the market. Maybe you think me hard, Anthea, but in time you will realize that I am doing what is best for both of us.''

''Very well, Mother,'' Anthea managed to say calmly. ''Now I'll go out with Beau.''

She held her head high, picked up her coat, and hurried out of the room through the kitchen. She caught sight of a figure in one of the greenhouses and saw that it was Ron, but at present she could not face speaking to anyone. She undid Beau's chain and headed for the fields where she could be sure of being alone.

This second blow was almost worse than the shock of losing her father. She felt that she almost hated her mother. How could anyone be so selfish and so unfeeling as to make her suffer as she was doing only a few hours after burying her father? Was it because, as Aunt Ellen said, she had been jealous of the bond that had been between them? Was she deliberately punishing Anthea for being so close to her father?

Her mother had shut herself out of their world. She had shown no interest in what they did, not even in the business that had provided her with many of the luxuries she had demanded. Her father had denied her so little. She had been able to go away whenever she wished, had plenty of expensive clothes, had been able to do whatever she liked in the house, and even last week had been told that she was to get a new car.

Suddenly the tears ran unheeded down Anthea's face as she thought of her father's patient loyalty to the wife who must have disappointed and hurt him a dozen times a day.

Obviously it was useless arguing with her. She had complete possession of everything. If only her father had remembered to make another will giving her a share in the decisions, but obviously he had never thought of it nor envisaged that he would go so suddenly.

There was absolutely nothing that she could do except carry on until the place was sold, but all the joy of the work would be gone. For her father's sake she would get the place in as good order as possible after the storm, but there would be no point in planning further. And what about Ron? He had been so faithful and worked so hard. Maybe she ought to tell him what her mother had planned. It was only fair that he should be free to accept another job if he had the chance.

Beau came dashing back, and Anthea felt a sudden stab of pain. Even Beau would have to go. Her mother detested him, and it would not be fair to try to take him into town. It would be difficult to get someone to take him, because he was so definitely her dog and would be a long time accepting anyone else.

A sob almost choked her as she thought of all she was losing—her father, her home, her work, her good friend Ron, the friends in Bewdley, her dog, and even Mark, who had no use for her now.

Years later Anthea looked back to that evening as the blackest moment of her life. There seemed nothing to live for. Suddenly as if she were beside her, Aunt Ellen's words came to her: "When God closes one door, He opens another."

"Oh, Lord, this door is certainly closed," she said out loud. "At present it doesn't look as if there is any sort of door in front of me, but I've got to go on. I need help. Please give me strength and patience."

Eventually she returned to the kitchen, where Aunt Kathleen was heating milk on the stove. She turned and looked at Anthea's white face and reddened eyelids and said, "Sit down. I'll get you something to eat. You look all eyes. Eleanor has gone to bed. This has been a big strain for her, and you know she isn't as strong as she looks. Try to understand that she is doing what she thinks is best for both of you, Anthea. Andrew never understood her; in fact, they made a mistake in ever getting married. Their temperaments were so different. You took after him, and she has felt lonely and deprived for years. Now she wants to make a happier home for herself and for you. She deserves to have what she wants for the years she has left."

"I haven't any choice but to agree, have I?" Anthea said quietly. "Father was one of the best men who ever lived, but he too must have suffered."

"Probably, but it was his own fault," her aunt said tartly. "Eleanor had it forced on her, and no one can ever say that she didn't do her duty to you both. Andrew became a very different man from the one she thought she had married, but all that is water over the dam now. It is no good dwelling on mistakes of the past. We have got to think of the future. What sort of job would you like?"

"I have no idea. Probably I won't stay in Newbridge. I'd like to work in another nursery, or nature reserve, or something where I'll be out-of-doors."

"Well, it may be some months before you have to leave

here; you should have a good break before you start something else."

"You forget that I'll have no money," Anthea replied.

"Eleanor will settle on something with you when the place is sold so you won't be destitute. You are young and strong and will be able to pick and choose."

Anthea pushed her cup away. Her head was thumping, and she felt that she could not stand any more discussion, so with a hasty good night she hurried up to the peace of her own room and stood for some time staring out the window.

A block of solid ice seemed to have formed in her chest. There were no more tears, and for the time being her mind had gone blank. Automatically she prepared for bed, laying out her working clothes and setting her alarm clock as usual. At least she would have work to do tomorrow, and for the moment her mind could project no further than the urgency of repairing the damage left by the storm. Thanks to the unpaid, unofficial help given so unstintingly, the place did not look too bad on the surface.

6

The next day Anthea told Ron what her mother had decided, and the expression on his face said clearly what he was thinking.

"She has surely decided in a big hurry. Don't you have any say, Miss Anthea?"

"No. Dad never altered his will. The only one was made during the war, just after he married and long before I was born."

"That's a pity after all the work that you and he put into it."

"And you, too, Ron. We owe so much to you, but I wanted to tell you right away so that if you are offered a good job you'll take it. Jack Dalton was saying that he had tried to get you to work for them, but you wouldn't leave us."

"And I won't leave now as long as you are here. I'll wait to see who gets the place before I decide. Somehow I'd like to go on with what we've done between us."

"Could you and Mollie stay here for a couple of weeks while my mother is away? It isn't that I mind being on my own, but I can't do the work and look after the house as well."

"I guess so. Mollie always enjoys a few days up here. Now that Billie is married, she says that she hasn't enough to do. Anyway, I'll ask her."

"And Ron, please don't say anything to anyone yet about selling the place. I am still praying that Mother may change her mind."

Ron nodded, but as he related the news to Mollie over his evening meal he said, "Fat chance there is of 'her ladyship' changing her mind. She's just been itching for the chance to get away from the place—thinks gardening is a lowly job—beneath her dignity. Poor Miss Anthea—lost her young man, her father, and now her home and the place she worked so hard on. You'll come up and look after her for a couple of weeks, won't you? Give the lass a bit of mothering, for that's what she's never had."

"And what about your job?" Mollie demanded.

"I'll stay until the place is sold. Far too much work for Miss Anthea on her own. I'm not worrying after that. Plenty of jobs I can get around here."

"Pity we never managed a daughter," Mollie said, putting a huge helping of rice pudding in front of him. "You are like a hen with one chick over Miss Anthea. I feel the same, and it's no wonder that old Mr. Gordon doted on her, especially when she came to them so late in life."

"Well, Billie didn't turn out so bad, and it wasn't your fault there weren't any more. Maybe Billie and Bridget will give us a crowd of grandchildren to make up."

"Maybe, but mind, no spoiling them. I'll give this place a proper tidy up tomorrow and come up to the nursery the day Mrs. Gordon departs. Couldn't stand being in the house with her. Billie will have to look after the hens—he gets most of the eggs anyway."

The next day Mrs. Gordon and her sister left for Newbridge. "I have papers to sign and arrangements to make about the appraisal," she said crisply when Anthea answered the summons of the dinner bell. "I can't settle down to anything here, and I feel I must get things arranged as

92

soon as possible. I am not sure when I'll be back, but I'll keep in touch. Please see that Mollie keeps the place clean and ready for possible inspection. If I know that anyone is coming to appraise I'll phone you, and I know you'll give them all the information you can. First impressions mean so much, so try to be reasonably dressed and have your hair tidy.''

''Very well,'' Anthea replied, determined not to let her mother guess at the seething emotions that filled her. She was being treated as a servant or a wayward child, but there was nothing to be gained by losing her temper.

''Good-bye, Anthea,'' Aunt Kathleen said when they were in the car. ''Try to get some rest. I'll take care of your mother and help her to unwind.''

''Good-bye,'' Anthea replied and looked at her mother's cold, almost hostile expression.

Was there something wrong with her? Was she ill, or had she transferred the bitterness she had felt against her husband to her daughter?

Aunt Kathleen waved her hand as they moved off; her mother made no sign, but simply looked straight ahead.

Anthea walked back into the spotless kitchen and listened to the empty house. Why did she mind so much if it were sold? Without her father it was only an empty shell, but it was a relief to feel that she was free from her mother for a few weeks. Nothing could be as bad as living with someone who obviously had no love for her. Perhaps her mother did need medical treatment as Aunt Kathleen suggested, but it would obviously be impossible for them to live together unless there was a drastic change in her attitude.

She took a long drink of water and went to find Ron. ''Mother and her sister have gone,'' she said. ''I'll drive down this evening and bring Mollie back. Would eight o'clock do?''

Ron nodded. "What about your evening meal?" he asked.

"I can see to that," Anthea replied. "There are leftovers or eggs in the refrigerator."

They went about their work, but they said very little to each other. Ron had never been talkative, and although there was plenty of work that demanded their attention, all the pleasure had gone. There was no point in doing more than tidying up the place if someone else was going to take over.

As soon as Mollie got into the house Anthea felt a lift in her spirit. She was plump, with a good-natured face and twinkling blue eyes, and she calmly took control. When Anthea returned after giving Beau his nightly run, the house already felt different. The stove burned brightly, the curtains were drawn, and the table was set for their evening snack.

The room looked so much more homey, but her mother would have hated what she called the extra clutter. Ron's newspaper was on the floor, and Mollie's knitting was in the basket chair, which her father had always insisted on using. The stove gave off a good heat, and the kettle was boiling on the top.

"I made some cold meat sandwiches. Tomorrow I'll have a good bake. There doesn't seem to be much in the pantry. What do you like for breakfast, Miss Anthea?"

"Dad liked porridge and eggs, but usually I only have toast."

"Not while I'm here," Mollie said firmly. "You can't work out in the cold all day without a good breakfast inside you."

Anthea summoned up a smile. "I can see you and I are going to have to do as we are told, Ron," she said.

"Well, I've been doing it for nigh on thirty years, and I've survived."

"And you look mighty well on it," Mollie said with a chuckle. "Now you go get your rest, Miss Anthea. I'll clear up. Ron will see that all the lights are off and lock up. Do you want a hot water bottle?"

"No, thank you, Mollie. We have electric blankets on all the beds."

Mollie nodded. "OK for them that fancies them, but I like a boiling hot bottle best. I brought ours with us. Now off you go, and try to have a good sleep."

"Good night, Mollie. I do appreciate your coming like this."

"Makes a nice change for me," Mollie said breezily. "Good night, dearie."

If only her mother had been like Mollie, what a happy home she and her father could have had. Maybe the place wouldn't have been so immaculate, nor the meals so well-cooked and regular, but what did those details matter if there was love in the house?

In the days that followed Anthea missed her father at every turn, but at least her mother was not there to criticize. Even if the meals were haphazard and not so meticulously served, at least the atmosphere was peaceful and sometimes almost gay. Mollie could never be quiet for long, and she had a ridiculous sense of humor.

Mrs. Gordon phoned to tell Anthea that she was going to London for several days and then probably on to Brighton. She had arranged for the appraisal to be put off until after her return. Three weeks later she came home unexpectedly, and the expression on her face showed clearly what she felt about the way Mollie had kept house.

"I've enjoyed being here," Mollie said calmly. "We've managed fine. Probably not as spic and span as you keep it, but you'll soon put it back as you want it. Ron and I like our comfort, and Miss Anthea hasn't complained. I'll get our bits and pieces together and get back to our place. It's small, but it's cozy."

"Anthea will drive you back," Mrs. Gordon replied. "Thank you for your help. I feel much stronger and able to cope now."

"I wish Miss Anthea looked better. I've tried to tempt her with all my best recipes, but she eats like a bird. She looks so frail that I'm afraid she'll blow away."

"We must see that she has a good holiday once this place is sold," Mrs. Gordon answered coldly.

Mollie was busy collecting her geraniums, her knitting, her magazines, Ron's slippers, his tobacco and pipe, and other odds and ends that were scattered around.

Mrs. Gordon shuddered inwardly at the clutter. "I'll go up and unpack," she said. "You arrange with Anthea when you want driving home."

"I'll have to wait until Ron has finished work because he hasn't got his bike here, so I may as well get the supper before I go. I've got a big stew on the stove, and I'm making pancakes."

"Then I think I'll just have a tray of tea and toast in my room," Mrs. Gordon said flatly. "My head aches, and I'd be glad to be quiet."

Mollie made a face at the door as it closed.

"Stuck-up misery," she muttered. "Doesn't deserve a daughter like Miss Anthea. I wish I'd left the house like a pigsty. She'll probably think it's like that anyway. I bet she'll go around polishing every bit of furniture and scrubbing the floors in case there is a crumb anywhere. I wouldn't stay and work for her if she paid me a hundred pounds a week, and the sooner Ron gets away, the better."

She took a tray upstairs, pushed their stuff into their

suitcase, put clean sheets on the beds, and went downstairs again. She set the kitchen table, mixed up the pancake batter, set the pan on the stove, and rang the supper bell.

Ron and Anthea came in almost together, kicked off their dirty boots, washed their hands, and sat down at the table. Mollie ladled out huge platefuls of stew and poured the batter into the pan.

"I can't eat all this, Mollie," Anthea protested.

"Well, eat as much as you can. You need filling up, girl, or the next strong wind will blow you away."

She busied herself at the stove and waited while Anthea ate most of her stew and a small pancake. Finally she said, "Your mother is back."

"But where is she, and how did she get here?" Anthea demanded.

"Her sister brought her, but she had to get back to some sort of social or concert or something. She's having a tray with tea and toast in her room. She couldn't face my cooking and said she wanted peace and quiet. You are to drive Ron and me home as soon as I've cleaned up."

Anthea flushed. "But, Mollie, surely you need not go tonight. Why not wait until tomorrow?"

"Bless you, Miss Anthea. Don't you worry about me. I'm not upset. I've enjoyed being with you, but your mother and I don't exactly click, and I'd rather be in my own house. I like being my own boss."

"Best for us to go now that she's back," Ron said calmly. "You know that we'll always come anytime you are on your own."

"I'll help you clean up then," Anthea said, her heart heavy with dread at what she had to face.

"I'll be through in a few minutes," Mollie said firmly. "Ron, bring down our case and put the stuff in the car. You go up and see your mother, Miss Anthea. By that time we'll be ready."

Anthea straightened her shoulders and went upstairs feeling as if she were going to be executed. She tapped on her mother's door and went in.

The tray was untouched at the bedside table, and her mother was busy with a dust cloth and polish.

"Hello, Mother, this is a surprise," Anthea said, going toward her mother who offered her cheek to be kissed. "I did not know you intended to come back today."

"That is fairly obvious," her mother said tartly. "I decided to come tonight as a man is coming from the estate agent tomorrow to appraise the house and business. I was afraid that if I did not come myself, the place would be in a mess, and it certainly is. I'll have my work cut out to make it look respectable by tomorrow afternoon. I don't know how you can live in such slovenly surroundings."

"Mollie doesn't clean and cook like you, Mother, but she has looked after us quite well."

"Maybe, but it is a good thing I came back when I did. I hope you will drive them home as soon as possible."

"They are leaving now. I'll finish anything else that has to be done when I get back. I hope you feel better."

"Perhaps a little, but there is so much to do and arrange. I'll be glad when all the upheaval of the sale and the move are over."

"Can I get you anything before I go?"

"No, thank you. I'll make myself fresh tea later. I don't fancy what Mollie brought me. I don't believe that the cup is properly washed. Has business been good?"

"Very good. I believe people have even bought plants and ordered stuff they don't really need just to show their sympathy."

"Good. The larger the takings, the better."

Anthea went out hurriedly, afraid of exploding at her mother's lack of gratitude for the kindness that had been shown by people who were almost unknown to them. She hadn't even the good manners to come down and say good-bye to Mollie and to thank her for her help.

A wave of bitterness was tying her in knots, and she was appalled at some of the thoughts that filled her mind. She would have to pray continually for patience and strength to guard her tongue. More and more she realized that this was the only way her father had managed to keep peace in the home.

When Anthea returned, her mother was mopping the kitchen floor, and a smell of disinfectant pervaded the house.

"It will take ages to get rid of the smell of Ron's pipe. He knows I have always objected to him smoking inside. I don't mind cigarette smoke, but pipe tobacco is so strong."

"I'll finish outside and let Beau have his run," Anthea said. "I can help you when I come back if you like."

"I can manage. I can work faster on my own."

Anthea pulled on her old duffle coat and a pair of warm gloves; it was bitterly cold outside. She sighed as she thought of the warm, cozy evenings she had had with Ron and Mollie. She would be back to "martial law" from now on, and the less time she spent in the house the better.

The next day, with the house back to perfection, her mother welcomed the estate agent graciously, showed him around the house while he took copious notes, and introduced him to Anthea as Mr. Matthews. She asked Anthea to show him the nurseries, the greenhouses, and to explain the layout and methods of working.

He was a short, thin man, with rather a long nose and eyes that missed nothing. Anthea escorted him around, then took him back inside where her mother had coffee and drinks set out in the lounge. Anthea did not offer to stay. She was in her working clothes and knew her mother's views on sitting on her precious furniture unless properly dressed. As she left she heard Mr. Matthews say, "Fine place you have here, Mrs. Gordon. I realize that this won't be the best time of the year to sell a place like this, but we will start on the advertising. Probably it will be spring until we get a really good offer and the new owner can take over. I'll send one of my assistants to take photographs and measurements."

Anthea deliberately lingered in the hallway. She needed to hear what was happening and when the sale was being planned.

"I hope we won't have to wait too long. I'd like to leave here as soon as possible, but on the other hand I need to get a good price. I must buy another house, and I'll have to live on what capital I have left."

"Will your daughter and the gardener be able to carry on so that everything is in good order?"

"My daughter would like to keep the place just as it is and try to run the business herself, but I cannot stand the isolation now that my husband has gone. I want a small, modern, easily-run house, and it will be better for Anthea to be free."

"She is young and very attractive," Mr. Matthews replied. "Not many girls would care for so much hard work, especially in the winter. However, I am glad that the grounds will be kept in good order. So often when the owner dies, a place gets run-down, and that reduces the value. Now I must go. I'll let you have my rough appraisal as soon as possible, and we'll work from there. Call me at my office if you have any questions, and I'll let you know about my assistant's visit or if any prospective customer turns up. Good morning, Mrs. Gordon."

Anthea was back in the greenhouse when Mr. Matthews drove off, but for several minutes she could not see the plants as tears streamed down her face.

What a farce for her mother to pretend that she was only selling because she missed her husband, and all that she seemed to need her for was to keep business going so that it would fetch a big price. Only the thought that it was her father's work that would suffer kept her from packing up immediately. For his sake she and Ron would carry on until someone else could continue what he had begun.

7

The weeks went by with cold, bitter winds, and most of the work was done in the greenhouses, although leaves had to be swept up continually, paths kept tidy, and beds prepared for spring planting when the soil was soft enough to work.

Occasionally someone came to look over the house and grounds, and one or two tentative offers were made, but nothing was finalized.

Christmas passed with very little festivity. Anthea attended church and sang as usual in the choir. In the afternoon she drove her mother to Kathleen's while she herself went on for tea with Great-Aunt Ellen, as she and her father had always done.

She was glad when the season of so-called "goodwill" was over, and she was back into the routine of work. Still in her heart she hoped that something would happen to change her mother's mind. Perhaps no one would offer what she thought a big enough price, or she might decide to move in with Aunt Kathleen and let Anthea and Ron carry on. The subject was never raised between them, but after Christmas she sensed a change in her mother. She was out more often, had more new clothes, and there was a sparkle about her that Anthea had never seen before.

As spring approached and the ground began to take on more color, there was quite a stream of prospective buyers. Mr. Matthews or one of his assistants often asked Anthea to show them over the grounds. One man, Mr. Jennings, came several times. Mrs. Gordon was certain that he was seriously interested but was going to try to get the price reduced if he waited.

Anthea began to dread his visits. He pretended a great interest in all that her father had done and asked innumerable questions, but he was too familiar and never missed an opportunity to touch her when they were alone. He had a nursery on the other side of Newbridge, which his father had run for years.

"Dad is like you, Miss Gordon. He likes experimenting with plants and spends far too much time on what doesn't bring any profit. Now I'm all for the business side. I employ men to do the work while I go out and sell. I have booths in the markets in Newbridge, Ansbury, and Linton. But our place is too small. We could do so much more with all the land you have here."

Anthea listened but showed no interest. She asked, "Is there anything else I need to show you, Mr. Jennings? I have to drive into Newbridge for various supplies."

"I have my car here. Let me drive you, take you to lunch, and bring you back."

"No, thank you," Anthea replied firmly. "I would rather go at my own pace. Besides, you would have to make a wasted journey back."

"Believe me, it would not be wasted. I would enjoy your company."

"I am sorry, but it is still no. I am going to spend some time with my great-aunt."

"Well, I'll hope for better luck next time."

"Now I must change and get going," Anthea said. "Good morning, Mr. Jennings."

"George is the name. It would sound more friendly as we are both in the same trade and may be doing business together in the future."

Anthea shook her head. "I won't be in this business much longer."

She walked firmly to the house, leaving George Jennings to find his own way out. She hoped sincerely that he would never get his hands on the place. There was something about him she detested.

Two days later he was back again, and he caught Anthea in the large greenhouse before she saw him arrive. "Morning, Miss Anthea. I'm here again, you see. I want to bring my father to see this place. Can you arrange a suitable time?"

"Better ask my mother about it. She is attending to the sale."

"But you are the one who knows most about the business, and it is that, not the house, that we are really interested in."

"I am here any time," Anthea said, trying to move to the door. "If I am not, Ron, our helper, knows more than I do."

Suddenly he grasped her hands. "Anthea, I'd like us to carry on this business together. I've fallen for you and want to marry you."

Anthea turned pale and tried to pull her hands away. "Please let me go," she said angrily. "You must be crazy."

"Why should I be? I've never met a girl like you before. We could make a good partnership. We'll sell our place, give your mother her share, and you won't have to part with anything. Your mother told me how upset you are at having to sell the place your father and you have worked on for so long."

"I certainly have no intention of marrying just to keep the nurseries," she said hotly.

"But you don't know me. Why turn me down flat? Let me take you out to dinner, and we'll get acquainted. Maybe I've rushed you, but I knew the moment I saw you that you were the girl that I wanted for my wife."

"I think you have made a mistake," Anthea said cuttingly. "I have no share in the business or house. Everything belongs to my mother. I will have nothing besides what I can earn at whatever job I can get."

"I don't believe that. Your mother led me to understand that you would get your share."

Anthea caught sight of Ron pushing a wheelbarrow just outside, and she called loudly, "Ron, will you come here a minute?"

Mr. Jennings dropped her hands and flushed angrily.

"Ron, will you answer any more questions Mr. Jennings has to ask. I need to take that stuff to Bewdley."

"I know all I want to know," the other replied rudely and stomped off to his car.

"If that man ever comes here again, Ron, don't leave me alone with him."

Ron looked at her blazing eyes and gave a half smile. "Nasty bit of work, he is. Mollie's cousin used to work for him. Said he expected the men to work like slaves but did nothing except drive about himself. He was married and had two kids, but his wife left him because he was always chasing other women. He's a bad-tempered brute when he's had a few drinks."

Anthea nodded, then managed to laugh. "He asked me to marry him."

"Blooming idiot!" Ron muttered.

"I'd rather scrub floors," she said putting her shoulders back. "Anyone would be desperate to take him on."

When she went for lunch her mother looked at her questioningly. "Wasn't Mr. Jennings here?"

"Yes."

"Why did he not come to talk about the sale to me? I felt he was the most likely prospect we have had yet."

"He wanted to be your son-in-law."

She stared at Anthea's face, then said calmly, "Very flattering. I hope you did not turn him down flat and so terminate the business negotiations."

"I certainly did. If that man comes here again I'll disappear immediately. Do you know that he has been married and had two children but was so impossible that his wife left him? Also he drinks heavily."

"How do you know all that?"

"One hears things about people in the same line of business."

"And I suppose you lost your temper?"

"Not exactly, but he knows how I feel."

"You are so naive, Anthea. You could have gone out with him once or twice or strung him along until the sale had been finalized."

Anthea stared at her mother, then said coldly, "The house and grounds may be on display and up for sale, but I am not. If he ever comes again, you must deal with him. I refuse to have him near me. I hate men who maul me and are so free with their hands. Besides, he had the idea that I had half share in the profits. He was certainly deflated when I informed him that I would only have what I earned from whatever job I can get when I finish here."

Anthea pushed her chair back quickly and without touching the dessert her mother had put in front of her she said, "I am going to Newbridge to see Aunt Ellen tomorrow. Can I take the car?"

"I suppose so. I have been invited out for dinner, and I'm being picked up. You might leave a parcel at Kathleen's for me if you are going to Newbridge."

Anthea had noticed that her mother had been out to dinner or lunch several times lately, but she had never said who her friends were or brought them to the house.

One day when Anthea returned from Newbridge where she had gone to collect various items they required, Ron said, "That Mr. Towers from Tall Timbers was here with the agent while you were out. He poked around a bit, but he knows the place pretty well anyway. Then his daughter came and both of them were in the house a long time."

"I wonder why they are interested," Anthea said slowly, but it was as if an icy hand gripped her heart. Gerry and Mark were still looking for a house, she knew, and she had been told by Mark's mother when she had met her that morning in Newbridge that the wedding was to be in June. Surely they weren't interested in the Rookery Nurseries. What use would they be to them?

Three days later Mrs. Gordon announced with great excitement that she had been offered even more than she had hoped for, and it only remained for the various papers to be signed.

"Who is the buyer?" Anthea managed to ask.

"Mr. Towers. He is buying the house and grounds as a wedding present for his daughter."

"But what on earth will they do with all the plots and greenhouses?" Anthea asked flatly.

"Well, that is really their business and can be gone into later. He wants you to sell as many of the young trees and shrubs as you can. They will have a landscape gardener come to plan the grounds for them. They will keep one greenhouse at least, but Gerry wants a tennis court and land for the horses she hopes to breed. This is the best place they

107

have found. It isn't too far for Mark to travel each day either and is quite near Tall Timbers.

The color had drained from Anthea's face, and her mother turned away from the stricken look in her eyes. "You mean all Dad's work will be destroyed?"

"I don't see it like that. Because of his work the value of the property has increased enormously. Many of the plants will be used in the landscaped garden, but new owners have the right to do what they like with what they buy."

"Then Ron and I have just been wasting our time all winter and spring."

"Ron has been paid, and you will get a share of what I receive."

"When do we leave?" Anthea asked, and her mother dropped her eyes.

"As soon as we can. Gerry and Mark hope to be married in June, and they want the alterations in the house finished by then. The grounds can be done by degrees."

"And where will we live?"

Again Mrs. Gordon looked away and said hurriedly, "Alan Towers has asked me to marry him, and I have accepted. We will live at Tall Timbers for the present, but both of us hope in time to get a smaller house in the vicinity and an apartment in London. We will probably travel a great deal as Alan still has many business interests, but there will always be a home for you, either in our house or apartment. It is the beginning of a completely new life for me and freedom for you."

Anthea stared at her mother's back, unable for some time to take in what she had said.

"Are you not going to say you are glad for me, Anthea?" her mother said, turning to look at her.

"I hope you will be happy, Mother," Anthea managed at last. "It is a shock, but I guess I'll get used to it in time."

"It need not affect you, except that life will be much more happy and easy for you. You know how I've always longed to travel again as I did during the war, and how I love a busy social life. I'll have all that with Alan, and I mean to enjoy every minute before I get too old. I am only fifty-six. Alan is sixty, but we should have many active years left."

"I think we ought to tell Ron what has happened," Anthea said after a few moments of awkward silence. "He should have the chance to look for another job."

"Alan suggested that I ask him to stay on here as gardener. They will need someone who knows the job; whatever else Ron lacks, he is a good worker. Perhaps you would put it to him, Anthea. You understand him better than I do."

"Very well," Anthea said, getting up and moving like an old woman. Her legs were weak, and she felt that she had aged twenty years since she had entered the house. She collected her tools and went on potting plants in the big greenhouse, but her hands worked automatically. What was the point of doing anything? These very pots would be sold off cheaply, the greenhouse which had cost so much pulled down, and all the plants her father and she had collected and loved would be scattered or thrown away. In their place would be manicured lawns, a tennis court, stables, and land for Gerry's horses. Worst of all was the thought that Mark, whom she had loved for so long and with whom she had shared all her growing-up years, would be sharing her home with Geraldine Towers. If her mother had plotted deliberately she could not have devised anything that would cause Anthea more suffering.

She threw down her trowel, pulled off her gloves, and scrubbed her face with a tissue. From now on she would have only two ideas in view—first, that no one would guess what this arrangement meant to her, and second, that she would move away and start her own life, free from her mother and any reminders of Mark, as soon as possible.

Ron looked at her pale, drawn face when she tracked him down where he was digging a bed ready for planting. He stuck in his spade and came toward her.

"Anything up, Miss Anthea?"

"Mr. Towers has bought the house and land as a wedding present for his daughter."

"You mean that she'll run the nurseries?"

"No, everything will be scrapped," Anthea said briefly. "A landscape gardener will lay out the grounds with a tennis court, lawns, and at the back there will be stables and land for the horses Miss Towers hopes to breed. My mother is going to marry Mr. Towers and live with him at Tall Timbers until they get an apartment in London. I am to ask you if you would stay on as gardener."

"Not likely," Ron said vehemently. "I'll be giving in my week's notice on Saturday. I have only stayed on to help you, and I wouldn't work for them if they offered me three times the wages I am getting now. But where will you live?"

"I don't know yet. I'll probably stay with Great-Aunt Ellen until I decide on a job. I'll have to stay here until the plants are sold; then I'll be free to make my own life. I certainly won't live with my mother and Mr. Towers."

"Mollie has been at me to tell you that if you are ever stuck, we've got a spare bedroom since Billie married, and she'd love to look after you."

Anthea gulped and finally managed to say "Tell Mollie that I'll not forget. I may need that room one day; even if I don't, I'll call to see you whenever I am near Bewdley. You've been a wonderful friend to Dad and me, Ron."

110

"Did you ask Ron about staying on to work for Gerry and Mark?" Mrs. Gordon asked as Anthea sat down to a supper that she felt would choke her.

"He is handing in his notice on Saturday."

Her mother flushed angrily. "I don't suppose you encouraged him to stay. However, Alan may be able to persuade him. Jobs aren't that easy to get."

"Ron has been offered several, but he wouldn't leave as long as we needed him."

"Oh, well, there will be plenty of others glad for the place, especially if they fix up a flat for a married couple—a woman to do the housework and cooking and a man for the grounds and to help with the horses. These things are easily managed when there is plenty of money."

"Mark won't have much," Anthea said bluntly.

"Alan is settling a good allowance on Gerry. They won't have to manage on Mark's small salary."

"Poor Mark!" Anthea said, then immediately regretted her remark.

"Poor Mark, indeed!" her mother snapped back. "He's a very lucky young man. How many years would it have taken him to be able to afford a property such as this will be when they have modernized it? He is also getting an unusually attractive wife. Personally I think Gerry could have done better for herself, but that is her business. I am sure that Mary Latham won't be allowed to interfere. She is preening herself like a peacock at present, but Gerry will be the ruling force in that marriage."

Anthea did not reply. It was better to keep her thoughts to herself, but she was seeing Mark in a new light these days. He had always been dominated by his mother; now it was to be his wife who would take over where his mother left off.

At present he was so infatuated that everything in his life was lovely, but how long would he be able to tolerate playing second fiddle? Gerry would always be able to call the shots as the house and land were hers, and she would not have to depend upon Mark for money.

She imagined what her father's remarks would be about the struggle Mark would have when pushed on one side by his mother and pulled on the other by his wife and father-in-law. He would be a puppet on a string.

Had he always been weak? Looking back she thought of how close they had been and realized that until Mark had moved to Newbridge they had always seemed to have the same ideas. They had never quarreled, and she had thought that Mark was the kindest boy in their class. Now she realized that it might have been weakness even then. Perhaps he hadn't the strength of character to stand up for himself and had been too easily persuaded instead of deciding for himself.

If I ever marry, Anthea thought wryly, *I want a man I can admire, someone who might not always agree with me, but with whom I can argue yet retain my own personality.* She remembered her father's words, *"I don't want you to make a mistake like I did."* Whose fault was it that his marriage had been such a travesty? Was it because her mother had wanted to change his nature and his way of thinking? In their own way both had been strong-minded. Her mother had become cold and bitter, while her father had refused to change but had grown quiet, and there had been no real link of affection between them. Would Mark become like that in time, or would he allow Gerry to force him into a brilliant social world for which his kindly nature was never designed? Even if there was a weakness there, Anthea knew there were depths of kindness also. Mark was following in his father's footsteps, marrying a woman who would never make him happy but would push him or force him up and on in the social scale.

112

"Anthea, you aren't listening," her mother said irritably.

"Sorry, Mother, I was miles away," she replied. "What was it you said?"

"I was suggesting that we put an advertisement in the local newspapers concerning the sale of the shrubs, trees, and bedding plants. This is a good time to sell. Will you draft one, and I'll take it in tomorrow?"

"What about the tools and machinery?" Anthea asked.

"We'll wait until we ask Alan and Gerry what they want to keep. They will probably prefer new electric lawn mowers and hedge trimmers. Some of ours, I imagine, are rather outdated."

Anthea nodded. "Yes, I imagine they'll want to start with everything new. What about the van and the car?"

"The van can be sold, and you can keep the car if you like when Alan and I are married. He is buying me a new one for my wedding present."

On Saturday morning the place was beseiged with customers who had seen the advertisement. Even Mrs. Gordon condescended to go into the office and take the money since Anthea and Ron were so busy outside.

By late afternoon the stream of cars had slackened, but there were still customers walking around, picking out what they thought were good buys.

Anthea was helping to carry some azaleas to a waiting car when she noticed Alan Towers, Gerry, Mark, and Max Sinclair drive in. She gave a brief wave and hurried back to some people who were choosing hydrangeas.

"I must go in now, Anthea," her mother said. "Anyway, we are going out for dinner. I did not realize it was so late, and I must have a bath. I feel filthy. Will you be able to manage?"

"I don't suppose there will be many more."

She went on doggedly until it was almost dark. Ron left, and she started to lock up but hesitated as a tall figure walked up the drive.

"It is only me," Max Sinclair said.

"I thought you had gone out for dinner."

"Not me. I only came because my stepfather wanted me to see what they propose doing with the house. You must be tired out after today's rush. What about a quick cleanup and going out for a meal instead of having a snack on your own?"

"I am too tired, and I still have to take Beau for his nightly run. But thank you for inviting me, Mr. Sinclair."

"That's a bit stiff isn't it, considering we are going to be relations of a sort?"

"It's hardly likely that we'll see much of each other. I won't be around. I'd like to move miles away from here where there are no reminders. Do you realize what it has meant today—to see plants we have grown and cherished bundled off as if it were a rummage sale? My father spent years making this place what it is; now it will all go under the bulldozer, but I hope I will not be here to see it."

"Have you another job lined up?"

"That is my business."

"Maybe, but we are going to have to bump into each other at times, unless you cut yourself off from your mother altogether. Believe me, someday she'll need you."

"What do you mean?"

"My stepfather is not a comfortable person to live with. There will come a time when she will need her daughter."

"I don't know how she can marry a man like Mr. Towers after having my father for her husband."

"He can be very charming when he chooses, and he has quite a lot to offer to attract a woman who has had rather a restricted life. He is losing his beloved daughter and probably feels that your mother will be easily molded to take her place.''

''Why do you visit him if you feel as you do, Mr. Sinclair?''

''Don't you think you had better call me Max as we are going to be part of the same devoted family?''

''Because my mother is marrying your stepfather does not really mean anything to you and me.''

''Have you any other relations to go to?''

''I don't want to be rude, but I've already told you that what I do is not your business.''

''OK, but don't forget that I'm willing to help you, and no strings attached.''

''Why?''

''Because I know what my stepfather can do to people. I saw what he did to my mother.''

''I still don't understand why you visit him if you feel so bitter.''

''Not bitter, only realistic. I have tried to keep an eye on Gerry, but she is tough and can take care of herself. Besides, her father has always given her whatever she wanted.''

''Yes, even another person's home,'' Anthea said bitterly.

''Someone else would have bought it if my stepfather hadn't.''

''Someone who would have carried on the business and not destroyed all my father's work. I could have done it myself if my mother had not been tempted to sell because she was offered such a big price.''

''But you don't want to spend all your life in isolation struggling to pay expenses, do you? What would happen if you become ill or want to get married?''

115

"There is no point in going on with this conversation, since I have not been consulted."

"Well, I repeat my offer. If you need help I'm available, if only because I'd like to even up what my stepfather is doing to you. Good night, Anthea."

Anthea turned away quickly, her eyes suddenly full of tears. She would hate to accept help from any of the Towers family, but the only person who seemed concerned about her was someone connected with the people who were taking everything and everyone she cared about.

8

On Sunday morning just as Anthea was leaving for church, Alan Towers arrived with Gerry, Mark, and an architect named Rowlandson.

"Only day we could all get together," Mark explained, stopping to speak to Anthea as she was driving out of the garage. "Didn't your mother mention that we were coming?"

"No. I expect she hoped I would have left."

"I'm sorry if you are upset, Thea, but this is the most suitable place we could find."

"I have no say in what happens," Anthea said coldly. "I hope you'll be happy here, but you, more than anyone, knew what the nurseries meant to Dad and me. I'm late, Mark, so good-bye."

"Mark, are you coming? We need your opinion," Anthea heard Gerry call and saw in the mirror that she put her hand possessively on his arm and propelled him inside.

Anthea found it almost impossible to concentrate on the service that morning. *What is being planned? How soon can I get away from these painful reminders? Why should I bother to go on?*

When she got back, her mother looked radiant.

"This house will be wonderful when all the alterations are finished. It will be just as I always wished I could have it."

117

"When will you be married?" Anthea demanded.

"Alan would like me to stay here and superintend the work to be done. He thinks that someone should be on the spot, so probably we won't be married until after Gerry's wedding."

"But that isn't for two months. I must get a job before that. There is no point in going on with the work here after we've sold the plants and stuff. Ron is leaving next Saturday, so I'll be looking for another job then. Surely Gerry can drive over every day and see that her wishes are carried out properly."

"Probably she could, but Alan thinks that I have more experience in dealing with workmen. Besides, we want to be free when we are married. You can take a break until I am ready to leave. I can hardly remain here by myself."

"Aunt Kathleen could stay with you."

"Not when the house is all messed up. No, I need you here."

"I'm sorry, Mother, but if I hear of a suitable job I'll have to accept it."

"Where do you propose to live?"

"Probably with Aunt Ellen for a time."

"She'll be delighted to have an unpaid servant. You'll probably end up being a nurse as well, and believe me, she is a difficult, crotchety old woman. She'll be glad to have you, if only to spite me. She has always hated me for marrying your father, and she'll be glad to tell you that I ruined his life. She never forgave me for coming between him and the girl she had picked out for him."

"She has always been kind to me."

Her mother set her lips in a tight, thin line, and Anthea said hastily, "Can I have the car for the rest of the day?"

"Yes, but I need it tomorrow. You can always use the van."

118

Anthea had several advertisements for job vacancies she had cut out of the *Newbridge Gazette,* but Sunday was not the day for making inquiries. Only one really appealed to her. A woman was required to sell flowers and plants in a florist's shop. She knew the shop but had not visited it because they had not needed to buy from an outside source. On impulse she drove over to look at the location. The window display was not as good as it might have been, as the flowers and colors were all jumbled together, but it was hardly fair to judge on a day when the place was closed.

Evidently someone lived on the premises, and after a quick prayer Anthea decided to ring the bell.

The door at the side of the shop was opened by a man of about forty who had once been handsome but now was flabby and unkempt.

"I know I ought not to disturb you on Sunday afternoon, but I wonder if the vacancy you advertised is filled. I could not get here sooner."

"No one suitable has applied. You'd better come in and meet my wife."

Anthea followed him down a narrow passage and into a room at the back of the shop that was obviously their living room. A woman was propelling herself in a wheelchair between the table and the sink.

"Jean, this young lady has come about the job. Maybe you'd like to talk to her."

"I ought not to have come at such an awkward time," Anthea said, feeling very embarrassed. "But I was not free yesterday, and I was driving past today so I thought I'd call to inquire if the vacancy had been filled."

"Sit down," the woman said, pointing to the worn settee while her husband flopped down in an old armchair.

"Have you had experience in this sort of work?" he demanded.

"Not exactly in a shop," Anthea replied. "I am Anthea Gordon, and until my father died some months ago we ran the Rookery Nurseries near Bewdley. Now my mother is selling the place and is getting married again, so I am out of a job."

"That's tough," the wife said. For the first time Anthea looked into her face and saw how tired but kind her eyes were. "At any rate you must know a great deal about flowers and potted plants, and those are our main trade. We do wreaths for funerals and bouquets for weddings too."

"I am afraid that I haven't had any experience in that area," Anthea replied.

"That's OK. Jean sees to all those. She can manage if the stuff is put within easy reach."

"Yes, fortunately only my legs are crippled. I can still use my hands."

"Is it arthritis?" Anthea asked sympathetically.

"No. I was in a car crash, and my spine was damaged, but I'm thankful that I am not absolutely helpless."

"She's a marvel," her husband said glibly. "She can do almost everything in the house besides doing the floral arrangements for bouquets and wreaths. Of course I can't leave her for long, and we've got to have someone for the counter work. We've got to discuss wages, but when could you commence work if our terms are agreeable?"

"Not for two weeks—until we have sold the rest of the nursery stuff."

"Isn't the new owner taking that over?"

"No. He is having the property completely gutted. The business is finished. Tennis courts will be laid out instead of the nursery beds."

"That's a shame," Jean said. "I guess we could manage another two weeks, Bert. There won't be many folks who will know as much as Miss Gordon. We supply overalls, and you can take your midday meal with us. Have you got someplace to live?''

''I will be staying with my great-aunt, and I think I'd like to go to her for my meal. It would mean she would get more regular food. I am sure she doesn't look after herself properly at present.''

Mr. Thompson stated the salary that they had paid other assistants but offered to increase it as he found her work satisfactory.

The amount sounded very meager, but Anthea agreed to come on a month's trial and stated that if she proved satisfactory she would expect her salary to be at least three pounds a week more than he had offered.

Jean said quickly, ''We'll gladly pay that for the right person. I'm glad you can stick up for yourself.''

Her husband flashed her an annoyed glance. ''We'd be bankrupt tomorrow if you had to run the business,'' he said sharply.

''Then we'll expect you two weeks from tomorrow,'' his wife said hastily. ''I think I'll enjoy having you about the place, my dear. You are different from the usual type we get—more superior—and I'm sure that we'll suit each other.''

''Thank you,'' Anthea said, getting up and making for the door. Mr. Thompson followed her and held out his soft, pudgy hand. ''We'll seal the bargain. I agree with Jean, poor soul. We'll enjoy having you join our little family. Call or phone if you want to know any more.''

''Thank you,'' Anthea repeated and hurried to the car, while Bert Thompson stood watching her from the doorway.

Had she done the right thing in agreeing to their arrangements? She felt sorry for the wife and believed that they could be friends, but she was certainly not attracted to the husband. At present, however, she could not afford to pick and choose. If she could not stand the job she would have the opportunity of looking around. Her mother would be annoyed, but she only needed her to suit her own and Gerry's convenience. When her usefulness was finished, they wouldn't care what happened to her.

She had not seen Aunt Ellen for over two weeks as they had been so busy with the sale. It was a long time before she heard the faltering steps come to open the door. She was shocked at the change in the old woman, who had always been so energetic and independent.

"Aunt Ellen, have you been ill?" Anthea asked, closing the door and putting her arm around her shoulders, which felt as if all the flesh had gone from her bones.

"I've not been myself, and last night I was bad."

"But why did you not phone?"

"You had enough trouble at present, lassie."

"Lie down again," Anthea said, pushing her onto the couch where she had been lying and pulling the throw rug over her. "Can I make you some tea? Have you had anything to eat today?"

"As much as I want," she replied. "But I'd love a drink of tea now, although maybe I'll not be able to keep even that down. I've been sick these last few days."

"Have you seen a doctor?"

"Awhile back. He gave me some medicine and tablets, but I know that it is only old age, and I'm not going to be put in the hospital and let them experiment on me at my age."

Anthea made tea and toast, but after a few sips Aunt Ellen shook her head. "I don't want any more."

"I think that you ought to be in bed," Anthea said firmly. "I'm going to get your bed warm and put you there. Is the pain easier when you undress and lie down?"

"Sometimes, but sometimes I'm glad to get up."

Anthea ran upstairs and looked at the crumpled bed. Aunt Ellen had always been so particular, even fussy; how it must irk her to be unable to look after herself. She changed the sheets, switched on the electric blanket she and her father had given Aunt Ellen several Christmases ago, and found a clean nightdress.

"Let me help you upstairs, Aunt Ellen," she said, bending over the emaciated figure who was lying with her eyes closed. "I am going to stay with you tonight and call the doctor tomorrow. You can't stay on your own like this."

"But your mother will be annoyed, and what about your work?"

"Mother is on top of the world at present, and the work has almost left me. My only worry is Beau, but Mother will have to let him out even if she doesn't like the poor animal."

She helped Aunt Ellen into bed, sponged her face and hands, put a basin nearby, and went to the phone. There was no reply, so reluctantly she called Tall Timbers, and it was Gerry who answered.

"This is Anthea Gordon speaking. Is my mother there?"

"No, she and Dad are out but will be back for dinner."

"Could you tell her that I am at Aunt Ellen's? I am going to stay the night as she is very ill. I will call the doctor in the morning if there is no improvement. And could you ask her to let Beau off his chain for a spell?"

"OK, Anthea, I'll do that. By the way, what do you intend doing about the dog?"

"I don't know. Probably he'll have to go back to the kennels to be retrained and sold."

"Then would you mind if Mark and I keep him? I'm not really keen on Dobermans, but we'll need a watchdog, and I

123

guess that he'll get used to us after you have gone, as Mark says he doesn't really want anyone except you at present."

Anthea clutched the receiver and held her breath. One more of her possessions that Gerry and Mark would take over, but maybe it would be better for Beau to stay in the place he was used to.

"Talk to Mother about it," she heard herself saying. "He's a very affectionate animal once he accepts you, and I can't bring him into town. He needs plenty of space. Please tell Mother I'll phone her tomorrow after I have heard the doctor's opinion."

Anthea, however, could not wait for the morning. About midnight when she looked in, as she did every fifteen minutes, Aunt Ellen was obviously hemorrhaging.

Anthea held her until the worst was over, then laid her back on the pillows. She ran down to the phone, called the night emergency number, and sat beside Aunt Ellen's bedside, longing for help.

After what seemed like hours, but was really only ten minutes, the door bell rang. She had left the hall light on, and she raced down the stairs and opened the door saying, "I'm so grateful to you for coming, Doctor—" then stopped, her mouth half open.

Max Sinclair stared at her, and she stared back in amazement.

"What are *you* doing here?" Anthea gasped.

"I am the doctor on call tonight. What are *you* doing here?"

"Miss Denham is my great-aunt. Doctor Emerson is her regular doctor."

Max nodded. "We take night duty in turns. There are five of us who share the practice. But let me see the patient; we'll continue our discoveries about each other later. When did you realize that she was ill?"

124

"I haven't been able to visit her for two weeks. I was shocked when I saw her today. I got her to bed, decided to stay the night, and call Dr. Emerson in the morning. She has been very sick and started hemorrhaging; I dared not wait any longer."

Aunt Ellen opened her eyes as they went in.

"Who are you?" she whispered.

"Dr. Emerson's partner. It was my turn on duty tonight. Tell me where the pain is."

Anthea stood by while he took her temperature, pulse rate, listened to her heart, her lungs, and very carefully prodded her body.

"Mighty painful, isn't it?" he said gently. "I'll give you something to help you get some relief. We must see what Dr. Emerson says in the morning."

He prepared a syringe and injected it into her arm. Gradually her eyes closed, and her breathing became more regular.

"She'll sleep for a few hours. Can you manage to rest yourself?"

"I'll pull a mattress in here on the floor so that I can hear immediately when she awakens."

"Let me help you carry it in."

Anthea led the way into another bedroom, and together they lifted the mattress, pillows, and blankets. She followed him downstairs where he pulled on his coat.

"I had no idea you were a doctor," she burst out as he put his hand on the door.

Max stared. "You mean nobody told you? What did you think I did?"

"I had no idea, but somehow I had a notion that you were in business with Alan Towers."

"Perish the thought. No wonder you looked so shattered

125

when I walked in the door at one o'clock in the morning."

"I guess you also got a surprise to find me here."

"I certainly did. Do you mind being here on your own? I'll come in again about seven o'clock before I go off duty. I'll leave my report for Dr. Emerson."

"Is my aunt seriously ill?"

He looked her straight in the face. "Yes, I am afraid that she is. She needs treatment immediately, but probably all we will be able to do will be to ease the pain. Remember that she is an old woman. Does she mean a lot to you?"

"She is the only person who means anything now."

The other nodded. "You and I both seem rather poorly supplied with worthwhile relations. If you need help before I come back, don't hesitate to phone."

"Thank you, Max."

"Try to get some sleep," he said with a smile and ran down the steps.

Anthea closed the door and stood with her back to it for a few minutes. Why was it that however much she wanted to avoid Mark's future relations, they kept invading her affairs? She had called him Max without even meaning to. Why had her mother not bothered to mention that he was a doctor? Probably because he really did not count in the Towers empire, but she would have imagined that Alan Towers would be proud of a doctor in the family.

9

About five o'clock Anthea wakened from a light doze to hear Aunt Ellen moaning. She jumped up and said quietly, "How do you feel, Aunt Ellen?"

She opened her eyes and stared as if she did not even remember who Anthea was. "The pain——" she muttered.

"The doctor will be back soon," Anthea said, holding her hand and feeling her feeble pulse. "Shall I make you a hot drink?"

"Yes, and bring some of my pills," she whispered.

Anthea took up a tray of tea, gave her two of the pills that were in a bottle by the bed, and held her up to drink the tea, but after a few sips she shook her head. "No more," she said. Anthea sponged her face and hands, gently brushed away her wispy gray hair from her damp forehead and tried to make the pillow more comfortable.

"Don't let them operate," Aunt Ellen muttered. "I'm too old and too tired."

"I know," Anthea said softly. "We'll do what is best for you."

Aunt Ellen's eyes opened, and with a sudden spurt of energy she said, "Who was that young doctor who came?"

"Dr. Max Sinclair."

"Have you seen him before?"

"He is the stepson of Alan Towers, the man my mother is going to marry."

"What a pity. He is the kind of man I would have liked for you. I wish you had someone to share you life with, Anthea. You're lonely without your father."

"You are going to get better, and I am going to stay with you, Aunt Ellen."

"Your mother won't let you do that."

"She'll be too busy with her exciting new life to worry about me."

"Poor Andrew. He had so much to give," she said, and again a spasm of pain crossed her face, and she gasped.

"Try to rest and not tire yourself," Anthea said gently. "Maybe you can have another little sleep."

At six thirty Max Sinclair appeared again and went through the routine examination, then motioned Anthea outside, and they went downstairs.

"She is weaker, and I think that we should get her to the hospital immediately. I could call Dr. Emerson if you'd like his opinion, but I don't feel that we should waste any more time."

Anthea looked at his serious face. "She has begged me not to let anyone operate."

"I don't think that there is any question of that. Unless I am very much mistaken the growth has gone too far, but we could ease the pain by reducing the fluid which has collected. Will you try to explain that to her while I call an ambulance?"

"Aunt Ellen, Dr. Sinclair wants you to go into the hospital."

"I won't have an operation."

"They won't operate," Anthea assured her. "The doctor says they'll just reduce the fluid which is causing you so much pain. Then you can come back home."

"You mean that, Anthea?"

"I promise you. I'll not let them do anything which will prolong the agony, and I'll come here to live with you when you get back from the hospital. It would be wonderful to have less pain, wouldn't it?"

"Very well. I'll go, but Anthea I want to die in my own bed."

Max glanced in at the door and saw the look of tenderness on Anthea's face as she bent over the old woman. At that moment he knew that for the first time in his life he had found a woman with whom he would like to share his life. His face was expressionless, however, as Anthea looked up. "The ambulance is on its way. Are you ready to let us help you, Miss Denham?"

"Yes, if you promise not to cut me up," she said with a sudden flash of her old spirit.

"Anthea will see to that. Dr. Emerson will be in to visit you this morning. Tell him how you feel."

Anthea climbed into the ambulance with her aunt while Max followed in his own car. She saw her aunt settled in a small ward and was asked to wait outside for a while. About half an hour later she went in again; Aunt Ellen smiled feebly but looked much more like herself.

"Is the pain easier?" Anthea asked.

"Never thought I'd have tubes pushed in me like that. Wonderful what nurses can do these days. I always wanted to be a nurse, but in my younger days it wasn't popular for nice young ladies. Mother needed me at home after I lost the young man I was engaged to."

"I think you should rest," a nurse said as she held Aunt Ellen's thin wrist. "You've had enough excitement for one morning."

"I'll be back this evening," Anthea promised and bent to kiss her. She drove back to the house, did some cleaning up, and waited to phone until she was sure her mother would be up.

Her mother's voice was frigid. "I hope that you are on your way back, Anthea. I told you that I need the car today. I don't like being in the house on my own, nor do I like having to deal with your dog."

"Mother, Aunt Ellen was very ill. I had to send for the doctor during the night, and she was taken into the hospital. I have just seen her, and she is a little better."

"Then I hope you are on your way home. A hospital is the best place for her. The nurses will know how to treat her."

Anthea flinched. Had her mother no sympathy or feeling?

"I am going to wait until I see her doctor and hear what they plan and how long she is likely to be there. Then I'll bring the car back. I can always drive the van when I visit the hospital."

"Then please make it as soon as you can. I want the car this afternoon."

"Very well. I'll try."

"That is not good enough. I can't have my plans all messed up like this. I need the car by two o'clock."

"I promised to get back as soon as I can. Good-bye, Mother."

"Good-bye, and remember that your mother comes before an elderly great-aunt who has already had her life."

Anthea put down the receiver and sat on the bottom of the stairs until she could gain control of her feelings. Someday, somehow, her mother was going to have to pay for her selfish disregard for other people's feelings and sufferings. Long ago Great-Grandma used to quote: "The wheels of God grind slowly but they grind exceeding sure." She added, "I've seen it happen time after time. People have to pay for their sins even in this life. Unfortunately sometimes other people have to suffer with them because no man is an island and lives only to himself.''

Some time later she phoned surgery and asked to speak to Dr. Emerson. She was connected with him and explained her reason for calling.

"Yes, I have seen Miss Denham," he replied. "She ought to have sent for me weeks ago, but all she did was to ask for more pills on prescription."

"She is adamant that she won't have an operation," Anthea said.

"I guess it is too late for that anyway. All we can do is ease the pain as much as we can. She'll be in the hospital for this week anyway; maybe she can go home for a while if she is stronger and has someone to stay with her."

"I'll arrange to be there," Anthea replied. "I'll visit her when I can and move in when she is ready to come home. In the meantime, if there is any emergency will you phone me at my present home—Bewdley two-nine-three-six-one?"

"Very well. She is a wonderful old lady and has always been one of my favorite patients—not that she has needed my services often, but we have known each other a long time. I am glad that she has someone to depend upon."

Anthea arrived home before lunch.

"Here I am, Mother," she called brightly as she walked in.

"Good. Will your great-aunt be staying in the hospital?"

"For a few days until Dr. Emerson sees how she is."

Why had she not mentioned Max Sinclair? She had said that she had been obliged to call a doctor during the night, but she hoped that her mother had assumed that it had been Dr. Emerson.

"Then you will be at home for a few nights, I imagine."

"Yes, but I'll visit the hospital when I can."

"There will still be plenty to be done here. I hope you will do all you can to finish outside, and I'd like your help in the house. There are your father's papers and books to sort out. You can take any of those you want and destroy the others. The furniture is old-fashioned so I will send it to the sale room. If there is anything you value especially, you had better tell me."

"I would like Father's desk, my piano, the furniture you gave me for my room on my eighteenth birthday, and the photograph album."

Her mother nodded. "You are welcome to any of those, and I believe there are some boxes of china and old-fashioned ornaments that belonged to your grandmother in the attic. Sort out what you want and arrange for the removal. I imagine that you will take it to your great-aunt's house."

"Yes, for the time being."

"Next week Alan and I are going to London. I am going to choose new clothes while he is at various business meetings. The builders will be starting this week so I hope you will be here to see what they are doing."

"It will depend on Aunt Ellen. Did you settle with Gerry about Beau?"

"Yes, she insists that she will pay you what he is worth. When you leave she will have him retrained as you suggested. I personally think that it is very obliging of her, as he is not everyone's choice."

"I don't think that there would be any trouble selling him if she changes her mind," Anthea said coldly.

"Actually it is Mark's idea, not Gerry's. I don't think that she is really very pleased about it, so if Beau doesn't respond, he may be sold to someone else."

Anthea hurried to her room and changed into her working clothes. Before doing anything else she called Beau, made a fuss over him, and took him for a brief run, but he would not leave her for more than a few paces. He very clearly showed that he was glad to have her back. He pushed his head against her legs to be stroked again and again. Bending down, Anthea put her arms around him.

"Poor old boy. I hate parting with you," she said huskily. "But I swear that if ever I have a place where I can keep you, I'll buy you back. Now it's time I started to work."

All that week customers continued to drive in for the remaining plants, which were being sold very cheaply. There was very little of any consequence left by Saturday afternoon.

On two evenings Anthea had driven to the hospital, where she was amazed at the change in Aunt Ellen. On Thursday she was walking around the ward and declared that she was ready to go home. Dr. Emerson promised that she could go home on the following Monday, providing that she had someone living in the house with her.

Anthea arranged that Aunt Ellen would be brought back by ambulance on Monday afternoon, and she would be there to meet her. Her mother was leaving on Sunday for her week in London, so she would take Beau to the kennels, and Gerry could drive over to superintend the workmen. Her responsibility in the nursery was finished; her mother could arrange for the sale of whatever was left. A moving van collected her belongings before she left. With a feeling that this was really the end of life as she had known it, she drove off with no one even to wish her good-bye.

She might come back again, but it would be as a visitor, not as the daughter of the house. It was a lonely, heartbreaking parting, but at least Aunt Ellen needed her. She prayed as she drove that she would be given strength and patience for whatever lay ahead. At present all that she could do was to go a day at a time and not look too far into the future.

Aunt Ellen insisted on getting up each day and even tried to cook. "I can't sit twiddling my thumbs all day," she said when Anthea protested. "I'll do what I can, then rest. I've been wondering what your plans are, Anthea. I don't want to tie you down. Dr. Emerson insists that I have home help each day, and if I need her the district nurse will attend to the bandaging. If you want to look for a job, I can manage, but I'll be grateful to have you with me at night."

"I had arranged to start work at Thompsons', the florists, on Monday," Anthea said, "but I intended to tell him that I was not available now."

"No. I won't have you just hanging around waiting on me all day, and I know you'll need a decent wage since your mother got everything."

"I am only going on a month's trial," Anthea explained. "I'm not very keen, but nothing else seemed suitable. Maybe I can see how it works out."

Anthea had a long talk with Dr. Emerson, who told her frankly that her aunt might live eight weeks or eight months.

"We can't operate, but we can relieve the pain by taking her into the hospital when necessary. She is a strong-minded old dear and has a tough constitution, but it is no good dodging the truth."

"I had a job lined up, but I'm perfectly willing to cancel it, if I ought to stay with her all the time."

"I don't really think that is necessary. I am arranging for home help every day, and the district nurse will visit. She'll probably be happier to know that she is able to look after herself, and you'll be here at night. Where are you going to work?"

"Thompsons', the florists."

Dr. Emerson nodded. "Jean Thompson is another of my patients. A wonderfully brave woman."

"I have only arranged to try it for a month. But if my aunt needs me before that, I'll leave immediately."

The doctor nodded. "Between us we'll make her last months as easy as possible."

So for the next weeks their life fell into a new pattern. Anthea was up early and made breakfast, although Aunt Ellen usually had nothing but tea and a thin slice of toast. Later, when the home helper arrived, the old woman got up and prepared a light lunch. After they had eaten she went back to rest, and Anthea insisted that she would prepare the evening meal when she got home. As the days went on she could see that her aunt was having increasing pain, rested more, and often Anthea had to go to her during the night.

Anthea would have enjoyed her work in the shop if she could have avoided Bert Thompson. She and his wife, Jean, got along well together. She admired the skill of Jean's clever fingers and the patient way she accepted her limitations, but she detested her husband. He was too smooth and far too familiar when his wife was not around, especially when he had had a few drinks. Anthea insisted on driving her old van back to Aunt Ellen's at midday, as this saved her having to share a meal with him. When she returned he was always missing for about an hour and came back smelling of alcohol.

"Take no notice of Bert, Anthea," Jean Thompson said one day when she noticed that Anthea was upset. "We'd be a lot better off if he would stop wasting money on drink, but nothing I say makes any difference. He only shouts that he has got to have some sort of pleasure when he's tied to a useless woman like me."

"You certainly are not useless," Anthea objected.

135

Jean reddened. "Well, from his point of view as a wife I guess I am."

"How did the accident happen?"

"Bert was driving. No one knows except me that he had been drinking. He drove too fast around a bend and went off the road. It was two hours before we were found."

"Wasn't he injured?"

"Only a broken arm, but it mended all right. My legs were trapped, as the car had gone over on my side. They thought that I was dead when they took me out. I guess drink has been the cause of all our troubles, but Bert won't change now. He is at the public house every night and has to have a few drinks at lunchtime as well. He and a couple of cronies can always manage to get what they want even if the pubs aren't open. Just keep him at a distance when he's had a few pints."

"I may not be able to stay much longer," Anthea said, feeling it was only fair to give Jean warning. "I can see that my aunt is getting worse again. Probably she'll have to have another spell in the hospital, but there will come a time when she'll need me constantly at home."

"I'll be sorry to part with you. You are the best assistant we've ever had. Perhaps we could arrange to make do until you could come back to us."

"I'd like to, for your sake. I really enjoy working with you, and you've taught me a lot already."

The next afternoon Jean was in the kitchen clearing up, while Anthea was in the place behind the shop where they made up the wreaths and bouquets, and where the office work was done. Anthea was behind the old desk writing out some accounts, when Bert Thompson came in, turned the key in the lock, and came unsteadily across the room. Anthea looked up, saw the expression on his face, and got up hastily.

136

"Not often do we have the place to ourselves, duckie," he said. "Jean keeps her eagle eye on me most of the time. What about having a bit of fun? Come on, honey, give me a kiss."

He reached for her, and Anthea shrank back from the smell of his breath. "Don't you dare touch me," she said, moving to one side.

"Aw, don't be so stuffy. I like you, Anthea. We could have fun."

He reached for her again; in desperation Anthea snatched up a pail which had held gladiola blooms, threw the water at him, and hit him hard with the pail.

He sputtered, and she ran around the back of the desk, across the room, and turned the key. Burt lurched toward her, caught his foot in the worn linoleum, and went sprawling.

Without waiting to see what had happened to him, Anthea grabbed her coat and handbag from the hall, dashed out of the shop around the back lane, and climbed into her car. She drove home in a panic, not bothering to consider where she was going until she had left the town and reached a quiet lane. Finally she pulled into a driveway and dropped her head to her hands, still gripping the steering wheel, sobbing violently. Why did she have to come across such horrible men? That was certainly the last time she would go near Bert Thompson. What a terrible life his poor wife must have lived.

Gradually she quieted down and got out of the car. She was still wearing the pale blue nylon overall, but she tore it off and threw it into the back of the car. She bathed her face in a stream and wandered along its banks to fill in time. She would not go home until her usual time so that her aunt would not guess that there had been trouble. She would

137

simply tell her that she had decided to give her notice as she felt she needed her at home until she was better.

Aunt Ellen said very little. The pain was becoming unbearable again, and it was impossible to hide it any longer. Two days later she went into the hospital for further treatment. Anthea had phoned Jean Thompson, explained that she had been called away hurriedly and would not be able to return since her aunt needed her. She mailed the overall and thought that that was the end of yet another episode.

"I've given my notice and am not going back to Thompson's until you are a bit better, Aunt Ellen, so as soon as you have finished the treatment you can come home," she explained when she visited her.

"But, lassie, I did not want you to do that."

"I didn't like the job anyway," Anthea said lightly. "I'll find something better later."

That evening Anthea had a phone call from her mother who had only contacted her once since her return from London.

"Hello, Mother. It is good to hear your voice. I was hoping to drive out to visit you tomorrow."

"I thought that you were tied up all day."

"I gave my notice. I did not like the job, and Aunt Ellen has had to go into the hospital again."

"Then perhaps you will be able to come home for a few days?"

Anthea hesitated. "I'll have to find out how long Aunt Ellen will be in the hospital. I can stay until she comes back. Do you need me for something special?"

"I cannot bear being here on my own. The house is such a mess that Alan and I have decided to get married next Saturday, have our honeymoon, and be back in plenty of time for Gerry's wedding. If you are free I'll come to Newbridge tomorrow to buy you a dress. It will be quite a small affair. Kathleen will by my witness, but of course I want my daughter there. We are being married at the Bewdley Church by special license, and we will have the reception at the country club. I bought my dress in London, but I am sure that there will be something suitable for you at Eltons or in one of the Newbridge stores."

"Very well, Mother. I'll be ready when you arrive. I'll visit Aunt Ellen this afternoon and make arrangements for her to stay in the hospital until after Saturday."

"Alan realizes that it isn't fair for me to be in a place like this on my own. We are upset that you have left me so hurriedly. I had done my duty so faithfully to you and your father."

"I am sorry you feel like that," Anthea said, trying to hold on to her temper. "But you are making a new life now, and I had to face a different future. Everything changed for us both when Dad died."

"Well, obviously it was useless to appeal to your sense of duty to me, so Alan has moved our wedding date forward. I'll arrive tomorrow morning, and we'll call at Joslins, the attorneys, as I have papers to sign. I am arranging that a certain sum will be paid to you each month, but I will keep the capital, although it will go to you when I die. You will be independent to a certain extent, and I expect that when Aunt Ellen dies she will leave the old house and all that she has to you."

"I don't want anyone to die so that I can inherit their money," Anthea replied firmly. "I will be grateful if I am not absolutely dependent on my wages, though."

"Good. Then I will see you tomorrow."

Anthea put down the receiver and went thoughtfully into the kitchen to make some coffee. She hated the idea of letting her mother buy her a dress, but she needed what small amount of money she had—especially as she had no job. Her mother would insist that she had something more stylish than she would be able to afford. Her mother pretended that she had been slighted and neglected, but Anthea guessed that in her heart she was delighted to have the excuse to move into Tall Timbers as soon as she could. The visit to London would have given her a glimpse of the kind of life she would have with Alan Towers.

She dreaded the thought of attending the wedding ceremony and reception and having to pretend that she was happy about it, when she knew that the memory of her father would make every moment a travesty of pretense. This was just another hurdle to get over.

She visited Aunt Ellen who was told that she would have to stay in the hospital at least a week longer.

"Disgusting," she burst out when Anthea told her about the wedding. "It is only six months since Andrew died. I hope this Alan Towers will make Eleanor toe the line. Andrew was always too good to her and let her have her own way. A good spanking is what she needed many a time."

Anthea tried to smile. "I'll be glad when the wedding is over. Then I will not feel I have to visit Bewdley and have the unhappy memories stirred up again."

"Do you need money for clothes, dearie?"

"Mother says she is going to buy me a suitable dress tomorrow and is arranging for me to receive a small sum each month. I wish that I need not take anything from her."

"Nonsense! Half of whatever she got for the house and nurseries ought to be yours—in fact more, because they were bought with money from your great-grandmother, and she wanted you to inherit it. She had no more patience with your mother than I have. You accept whatever you are of-

140

fered. I don't suppose she will part with much anyway. Why have I got to stay here another week?"

"The doctor says he is doing further tests, and you need to get stronger."

"Well, I'm grateful when they relieve the pain, but I long for my own place and my own bed. Everybody *is* very kind to me. Could you bring your dress in for me to see, Anthea?"

"I'll do more than that. I'll come to visit you when I am wearing it on Saturday and bring you a piece of wedding cake," she said teasingly.

"Give it to the ducks. It would choke me," Aunt Ellen replied.

"Obviously you are feeling better. You are getting spunky," Anthea said, patting her aunt's hand.

The old woman nodded. "I am in less pain, and I'm better off than I ever thought I'd be. I know that Andrew would have done his best for me, but I never thought that I'd have you to myself. I couldn't have had a kinder daughter if I'd had her made to order."

Anthea flushed. "You have always been special to Dad and me," she said tenderly. "Being needed has helped me over this bad stretch."

"Now we'll stop being sentimental, but I want you to remember that whatever happens, you made life worth living for your father and for me. I am praying that someday you will meet a man who is worthy of you, but Anthea, first make sure that he. has a real, living faith in Jesus Christ. Andrew made that mistake and paid for it with a lifetime of loneliness. I missed a lot by not having a husband, but better to be alone than live with someone who has no sympathy with one's deepest feelings."

The next day Anthea drove back with her mother so that she could bring the old car back after the wedding.

"I am so thankful that I won't have to ride in this old rattletrap any more," her mother exclaimed as they set off. "If you can manage it, you should sell this as well as the old van and get a small, modern car."

"It will depend on what I am offered for them. Anyway, I do not need a car much while I am in town. I can always walk or take a bus."

"You are determined to stay on with your great-aunt then?"

"As long as she needs me I'll stay. After that I may move away. I'd like to get something like horticultural work in the country."

"You will find many changes in the house and grounds," her mother said calmly. "At present it looks a mess, but it will be a wonderful property when all the alterations are complete. I thought you could sleep in your father's bed tonight. At present his room and mine have not been too upset. Gerry plans to have them done next week. My room and your father's are to be knocked into one. They will make a lovely master bedroom with a private bath."

Anthea kept her eyes turned away. These days were going to be one long series of hurts, but she was determined that no one would guess how much these details upset her. In spite of her resolutions, however, she gave a little gasp when they drove in. All the nursery beds which they had kept so immaculate were trodden on and filled with weeds or rubble. One large greenhouse had been dismantled, and only the naked patch with broken bricks remained.

"Gerry is determined that the house will be completed before their wedding. The landscape gardener has the grounds planned out and will start very soon; he can go on with it while they are on their honeymoon. They are touring Europe for three weeks."

Anthea reached to the back of the car and gathered up the parcels. Had her mother forgotten that once Mark had been *her* special friend? Was she so insensitive that she was incapable of realizing how such remarks hurt her? Sometimes it seemed that she was deliberately making Anthea suffer. Was her mother still bitter against her dead husband and working out that bitterness on her daughter?

The house was almost unrecognizable. Windows had been enlarged, central heating was being installed, pipes, radiators, stepladders, and cans of paint were everywhere. All the carpets were pulled up, the curtains taken down, and in the kitchen a new stove and refrigerator had been installed. In the small back kitchen where she and her father had left their working shoes and washed, a freezer, washing machine, and dryer stood waiting to be connected.

"No wonder you cannot go on living in this upheaval," Anthea exclaimed. "How do you manage to find anything?"

"I am not here much. Either I am out with Alan, or I spend a night or two with Kathleen. The worst is almost over anyway. But think of central heating in the winter instead of shivering like we used to do. And the laundry will be so easy. The old coach house that you used to use for your tools and lawn mowers is being made into a flat for a married couple. If we had done that years ago it would have been so easy to get extra help when we needed it."

"But we never had money to spare for anything like that," Anthea replied. "Besides, Ron would always have preferred to live in the village."

"It is so wonderful not having to worry about expense. Tall Timbers is a marvelous house now. It is finished too, so Alan will be able to sell it for much more than he paid for it, and we can choose a really convenient apartment that will need very little upkeep. We saw some marvelous places when we were in London. We can have room service or eat in the restaurant; we will be able to have it without worrying about anything.''

Anthea glanced at her mother's animated face. She had never heard her so excited before. In fact she had never really heard her talk so much. Obviously life stretched out before her as one long round of social activities, but Anthea felt no pangs of envy. That sort of life did not appeal to her in the slightest. If her mother was happy then she would be glad for her, but living in an apartment complex, going from one party to the next, always dressing up and meeting new people who really meant nothing to her, was the last sort of existence that she would enjoy. This glimpse of her mother's real nature made her understand more fully how their old life must have bored and irritated her and also how little her parents had in common.

10

For the next two nights Anthea wept when she reached the privacy of the little room that had been her father's. Except for herself no one seemed to remember that he had ever lived here. Apart from his bed, everything belonging to him or connected with him had disappeared. She was glad that she had taken his desk, papers, and books. So far she had not had the opportunity to sort them out and classify what was of real value. At the back of her mind was the thought that she would offer his notes and illustrations for publication. When she returned to Aunt Ellen's and she had no job lined up, she would have time to see what could be done.

If a book under her father's name could be put in print, it would mean that his love of God's creation would be passed on to others. Maybe only children would read it, but he had amassed a wealth of knowledge during the years that could bring simple joy to anyone who was interested in the wonders of nature.

On Saturday her mother was as excited as any eighteen-year-old bride. There was nothing to do in the house, so she could spend plenty of time on her makeup and certainly made a very elegant figure in a long, dark turquoise dress, high-heeled black shoes, and a very flattering hat, which was deceptively simple but which Anthea guessed must have cost more than her whole wardrobe.

Her own dress was white with a silver pattern woven into it. It had a tight fitting bodice with tiny pearl buttons down the front, long, tight-fitting sleeves that were fastened with the same irridescent pearl buttons, and a full skirt, which fell in flattering folds to her feet. She wore silver shoes, carried a white and silver handbag, and her hat was a cap of white and silver flowers.

Her mother looked her over critically. "I've never seen you look so lovely, Anthea. I can certainly feel proud of my daughter today."

"Thank you, Mother. I think Alan Towers is getting a beautiful bride. He must be very proud to introduce you to his friends."

Her mother flushed slightly under her make-up. "I am sure that I can help him socially, and I think we will suit each other very well."

There was a knock at the door, and Aunt Kathleen arrived. Anthea was to drive her aunt and mother in the new car, which was already in the garage. No other guests were expected at the house, but all would drive straight to the church.

"My, but you both look outstanding," Kathleen exclaimed. Her face was overly made up, her hair too blonde, and she had tried to squeeze into a dress that was a size too small for her. "How you both keep so slim I don't know. I've eaten practically nothing this week but haven't lost an ounce. I get so tired of fighting the battle of the bulge."

Mrs. Gordon laughed. "You are too fond of cocktails and little nibbles, Kathleen."

"Well, you two will certainly make Gerry Towers and Mary Latham turn green with envy. Maybe when Mark sees you in that dress, Anthea, he'll wish he hadn't changed his mind."

"Don't talk so stupidly," Mrs. Gordon snapped. "There was never anything serious between Mark and Anthea. Anyway, it is time we were leaving."

Anthea picked up her handbag and the car keys. She was used to Aunt Kathleen's thoughtless remarks, but what she had just said was in shockingly bad taste.

"It's a beautiful car, Eleanor," Kathleen gushed as they set off. "You and I will have some good times in this when you get back, while your Alan is busy. You certainly have got a good bargain in husbands. I wish I could find one like him."

Anthea kept her eyes on the road and her mouth tightly closed. Did nothing matter to these two except money and self-gratification?

Anthea stood in the church and could scarcely see for the tears. How often her father and she had come here and felt the peace of God fill their hearts and minds after the busy work of the week. Except for the funeral, it was the first time she had ever remembered her mother's being there with her. What a mockery it was to make use of God's house for their own convenience—to expect His blessing on a marriage in which He would count for nothing!

The wedding party consisted of Aunt Kathleen and two of her friends, some business acquaintances of Alan Towers with their wives, Gerry, Mark, Mrs. Latham, and Max Sinclair.

After photographs at the church door the cars drove to the country club where Alan had ordered a sumptuous meal in a private dining room. They had stood about with glasses in their hands until the meal was announced; Anthea found herself seated between Max Sinclair and an older man who had been introduced as Donald Roper.

"So you are the daughter of the very charming bride," he said gaily. "Alan sure knows how to pick 'em. Will you live

147

with him and your mother when they return from their honeymoon?"

"No, I am living with an aunt in Newbridge," Anthea replied. "My mother and her new husband will probably travel a great deal."

Max Sinclair was watching her face and saw the spasm of pain that crossed it as she managed to say "her new husband." She was putting on a brave front, but he could imagine what an effort it was.

Different wines were served with each course, and Mr. Roper refused nothing. Anthea took only orange juice and was surprised when Max Sinclair did the same.

"Don't tell me you won't even take a glass of wine at your mother's wedding," Mr. Roper exclaimed. He was becoming increasingly talkative as the wine livened him up. "Is it because you are a doctor that you don't drink during the day?" he demanded, talking to Max across Anthea.

"I don't drink at any time," Max replied. "I have seen too much of the damage that it has done."

"But think of the pleasure that it gives. Wine in moderation is good for you."

His neighbor on the other side claimed his attention, and Max said in a low voice, "You and I are obviously in the minority. I guess one or two of these guests will be fairly lively before we have finished. I saw your aunt at the hospital yesterday since Dr. Emerson is away. She told me that you had given up your job at the florists."

"I found that it was not what I wanted. Anyway, Aunt Ellen needs me at home with her when she returns. How was she?"

"Quite chipper, but this disease is so unpredictable. You do realize that she may go suddenly or that she may live for months?"

"Yes, I realize that."

148

"I'm talking 'shop' as usual. Gerry says that I can never get away from my all-absorbing topic. Please forgive me."

"I asked you a question and you answered. There is nothing to forgive."

"We need a receptionist in surgery. Would you be interested in the job?"

"I really don't know anything about it. I think that I'd rather do something I understand."

"Nothing much to it as long as you can read and write, answer the phone, and have lots of patience."

Anthea shook her head. "Not at present. I am staying with Aunt Ellen as long as she needs me. Then I may try further afield."

"Oh, horrors! Here come the speeches and the champagne," Max said, with a groan. "Hope they won't go on for too long."

Anthea refused champagne and asked for grapefruit juice. At least that did not look so obvious.

"Bright idea," Max said, following her example. Anthea saw her mother's expression and saw that her eyes were fiery with annoyance. Sometime in the future she would be told off for showing such bad manners.

"Surely you aren't going to drink to the health of the happy couple in that stuff?" Mr. Roper's voice boomed out, and Alan Towers looked in his direction. Obviously Mrs. Roper told him to keep quiet, and he subsided.

John Baxter, who had been best man, made a short speech congratulating Alan on his choice of a beautiful wife, read out some congratulatory telegrams and messages, made some feeble jokes, and asked the assembled company to drink to the couple's future happiness. The champagne bottles appeared to refill the glasses, and Alan got up to reply.

"Not too bad," Max whispered. "I've heard him much longer. Well, that's over. Are you going back to Newbridge? Can I give you a lift?"

"Thank you, but I'm driving our old car back. It is mine now, since your stepfather's present to his bride was a brand-new car—something we have never had in our lives before."

"It will take more than a new car to sweeten that bitter taste before long," Max said with a wry grin. "Hi, Gerry, you look very ravishing," he said as Gerry approached.

"And you look as disdainful as ever," Gerry replied sharply. "You and your new sister seem to be on very friendly terms."

"Do I detect a note of jealousy?" Max teased. "Anthea refuses to accept any relationship, so you remain my one and only sister."

"Then don't forget to keep June twentieth free," Gerry said crisply. "You are all that I have in the way of brothers so I need you there. Your mother looks very charming, Anthea, and so do you."

"I agree with that," Mark said, putting his arm around Gerry's waist. "I've never seen you dressed like that before, Anthea."

Anthea smiled. "Well, I could hardly wear this dress in the nurseries, could I?"

"What do you think of the house?" Gerry asked.

"I guess we'll not be able to recognize it when it is finished," Anthea said calmly. "You are fortunate to start off in such a place, Mark."

"Don't I know it," Mark replied enthusiastically. "But as long as I can marry Gerry, I would have been happy in a cottage."

"Not for long," Gerry snapped back. "Love in a cottage

certainly wouldn't suit me. Besides, being able to entertain important clients will be a big help to your future.''

''A very lovely wedding,'' Mary Latham said standing beside her tall son, a look of fatuous complacency on her face. ''You look very young and sweet, Anthea.''

''Thank you,'' Anthea said looking her straight in the face. After a few moments Mrs. Latham dropped her eyes.

''I must say goodbye to Mother as I want to visit the hospital this afternoon,'' Anthea added, moving away.

Max followed her, and they walked to the parking lot together. ''How small-minded and catty some women can be,'' Max exploded when they left the front door. ''Give me hard-working women with big families and very little money every time. Mrs. Latham dotes on her wonderful Mark just like my stepfather does on Gerry. They don't stand a chance with parents like that.''

Anthea had reached her limit, and she made no reply. She took out her key and tried to put it in the lock but could not see to find the hole. Max took the key out of her hand, opened the door, helped her inside, and pushed a large, clean, white handkerchief into her hand.

''Mop up before the others come out,'' he said sympathetically. ''Or if you will come in my car, we'll go for a quiet cup of tea somewhere.''

Anthea gulped, wiped her eyes, and handed back his handkerchief. ''I'll be OK; thank you for your help. Here comes the first contingent. Good-bye, Max.''

He slammed the door and walked over to his own car while Anthea drove away as fast as she could.

Next day she met Max Sinclair as she was coming from the hospital. He stopped and said, ''Feeling better?''

''Yes, thank you.''

''Did you know that your late employer was killed last night?''

"You mean Mr. Thompson, the florist?"

"Yes."

"What happened?"

"He was involved in a car crash. He did not stop at a red light, and a truck smashed into him. He was dead when he got to the hospital. There was nothing we could do for him."

"Had he been drinking?"

"I am afraid so."

"But who will look after his poor wife?"

"Her sister is with her at present, but she has a family of her own so she cannot stay. Did you leave the job because something unpleasant happened? Your aunt suggested it, and last night Mrs. Thompson said the same."

"Mr. Thompson had been drinking and made advances toward me, so I threw water over him, hit him with a pail, and I ran away."

Max grinned. "Good for you. I wish I had seen it."

"How awful to think that he died without time to get right with God. I'll visit his wife now. She will need help in the shop."

Anthea found Jean Thompson sitting in her chair staring out the window that overlooked the untidy, neglected backyard. She looked at her blankly when she spoke.

"Jean, I'm so sorry," Anthea said, bending down beside her wheelchair.

"I'm not," Jean said bitterly. "I knew this would happen some day. I am glad no one else was injured, but he deserved what he got after what happened to me. Now at least I'm free of his drunken beastliness. But what is going to happen to me and the shop? Was it because he wouldn't leave you alone that you went in such a hurry?"

"Yes, but I hated leaving you."

"I thought as much. Every time we have had a decent, nice-looking woman the same thing has happened."

"I'll come back for the time being if that will help you," Anthea offered. "Does the property belong to you?"

"No, it is only rented. All I have to sell is the contents. I am sure that there are plenty of debts. The place will have to go. I can't manage on my own, but I don't know where I'll live. I can't go to my sister as she has a large family, and I can't look after myself. Dr. Sinclair says that he will ask Dr. Emerson to get me into a home for people like me, but it may be some time before there is a place available."

When Anthea went home that Sunday evening she walked around the rambling old house and wondered if they could offer a room to Jean Thompson until she could go into a home for the physically handicapped.

It would be better for Aunt Ellen too if she had her bedroom downstairs.

The dining room could be turned into a bed/sitting room for Jean, and the lounge could be used as a bedroom for Aunt Ellen. The kitchen would make them a comfortable living room as it was on the same level, so that Jean could move about easily in her wheelchair, and it would be better for Aunt Ellen if she did not have to go upstairs.

On Monday Aunt Ellen came home, and Anthea told her what had happened to Mr. Thompson.

"But you said that his wife was in a wheelchair. How can she manage?"

"I am going to help in the shop until it is sold."

"Where will she live?"

"I wondered if we could make the dining room into a bed/sitting room for her until the doctor can find a place in a hospital especially designed for people like her."

"Of course, if it won't be too much for you to cope with."

"I think at the same time we should have the lounge made into your bedroom. It will save you having to go upstairs, and we can live in the kitchen. It is big and roomy."

"That mind of yours certainly has been busy. Do you realize that you'll have two invalids on your hands?"

"I know," Anthea said with a smile. "I'm not trained as a cook or a nurse, but between us we'll manage. Jean Thompson needs help and kindness after the miserable life her husband gave her."

By the end of the week the business was up for sale, the funeral over, and a neighbor had offered to sleep in the house at night until the transfer was completed.

A week later the new owner moved in and took over the house and shop just as it was. Jean moved into the room Anthea had got ready and met Aunt Ellen for the first time.

"You are very good to let me share your home," she said as they gathered in the kitchen for their first meal together. "How pretty this room is."

Aunt Ellen nodded. "Anthea has worked like crazy this week. She has made our bedrooms very comfortable and sewn these new curtains and cushions to cheer the place up."

"I'll need help with the cooking," Anthea said gaily. "I can't do much beyond boiling eggs and making cups of tea or coffee."

"None of us need fancy food," Aunt Ellen said briskly. "Mrs. Thompson and I are not quite helpless, anyway."

"I'll be glad to do the cooking, Anthea. I can manage most things if the ingredients are put where I can reach them," Jean offered. "Please don't feel that I am useless."

"I know," Anthea replied. "I am depending upon you to teach me all sorts of new recipes."

That first evening they sat in Aunt Ellen's room to listen to the nine o'clock news after she was in bed. When Anthea switched it off, the older woman said, "Will you read this evening's passage, Anthea? My eyes are too tired."

Anthea picked up the copy of *Daily Light* and turning to Jean said, "We always read and have short prayers before we go to bed. Will you join us, Jean?"

"I'd be glad to."

Anthea read the verses slowly and clearly, prayed simply for blessing on each of them, and when she looked up saw Jean inconspicuously wiping her eyes.

"Now it's time you settled down, Aunt Ellen."

"I'll go too," Jean said quietly. "Will you help me to undress?"

"Of course," Anthea replied, and after she had given Aunt Ellen her pills and turned down the light she went over to Jean's room.

"I can't manage the belt and brace I have to wear," she explained. "If you can fasten it for me in the morning and take it off at night, I can do most other things for myself. I have had to learn how to cope on my own."

Anthea was appalled when she saw what Jean had to wear so that she could sit up. How tired her body must get having to remain in the same position for so long.

She helped her into bed, but Jean held onto her hand and her eyes filled with tears.

"If only I had had a daughter, what a difference it would have made. Yet often I was glad that we never had children with such a man for a husband. I believe that God sent you to me. Years ago I went to church and Sunday school. I had a good Christian home, but I met Bert and fell violently in love with him. He was such a handsome, attractive man then, and nothing or no one else mattered. After we married

155

he had no use for church and only used the name of Christ as a curse. I did not bother either. After the accident I was bitter against God, but in my heart I knew that it was my own fault. I should have listened to my parents and never married him. Now I feel that God is drawing me back. Pray for me, Anthea, that I may find peace of mine and heart, even if my body can never be healed.''

"God leads in so many different ways," Anthea said gently. "He knows how you have suffered, and He wants to comfort you. Tell Him that you are sorry you have forgotten Him for so long, but you want to accept His love and forgiveness.''

Jean nodded. "I wish that I had the quiet faith that you and Miss Denham have. She knows that she is dying, but she has no fear.''

"For her it will be a happy release," Anthea said gently. "She has more pain than she will admit. Soon the hospital treatment will not help any more, but I am praying that the Lord will take her before it becomes unbearable and she has to be kept sedated.''

"Not many girls would be willing to take on the care of two lonely, ailing women," Jean said huskily.

"For me it is wonderful to feel that someone needs me. Since I lost my father I need someone to love and to love me. Now try to rest, Jean. I hope that you will sleep well.''

11

For the next few weeks life went on almost like a routine. The house had a feeling of peace even though Aunt Ellen was obviously getting weaker, and she had brief spells in the hospital. She tired quickly and only got out of bed to sit in the chair for short spells.

Anthea had to summon up her courage once more to attend the wedding of Mark and Gerry on June twentieth. She had thought of making her aunt's condition an excuse but knew it would only cause gossip. Aunt Ellen and Jean insisted that she buy another new dress instead of wearing the same one she had worn for her mother's wedding.

"I am going to buy you the prettiest dress and hat that you can find in Newbridge," Aunt Ellen insisted. "No one is going to look down on my great-niece. Hold your head high, dearie, and don't let anyone guess that Mark Latham was fool enough to choose Geraldine Towers instead of you. But then what could you expect with a mother like Mary Latham!"

"He must have been mad," Jean exclaimed.

Anthea laughed. "You two are biased, but you are good for my ego. Very well, I'll waste your money if you insist, and I'll try to glue a smile on my face."

She set off on her shopping expedition feeling more like preparing for a funeral. She had got over her first unhappiness and was able to realize that Mark was not the ideal man that she had imagined, but no one else had filled his place. His rejection still hurt when she remembered how much they had meant to each other.

She chose a beautiful blue dress with a loose, matching coat and hat. She decided that this time they would be three-quarter length because she had little opportunity to wear long dresses. She had her hair styled and set and bought matching shoes and handbag.

When on Saturday morning she paraded in her finery before her approving audience, their loving admiration was helpful in sending her off with a lighter heart.

This wedding was very different from her mother's. The biggest church in Newbridge was packed, and almost four hundred people attended the reception, which was held in Newbridge's largest hotel. Anthea thought that at least it would be easy to melt into the crowd, but for some unknown reason her mother made it obvious that she wanted her near.

In the reception line she had to stand next to her and be introduced to dozens of people that she had never seen before and probably never would see again. At the table she found that she was placed between two of Mark's relations, while Max Sinclair was at the other side of the room. Why had he not been included in the immediate families?

Several times she glanced at her mother's face. Under the expert makeup she looked strained and tired. The animation was missing, and it seemed an effort for her to appear interested in the conversation around her. She was definitely thinner. Was she already finding life with Alan Towers a disappointment?

Aunt Kathleen pushed through the crowd as they waited for the bride and groom to change. "A lovely wedding," she enthused. "Don't you think that your mother looks wonderful, Anthea? She is having such a marvelous life."

"I think that she looks tired," Anthea said quietly.

"There has been a lot to do, with all the final details for such a big wedding, the presents arriving, and visitors calling. She and Alan are going abroad again soon, so she'll be able to rest. How is your aunt?"

"Getting near the end," Anthea replied.

"Well, at her age you can't expect much else. It will be a relief to you when it is over, I am sure."

"For her sake I'll be glad, but I will be very lonely without her."

"What a crowd," Max Sinclair said, and after a brief greeting Aunt Kathleen melted away. She detested what she and Eleanor called his superior air and considered him stuck-up and big-headed. He was one of the family they could do without.

"Meeting at weddings seems to be becoming a habit," he said. "I hope this is the last; it's too expensive."

"Well, there aren't any more in the near future, unless you are keeping your affairs a deadly secret."

"Open as a book, I am," Max replied lightly. "What I've seen of marriage doesn't encourage me to rush into such entanglements. Here they come. Gerry definitely makes a blushing bride, but Mark looks a bit overawed."

There was a rush to the door, and Anthea found herself pushed forward with Max behind her.

"Good-bye, Daddy," Gerry said, kissing her father. "Bye, Eleanor. Thanks for all your help."

"I'm glad you were here to wish me luck," Mark said, taking Anthea's hand. "I guess I can claim a kiss for old times' sake." Before she could protest, Mark had kissed her in front of everybody.

Gerry's smile disappeared for a moment, but with her

159

hand through Mark's arm she exclaimed, "You must come and stay with us, Anthea, and see the house now that it is finished. Good-bye, Max. I hope to dance at your wedding soon."

She kissed Max lightly on the cheek and hurried Mark away.

Max had been watching Anthea closely and had seen how the color drained from her face and how she flinched from Mark's touch. Did he really mean as much to her as Mary Latham and Aunt Ellen had suggested? Had Gerry taken her fiancé as well as her home? Max had no delusions about his half-sister. She was attractive, but was spoiled and selfish, and in her own way could be as hard and arrogant as her father. She had always wanted what belonged to someone else. Maybe that had been part of Mark's attraction.

"I'm thankful that is over," he said, putting his arm under Anthea's elbow. "Come for a drive to get the smell of smoke and wine out of our lungs."

"I ought to get back to Aunt Ellen," Anthea replied half-heartedly.

"Phone and see if she and Mrs. Thompson are OK for another couple of hours."

Anthea nodded and made her way to the nearest phone.

"Aunt Ellen is not getting up today, and Jean says they are fine. The nurse has visited, and I have no need to hurry back. I walked to the church, so I don't have a car with me."

"Good, then let's disappear."

"I must say good-bye to Mother first."

"Then I'll wait in the car so that I don't have to endure any more insane babble."

"Good-bye, Mother," Anthea said when she managed to

attract her attention. "I hope that you will be able to rest now that all the excitement is over. It was a lovely wedding."

Her mother gave her a keen glance, then dropped her eyes. "I am sorry that I have seen so little of you lately, Anthea. I'll try to visit before we go abroad."

"I wish you would," Anthea replied. "Aunt Ellen would appreciate it, I know."

Her mother turned to shake hands with one of the guests, and Anthea slipped away.

"You look very sober," Max said after they had driven for some time in silence.

"I am thinking about my mother," Anthea said. "Somehow she looked unlike herself and appeared very strained."

"There is nothing you can do, except be ready to show you have no ill feeling when she needs you. Is it true that you and Mark had planned to marry, Anthea?"

She shot him a startled glance. "Who told you that?

"Various little hints have suggested it."

"Mark and I lived in the same village, were in the same class at school, and sang in the choir together. But we were not engaged or anything like that. We were very good friends, but Mark was perfectly free to marry whoever he chose. Can't we forget weddings and families?" Anthea questioned. "Could we stop and walk for half an hour? Since Dad died I have missed our rambles so much. I haven't even got a dog to take out these days."

"Great idea. I'd love some exercise and fresh air. We'll leave the car in the parking lot and walk along the river. I think there is a path, but you have dressy shoes on."

"They are comfortable nevertheless. I never sacrifice comfort for fashion."

"Sensible girl," Max replied. "I wish other women had

as much sense. The kind of crippling, ridiculous footwear that most girls hobble around in these days makes me shudder at the thought of future spinal complications.''

"These wouldn't do for a long tramp, but I can't go far as I don't like leaving Aunt Ellen alone very long. She is getting very weak.''

Max nodded. "I expect that Dr. Emerson will order morphine injections soon, as the pills are losing their effectiveness. Will you stay in Newbridge after she goes?''

"I have no idea. If Jean Thompson can find a home, I think that I will try for work in a nature reserve or at any rate some sort of job in the country. I'd hate to be boxed up in an office or shop all day.''

They walked on, but Anthea kept stopping to pick flowers, leaves, or grasses. "They are every bit as beautiful as hothouse blooms,'' she said holding up the variegated bunch. "Oh, Max, look,'' she whispered, putting her hand on his arm and standing still. At the other side of the river a kingfisher flashed in the sunlight, swooped down to the water, and darted into a hole in the bank.

"Wasn't that lovely?'' she said in a hushed voice, her eyes shining. "What gorgeous colors, but the nest will be filthy.''

Max smiled. "Good lesson there—fine feathers don't always mean good homemakers. The drab little sparrow makes a much more comfortable nest for its babies.''

They sat down on a fallen rock for a few minutes watching the hole where the bird had disappeared. They spoke in low voices and hardly moved. Suddenly the kingfisher darted out again, skimmed along the water, pounced suddenly, and held a small fish in his beak. With a quick flick of his flashing body he turned and vanished.

Almost immediately came the persistent notes of the cuckoo.

"Sh," Anthea whispered again and stared at a clump of reeds. A small head with beady eyes and a sleek shiny body slipped into the river.

"How Dad would have loved to see that otter," she said, her eyes misty.

Max could hardly take his eyes from her face. He was seeing the real person this morning—the girl who cared nothing for expensive clothes and social activities but who could find such joyful satisfaction in the simple wonders of creation. What would she say if he told her that he loved her and wanted to marry her?

She stood up, saying regretfully, "It has been wonderful, but I must get back."

Max shook himself impatiently. He believed that there was a feeling of increasing friendship between them. He must go slowly and not frighten her before she was ready. He realized that even if she was beginning to let down her defenses with him, the greatest barrier would be his connection with Alan Towers and his family.

"Will you take me straight back?" Anthea said when they reached the car. "I feel uneasy, but this break has done me good."

Max did not argue, and they said little on the way home.

"Will you come in for coffee?" she inquired as the car stopped.

"Thank you. I'd like that. I'll visit Miss Denham as a friend—not as a doctor."

Anthea opened the door with her key and walked inside with Max behind her. She put her head around her aunt's door and found her fast asleep. She heard a moan from the direction of the kitchen. She hurried down the passage, pushed the door open, took one look, and said, "Thank the Lord you are here, Max."

163

Jean Thompson, still strapped in her chair, was on the floor.

Anthea bent down on one side and Max on the other.

"Jean, what happened?" she asked loudly.

Jean opened her eyes, moaned, and closed them again. She was lying in a very awkward position, and there was blood from a gash on her head.

Max was feeling her gently.

"My arm!" she gasped.

"Don't try to move her," Max said quietly. "I'll phone for an ambulance. Throw a thick blanket over her and switch on the kettle."

Max did not stop to close the door, and Anthea could hear his crisp, professional tone. "Dr. Sinclair here. Send an ambulance immediately to forty-four Luxham Street. Inform emergency that a crippled woman has tipped over her wheelchair, probably broken arms and ribs, and maybe has a concussion."

He hurried out the front door and returned with a medical bag in his hand.

"Do you always carry it with you?" Anthea asked.

"I like to have it in the back of the car just in case of an emergency."

He placed a pad of cotton wool on the wound on the side of Jean's forehead. "If you can find an old towel or sheet, we could mop up the mess. Then make some strong coffee. I'd rather not try to lift Mrs. Thompson until the ambulance men come, but I guess we could both do with a drink."

Anthea knew that Max was thinking of the shock she had had, and with misty eyes she reached for the jar of coffee and took milk from the refrigerator.

"Put plenty of sugar in for yourself," he ordered.

"I don't take it in coffee."

"Doctor's orders," he said, tipping two big spoonfuls into her cup.

"Poor Jean. I suppose that she was trying to reach something and overbalanced," Anthea said, gulping down the over-sweet liquid. "I ought not to have stayed away so long."

"Now, don't start blaming yourself," Max replied briskly. "This could have happened when you were out shopping, or upstairs, or anywhere."

"Will she have to stay in the hospital?"

"Yes, I expect it will be several weeks in her condition."

"I'd better get together some things that she will need."

Max nodded and bent down again to take Jean's pulse and to change the pad. He was glad to get Anthea out of the room before the ambulance men came.

The men arrived, pushing a collapsible stretcher. "Anthea, stay in your aunt's room in case the noise disturbs her," Max ordered. Again she realized that he was only thinking of her, but it was impossible not to hear Jean moan. As they maneuvered the stretcher down the steps she came out and looked at what little of Jean's face was showing between the bandage and the red blankets.

"I'll be back as soon as I know what is happening," Max said, putting a hand on Anthea's shoulder. "I'll phone Dr. Emerson from the hospital. And remember, we will do all that we can to help her."

Anthea nodded. "I seem to be getting more and more in your debt."

"No debts between friends," Max replied and hurried to his car.

"What was all the slamming of doors about?" Aunt Ellen asked when Anthea returned to her room.

"Jean had an accident. She somehow tipped her chair sideways and was on the floor when we got home."

"Is she badly hurt?"

"It looks as if her arm is broken. Dr. Sinclair drove me back. He phoned for an ambulance, and they have just left for the hospital."

"You mean that young doctor who helps Dr. Emerson?"

"Yes, you remember that he is Alan Towers' stepson. He was at the wedding."

"I keep forgetting," the old woman said fretfully. "But I liked him. Poor Jean. Lying on the floor, and I was asleep."

"What a blessing you were. You could not have done anything to help her. Dr. Sinclair wouldn't let me try to move her until the ambulance arrived. Now I am going to get you some soup."

"Only tea," Aunt Ellen insisted, and Anthea did not argue.

She ate hardly anything now and was pitifully thin. This morning she was more alert, but there were times when she scarcely seemed to know what went on around her and only slept when she had been given very strong drugs.

Anthea held her up, but after a few sips she turned away. She muttered, "That's enough," and Anthea laid her back on the pillows. She closed her eyes, and Anthea wiped her face with a cloth dampened with water.

"That's refreshing," she said, suddenly opening her eyes again. "Anthea, when I'm gone this house will be yours. There isn't much money because my annuity and pension will stop, but you can sell the house."

"Aunt Ellen, you are tiring yourself out talking, and you need all your strength."

Aunt Ellen shook her head. "I won't need anything much longer. It will be wonderful to be finished with all the pain. Don't grieve for me. I'll be much better off."

"I know," Anthea said, holding her thin, skeletonlike hands.

"You have been so good to me. God will bless you for it, dear."

At the moment Max rang the bell and walked in. "How is she?" Anthea asked.

"Dr. Emerson is there now. They suspect a broken arm, several ribs, and probably a concussion. I left her in good hands. You'll be able to visit when she is more comfortable. Dr. Emerson asked me to look in on Miss Denham as he won't be in today. He feels we should arrange for the visiting nurse to administer a much stronger injection. Is she awake?"

"Yes, she has just had a few sips of tea."

Aunt Ellen's eyes opened. She looked dazed for a moment, but then she said, "So you drove my niece home. Will you look out for her when I'm gone?"

"Aunt Ellen!" Anthea blurted out.

"I promise I'll do that," Max said firmly. "Now let me have a look at you."

He put away his stethoscope saying, "We are going to give you something stronger to ease the pain."

"Is Jean hurt badly?" she asked, her eyes opening again.

"Not too bad. She'll soon be better."

After a few days Jean was moved to a special geriatric hospital some distance away, and Anthea was unable to visit her; but she wrote to her and got news from Dr. Emerson.

The night after the accident Aunt Ellen went into a coma and did not recover consciousness again. For three weeks Anthea sat by her bedside between the necessary jobs and slept on a settee in her room. Beyond the fact that her heart was still beating, it was hard to tell that Aunt Ellen was alive.

Anthea's mother visited in the second week and stood looking down at the twisted gray features.

"Could you not have taken her to the hospital?" she asked as Anthea stood beside her.

"I can do as much as anyone," she said quietly. "She is beyond nursing now, and I promised that she would die in her own bed."

"But you are on your own at night?"

"I don't mind," Anthea replied firmly. "I can call the nurse or Dr. Emerson any time I need them."

Her mother shivered. "You are braver than I am. I could not bear it. I wish we were not leaving tomorrow. I ought to have come before, but Alan had so many engagements arranged."

"Don't worry about me, Mother. You take care of yourself and try to relax when you are away."

Her mother gave her a rather wry smile. "Not much chance to relax with the kind of schedule Alan has lined up. You make a wonderful nurse," she added, going to the door.

Anthea walked with her to the smart little car and bent down to kiss her. "Good-bye, Mother. I am glad you are happy now."

Her mother hesitated but said hurriedly, "Good-bye, Anthea. I guess *you* are only happy when you are sacrificing yourself."

Anthea waved as the car pulled away, and walked inside. Whatever happened she wouldn't have to depend upon her mother for help. She would never forgo her own pleasures to help anyone, but Anthea sensed that the life she had chosen was not quite as glamorous as she had imagined.

Two weeks after her mother's visit Aunt Ellen died early one morning. Anthea phoned for the nurse who had promised that she would come if she called her at any time. They did what was necessary, and for the rest of the day Anthea was busy visiting the undertaker, the pastor of the church, and phoning a few old friends. In the evening Max Sinclair arrived. She had only seen him once since Gerry's wedding as he had been to a special medical convention.

"Dr. Emerson told me that Miss Denham has gone," he said, following Anthea into the kitchen, which she still kept as her all-purpose room. "Surely you are not staying here on your own?"

"Why not?" Anthea asked. "The house feels empty even though Aunt Ellen was unconscious for so long, but I am not frightened of loneliness."

"Your mother and her husband ought to have been with you," Max said impatiently.

Anthea smiled. "That would have been worse than loneliness."

"When is the funeral?"

"Two o'clock on Thursday at the Methodist church which Aunt Ellen has attended for over sixty years. Now it has a very small congregation, as most of Aunt Ellen's generation have gone long ago, but she loved it.

"May I help in any way?"

Anthea shook her head. "Everything is arranged, but you could have coffee with me."

"Have you had a proper meal today?"

"Not really," Anthea replied. "I did not feel like it."

"I guessed as much. Go and put your coat on. I am taking you out for a decent dinner."

"I can't leave the house."

"There is no one who needs you now. We'll go to a very quiet place, so don't think that you will be accused of being unfeeling."

Anthea flushed. Max Sinclair seemed to have the ability of reading her thoughts. Somehow she felt as if he could see right inside her mind.

"I really don't want to," she protested.

"Well, I'm hungry if you aren't, so either we go out, or you'll have to cook me a big meal. I don't suppose you have a lot of food stashed away. Come on, Anthea. I'm the only bit of family available, so accept gratefully."

"It will take me a few minutes to change."

"OK. I'll sit here and look at the newspaper."

Anthea pulled herself upstairs, wondering why she always felt powerless to stand against Max Sinclair. She was so tired she would rather have gone to bed immediately, but Max was right as usual. She had had only coffee or tea all day, and probably part of her tiredness was from lack of food.

They drove out of town to an old farmhouse that had been turned into a restaurant. There were several small dining rooms instead of one large one, so that it felt homelike and private. Max must have made special arrangements because they had a small room to themselves.

"What an unusual place," Anthea exclaimed as they sat down and a plump, middle-aged woman handed them the menu. "You seem to know all sorts of out-of-the-way spots."

Max smiled. "I hate restaurants where one is smoked like a sausage and one's ears are blasted with raucous noise—it upsets my digestion. They have a good filet mignon here."

"That sounds tempting."

After their order was given Max said, "Have you decided what you are going to do now?"

"Not really. I'd like to keep the house so that I have a home of my own. Aunt Ellen told me that she had left it to me, but I am afraid that there will be no money for its upkeep. I have wondered if I could make the upstairs into two apartments."

"Why not sell it and buy a smaller, modern bungalow?"

"I'll have to get a job before I make any decision."

"We need a receptionist again. The one we got has left suddenly after a few weeks to get married."

"I'd rather stand on my own feet," Anthea replied firmly.

Max grinned at her. "Stubborn little animal, aren't you?"

"Not really. I just want to be independent. All my life I have depended upon someone else, and it's time I made my own decisions. I can imagine what Gerry would say if I came to work in your office."

"Gerry has nothing to do with it. Have she or Mark bothered to call since they got back?"

"Not yet, but there is no reason why they should."

"Surely Mark knew Miss Denham."

"When we were kids he used to come here often as we were always sure of a free meal. Mark was a great favorite."

"Have you let them know she has died?"

Anthea's expression hardened. "If Mark had no time to visit when she was alive, there is no point in his coming now or going to the funeral."

"Have you called your mother?"

"A letter will reach her soon enough."

"Are there many relations?"

"No, Aunt Ellen was the last of her family. My grandfather was her only brother. She had no sisters."

"Strange how some families die out," Max said thoughtfully. "You are the last of the Gordons, and I am the last of this branch of the Sinclairs. Here comes the food."

Anthea bent her head to say grace and looked up to see Max doing the same. He smiled as he caught her looking at him. "My stepfather thinks I am a religious nut."

171

"My mother thought the same about father and me. How is it that you are so different from Gerry and her father?"

"Before she died my mother had become a Christian. I guess you understand what I mean when I say that. She begged me to make a decision for Christ, but it wasn't until I was in college that I started to think seriously about what people term "religion." I saw some of the men, especially the medical students, drinking and messing up their lives. Some of them flunked exams because they wouldn't take life seriously; but I saw others who were good fun but were in earnest about their profession. One especially attracted me. He was an outstanding athlete, could be hilariously funny, but he meant business. I found out that he did a lot of extra work with kids in the slums, helped in camps during vacations and was destined for the mission field. We got friendly—used to argue a lot—but finally he made me see that I needed to accept Jesus Christ as my Savior."

Anthea's eyes shone. "I'm glad that you told me, Max."

"How was it with you?" he asked.

"Nothing so dramatic," she replied quietly. "I feel as if I have always known God. Dad used to talk to me about Him so simply when I was child. I believed and grew up loving Him. I learned early that mother wasn't sympathetic, and there were some things that we did not talk about when she was there."

"How did they come to get married? They were so different."

"Dad was going into the ministry, but the war came and he was in the Officer Training Corps and was called up immediately. He was abroad almost four years, during which time he met Mother, who was in the women's service. They fell in love and were married after a very short acquaintance. I suppose in those days, as Aunt Ellen said, people were not quite normal, life was uncertain, and people grabbed at what happiness they could get. Dad was a major by then, and I suppose that his rank made him special; Mother was attractive, fastidious, and very charming.

"Probably he realized his mistake even before they were discharged. Mother refused to be the wife of a struggling clergyman, so Dad went back to the university and started teaching. I was not born until about twelve years after they married, and I suppose by that time Mother did not want her life messed up by a baby. Dad was delighted. I remember them as two people who lived in the same house but had very little in common. Mother looked after me but was always cool and withdrawn. It was Dad who supplied all the warmth and love.

"I wasn't very old when Dad had trouble with his voice and throat and was told that he would have to give up teaching and live as much as possible in the open air. His grandmother, who had brought him up after his parents were killed in a car crash, died about that time and left her money between him and his Aunt Ellen. He scraped together all that he had, bought the house and grounds near Bewdley, and turned them into the Rookery Nurseries."

"No wonder you hated to see the business wiped out. Now what about dessert?"

Anthea looked surprised. As she had talked, she had eaten slowly. She was surprised to see that her plate was almost empty.

"Goodness, have I eaten all that?" she exclaimed. "Why did you let me talk so much?"

Max laughed. "That was my subtle intention. Now admit you feel better."

Anthea smiled. "Much better."

"What about ice cream and coffee?"

"I don't think I have room."

"Nonsense, a growing girl like you needs filling up."

"There's only one way I can grow, and that is something I don't need."

"How much weight have you lost since you went to your aunt's house?"

"I don't really know as she had no scales."

"Then what about your clothes?"

Anthea grinned. "They are getting very loose. I'll have to start taking tucks in the waistbands."

"Don't you dare. Just you get some good, nourishing, regular meals into you."

"Very well, doctor," she said primly, tackling her large helping of ice cream.

Max drove her back and insisted on accompanying her into the lonely, silent house.

"Go straight to bed with a book if you can't sleep," he ordered. "I wish I could take you out again tomorrow night, but I am on call. Lock the door after me, and if you need anything, any time, call either to the office or my flat. This is the number. Good night, Anthea."

"Good night, Max, and thank you for your kindness."

"The pleasure was all mine," he said, and only Max knew what an effort it was to tear himself away and leave her alone, but he felt that he was making some progress. She had let down the barriers of reserve and talked more openly than she had ever done. One day when the time was ripe he would tell her how much he loved her, but she had gone through so many traumatic experiences in these last weeks that it was better to let her take their friendship quietly and not try to rush things.

12

Aunt Ellen's funeral was pathetically small; only a few elderly acquaintances, Mr. Joslin, the attorney, and Max Sinclair were present. There had been no flowers, by Aunt Ellen's special instructions, and as the coffin was lowered into the ground Anthea's heart ached at the thought of how few people were left to mourn her loss. Yet in the years gone by, how often she had helped others who were in need.

Her mother was still abroad, and there had not been even a card of sympathy from Mark and Gerry. Only Mr. Joslin returned to the house with her to read the will, which was perfectly straightforward. The house, the furniture, the jewelry, and whatever money that was left after expenses were paid were all left unconditionally to Anthea.

"I wish that there were more money, Miss Gordon," the attorney said sincerely, "but Miss Denham's pension and annuity ceased with her death. She did have a small insurance on her life. I know how much you have meant to your great-aunt. I hope that the house will at least bring a substantial sum. Property is very valuable in this area now, even if it needs a good deal spent on it. Do you intend to sell it?"

"I haven't made up my mind," Anthea replied. "I'd like to keep a home of my own, but I must also find a suitable job."

"Well, there is no immediate hurry, but if we can assist in any way please don't hesitate to consult us. Your great-aunt was a friend of my mother's long ago."

"Thank you," Anthea replied. "I will let you know what I decide."

Anthea searched the vacancy columns in the local newspaper and called or visited several of those listed. Very few involved the kind of work she wanted, and at two places she had to admit that she had left her last job at Thompson's without references.

The evening after the funeral she wandered around the house, wondering what was the best thing to do. Should she sell it or use what money was available and have it made into separate apartments? It would divide quite easily, two apartments upstairs and the ground floor for herself. The rents would pay for the taxes and repairs. She might even get somebody suitable to live in the bed/sitting room Aunt Ellen had used, who would be willing to help with the work and see that the boarders behaved reasonably.

If only she could find suitable work locally. Finally she decided to try it for the next few months. She would hardly admit to herself that she hated to cut herself off completely from Max Sinclair—he was becoming increasingly important to her and was the only person who had shown any real kindness in the recent weeks. Probably his kindness was only because he was sorry for her and because he detested his stepfather, but she longed that their friendship would have a chance to develop and mature.

She scanned the "Positions Wanted" section and was amazed at the number of people who needed somewhere to live—couples who stated boldly that they had no children or pets, students who needed bed/sitting rooms, and businessmen or women who wanted flats within easy distance of the center of town. There was obviously no shortage of would-be tenants.

As she folded the paper her eye caught an advertisement stating that there were vacancies for nurses to train in the hospital, and her mother's words came back to her: *"You make a good nurse, Anthea."*

These last months she had seen Jean Thompson and Aunt Ellen suffer and had been glad to do what she could to relieve them. Surely this would be worthwhile work, and she would be able to learn a great deal more because she had been continually conscious of her lack of knowledge of even the elementary skills of nursing.

She would wait until she had signed the final papers concerning Aunt Ellen's estate, then consult a builder and find out what it would cost to have washbasins put in the bedrooms, maybe central heating if she could afford it, and the house painted and decorated. The furniture was solid, even if old-fashioned. Paper and paint would make all the difference, but the decorating would all depend on how much Aunt Ellen had left. There might be some antique stuff that it would be better to sell and put less valuable stuff in the rooms strangers would use.

The next day she drove to the hospital where Jean Thompson was recovering. It was the first opportunity she had to go so far. Jean's ribs were healing, and her arm was out of the cast.

"Jean, you look much better."

"I've been longing to see you," Jean replied. "I am sorry about your aunt, but poor soul, one couldn't wish her to linger on like that."

"Is your arm almost better?" Anthea asked.

"It is a bit stiff, but I do exercises to make it more mobile. I have been waiting for you to come so that I can share my big surprise."

177

"It must be something good for you to look so excited."

"When the doctor and physiotherapist were examining me they decided that there is no need for me to sit strapped in a wheelchair all day. They started on treatment and exercises as soon as I got here, and my legs are already getting stronger. They are sure that if I persevere I'll be able to wear braces and walk about the house with a walker or canes and perhaps in time even drive an invalid car."

"Oh, Jean, I am so happy for you," Anthea said, her eyes suddenly moist. "Why did nobody think it could be done before?"

"This is a new treatment. Now my leg muscles are weak for they haven't been used for so long, but when I leave here the staff are sure I'll be able to move about."

"Will you be here much longer?"

"I'm not sure. The doctor says that I can go on with the treatment at a hospital nearer home, although I don't know where that home will be."

"If you can move about, couldn't you go to an ordinary rest home?"

"Maybe, but I don't like being with a crowd of women. I'd rather have one room and look after myself if I can. But what about you, Anthea? Have you got another job lined up?"

"Not yet," Anthea replied. "I am still not decided what I want to do or where I should live."

"Are you going to sell the house?"

"Probably I will have to. I can't keep up a place like that on my own with the taxes, and it needs so much spent on it."

"I wish you could stay somewhere near Newbridge," Jean said wistfully. "I have a few friends, but no one very close. I'd like to think you could visit me sometimes."

"It will depend on what Mr. Joslin, the solicitor, advises when things are settled and what sort of job is available. Now I am almost glad that you had that accident. If you hadn't, the doctors probably would never have found out that you could be more mobile."

"I have been thinking a lot while I've been here, and I realize how good God has been to me. If you hadn't come to us for those few weeks, I don't know what I would have done when Bert was killed. If Bert had not been killed, I would not have come to live with you and found the peace I needed so much. If I hadn't tipped the wheelchair I probably would have gone on completely crippled for the rest of my life. Sometimes what we think are terrible tragedies turn out to be blessings."

Anthea nodded. "God does answer our prayers, but not always in the way we imagine would be best. I can see now that He was good to take my father so suddenly without pain or a long, drawn out illness, and I know that He is teaching me many lessons, even if some are painful."

"And someday you'll see that He saved you from making the mistake of marrying Mark Latham."

"I realize that already," Anthea said emphatically. "Now I must go. I have an appointment with Mr. Joslin at four o'clock, and it is a good hour's drive."

"Anthea, I have a little money in a separate account. An old uncle left it to me, but I never told Bert. He would have just wasted it. I kept it a secret, because I believed that someday I would need it when I was desperate. I'll have my social security check, so if you need that money I'd willingly give it to you."

Anthea's eyes filled with tears. "I do appreciate your offer," she replied, a lump in her throat. "But we'll leave that money where it is. Is it enough to buy you a little home?"

"Only if it was a very cheap one," Jean smiled. "But I have no family; if it would help you keep the house I'd be glad to give it to you."

"Bless you, Jean, I'll not forget," Anthea said, bending down to kiss her. "I'll come again soon and tell you what I have decided."

Anthea hurried out to her car, her thoughts very busy. Surely this news was a seal on what she hoped to do. If Jean could move about and look after herself, she could have the bed/sitting room downstairs, live rent free in exchange for being the caretaker, and her social security check would pay for her food and necessities. With an adapted car, which would be supplied by the government, she would even be able to get out to the shops herself.

Mr. Joslin greeted her pleasantly. "We have a rough estimate of how things stand. There were no large debts, so with the insurance we figure that you will have roughly about five thousand pounds."

"As much as that?" Anthea exclaimed.

Mr. Joslin smiled. "That isn't a vast sum."

"Would it be enough to have some alterations done in the house?"

"What did you have in mind?"

"To divide the upstairs into two apartments, put washbasins in the bedrooms, maybe install central heating, and have the rooms redecorated. I thought that I might sell some of the antique furniture that I imagine may be valuable."

"Then you have decided to keep the house?"

"For the time being at any rate."

Mr. Joslin put his fingertips together and looked thoughtful. "Whatever you put into it will always improve the property and bring a higher price if you do decide to sell, but I would advise you not to exceed three thousand pounds. You ought to keep a little nest egg for emergencies."

Anthea smiled. "I feel like an heiress. To me even one thousand pounds sounds like fabulous riches."

"Your tastes must be very modest, Miss Gordon. Keep in touch, and remember that we are here to help you if we can."

"Thank you so much, Mr. Joslin. You have been most helpful."

Anthea walked out as if treading on air. That was far more than she had expected. She had looked up the names of several builders and decided to call at their offices. She believed that she could have a better idea from the reception she received than if she phoned.

Eventually she arranged with three different firms to send someone to take particulars and give estimates. Then she drove to the hospital and asked for an interview with the nursing supervisor. She realized that there would be a lot of work to do when the alterations were being done, but she would feel more secure if she had some sort of job in view. No point in deciding to stop in Newbridge if there was no work for her.

Her legs felt weak, and she grasped her handbag tightly as she entered the supervisor's office.

"You wished to inquire about training?" The woman said briskly. "Can you tell me what experience you have had as you are rather older than our usual beginners?"

"I really have had no experience. Until a short time ago I worked with my father in his nursery business in Bewdley. He died suddenly, the business was sold, my mother remarried, and I came to live with my great-aunt in Newbridge. I have cared for her for the last six months. Her name was Miss Denham, and she came to the hospital several times for treatment, but of course you have so many patients."

"I remember her. Certainly a remarkable old lady."

"I realized that when I was caring for her and another crippled friend, Mrs. Thompson, who was living with us, how little I knew about the most elementary nursing. I need work. I will be free soon, and I would like to learn a lot more."

"A very good attitude. Evidently you are not afraid of hard work, because no matter how one looks at it, nursing is hard work—long hours, unquestioning obedience, and great responsibility. You understand that you would have to start with a group much younger than yourself."

"Yes, I realize that, but I'd be just as ignorant."

The supervisor smiled. "That is good insight. Our next class begins in two months' time. Can you fill in your time until then?"

"Very easily. There is a lot I want to do to the old house my great-aunt has left me."

"Then you hope to live out—not be in residence?"

"Is that possible?"

"Yes, some nurses prefer it, although it takes up time and energy to travel each day. Will you live on your own?"

"The crippled friend I mentioned will be returning from the hospital where she is having physiotherapy treatment, and she will share my home, I hope."

"You can see how you get on. If you find it too much you can always transfer to the nurses' home. When you live out, you miss a lot of the community activities, but not everyone likes being in a crowd. Visit the student nurses' office, and you will be told about uniform. You can also fill out the necessary information. We will send you a formal recognition of your acceptance in due time."

Anthea sat down immediately when she got out of the office, feeling weak and deflated. No wonder she had always heard or read about nurses being scared of the supervisor. She had been pleasant and friendly enough, but there was something unnerving in the atmosphere and in the piercing eyes, which were assessing every detail. She hoped that she would never have to go to her for any mistake she made.

For the next weeks Anthea was kept busy every minute of the day. She had persuaded a builder and plumber to start immediately, so the house was in a continual upheaval. She was reminded of her old home and the mess it was when she last saw it.

Twice she went out for dinner with Max Sinclair, but for some obsure reason she kept her proposed nursing career a secret.

"What about that job you were looking for?" Max inquired on the first occasion.

"I have too much to do in the house at present," Anthea replied.

"What made you decide to keep it and to take in boarders? I must say that I wouldn't mind having you for a landlady myself."

Anthea laughed. "I suppose what really made me decide was Mrs. Thompson's need of a home."

"You mean the woman we rushed into the hospital when she fell in her wheelchair?"

"Yes, but it turned out to be the best thing that ever happened."

"Now you are talking in riddles."

"You know that she was sent to Greburn Geriatric Hospital. The doctor and physiotherapist decided that there was a new treatment that they wanted to try on her legs, so they worked on them as well as her arm. They are sure that she will be able to have braces fitted, be able to get about, and even drive an invalid car."

"That's amazing. You mean everybody had assumed that she would always be confined to a wheelchair?"

"I suppose that no one ever thought of anything different. Probably only experts dealing with that sort of condition would know of a new treatment."

"Makes you think, doesn't it?" Max said thoughtfully. "So you are going to keep the house and make a home for her?"

"Not altogether. I want to feel that I have a place of my own, and she and I get along well together. We will share the ground floor and rent the two apartments upstairs."

"I am glad you aren't vanishing altogether," Max said lightly, and Anthea blushed.

13

By the first of November when Anthea commenced her training many changes had been completed. Every room had been redecorated, a young married couple were living in one apartment, two medical students in the other. The outside of the house had been painted, the garden tidied up and replanted. Jean Thompson had returned from the hospital walking on braces with the promise of a car for the handicapped as soon as possible. The kitchen had been remodeled so that the work was as easy as possible, and Jean looked at everything with a beaming face.

Anthea had washed the old curtains and bedspreads or made new ones. Much of the heavy antique furniture had been sold for a far higher price than Anthea had expected, and new lighter stuff, which took less polishing and was easier to move, had been put in its place.

"How did you get it all done?" Jean asked as she moved around the ground floor and looked up the staircase.

Anthea smiled. "It has certainly kept me busy, but I hope we'll have a happy home here."

"You look tired. Can't you have a vacation for a few weeks now that everything is finished?"

Anthea shook her head. "I am starting my new job on Monday."

"And what is that? I thought that having people living in

185

the house would keep you busy enough and would pay the expenses.''

''Not quite,'' Anthea replied. ''It will help with the up-keep of the place, but I need money for extras. Besides, I would need more than this to occupy myself. I am starting to train as a nurse. I don't know if I'll be any good, but I'd like to learn how to look after people who are ill.''

''You can do that without training,'' Jean said emphatically. ''Look what you did for your aunt all those months and all the help you were to me when I was so useless.''

''It is because I felt uncertain and helpless so often that I have decided that I want to be better trained.''

''No one is more cut out for it,'' Jean said. ''Does your mother know?''

''No. She has called a couple of times and thinks that I am mad. She wanted me to stay with her at Tall Timbers before it is sold, but I made the excuse that I had too much to do and was too tired to dress up.''

''Does she know about the nursing idea?''

''No. I have told no one. I must make my own decisions and not consult anyone else.''

''Did you keep the house partly for my sake?'' Jean inquired.

Anthea smiled. ''Maybe a little, but I wanted a home and I needed you with me.''

''Bless you. I'll never forget it,'' Jean said, hastily blinking away tears. ''But, Anthea, I want you to remember that you are never to sacrifice yourself for me. I can always go into a rest home or even manage on my own in one room.''

Anthea nodded. ''I'm counting on you to look after the house for me. I am arranging for a woman to come in one day a week to do the heavy work, but there will still be plenty for you to do.''

Late that afternoon while Anthea was shopping she met Mark coming from his office.

"Hi, stranger," he greeted her, holding out his hand. "Where have you been hiding yourself?"

Anthea laughed and pulled her hand away. "I've been up to my eyes in dirt, having Aunt Ellen's old house made into apartments."

"Yes, your mother said you intended hanging onto the old place. Will this be enough for you without getting a job?"

Anthea hesitated. Sooner or later her family would have to know about her new work. "No, but the rents will pay for the upkeep of the house and give me a home of my own."

"I thought that you hated being in town and wanted to be in the country."

"We can't always have everything we want," Anthea said calmly. "I have decided to try nursing for a few months anyway. I am starting on Monday."

"What a change from growing plants! You'll have all the male patients and doctors falling in love with you."

"Don't be silly," she said sharply. "How is Gerry?" she asked as she saw a flush rise in Mark's cheeks.

"Not too good at present. She's upset because there is a baby on the way, and she hadn't planned for that to happen. I guess most girls are a bit unpredictable during the first months. I thought perhaps your mother would have told you."

"I haven't seen her recently. I believe they have been traveling again."

Mark nodded. "Alan Towers is like a cat on hot bricks. He just can't relax. He said he wanted to retire, but he is busier than ever. I suppose that is one of the things Gerry thinks that she will miss. She won't be so free to dash all

187

over the place or do all the riding and show jumping she had planned.''-

A horn sounded, and Mark jumped around. ''There she is now; she said she would pick me up at the office at four o'clock. Good-bye, Anthea. Lovely to see you.''

Anthea walked into the nearest shop, trying to forget the way Gerry had looked at her.

When she got home her mother's car was outside the door, and unconsciously she pulled her shoulders back and put a plastic smile on her face.

''Mother, how nice to see you,'' she said, finding her mother standing in the hall talking to Jean.

''I was just leaving as you were not here,'' her mother replied. Anthea recognized that cold, complaining note in her voice.

''Stay for some tea,'' she said gaily. ''I am dying for a cup, and I know that Jean will have the kettle on.''

Jean nodded. ''I've had mine, so I'll go to my room.''

''Let me take your coat, Mother,'' she said, hanging her own in the hall closet.

''No, thank you. I can't stay. Alan and I are going out to a dinner and theater, so I must get back in plenty of time to change. Is that woman here all the time, Anthea?''

''She is acting as caretaker and helps me tremendously,'' Anthea replied.

''I suppose you realize that you will be saddled with her for life. What about the rest of the house?''

Anthea put boiling water in the teapot and laid the tray on the kitchen table.

''A married couple are in one apartment and two medical students are in the other.''

''Alan thinks that you are crazy. You are too young and pretty to settle down like this. What about your great love of the country?''

188

"I wanted my own home, so I am trying this for a time. If it doesn't work out I can always sell. Mr. Joslin said that whatever I put into the house would improve the property."

"Yes, if tenants don't knock it about too much. I never thought my daughter would condescend to keeping a boardinghouse."

"I did not need a home this size for myself," Anthea said trying to keep her temper.

"I came to ask you to spend the weekend with us. We are having several guests, and I'd be glad of your help."

"I am sorry, Mother, but I will not be free."

"You mean you have another engagement?"

"Not exactly. I will be working. I am beginning nurses' training at the hospital tomorrow, and I don't know what my hours will be."

"Oh, Anthea! Running around like a maid cleaning lockers and emptying bedpans is even worse than grubbing in the nursery. I wonder why we bothered to give you a decent education."

Anthea laughed. "It can't be as bad as all that. Anyway, I guess it will be useful to know how to take care of myself and other people if they are ill. I learned when I was looking after Aunt Ellen that I knew very little."

"Well, I hope you'll arrange to be free at Christmas as we will be leaving Tall Timbers soon after. Gerry is planning a special housewarming now that the place is all finished."

"I hear a baby is on the way."

"How did you know? I suppose Max Sinclair told you. Gerry says you are very friendly with him."

"No. Mark told me this afternoon. I met him while I was shopping."

"Poor Gerry is very upset. Mark ought to have been more considerate. Alan is thrilled at the thought of a grandson, but I can understand that she does not want to be tied down right away. I am sure that if it is a son it will be the only one.''

Anthea turned away quickly. How could her mother and Gerry be so callous and selfish? She longed for children of her own. How often she had dreamed of the time when Mark and she would have their own family.

"I can't promise for Christmas; I can't leave Mrs. Thompson on her own.''

"You mean you will consider her before me?''

"You will have so many people with you, and she has no one. And I may have to be on duty in the hospital.''

"Very well,'' her mother replied coldly. "Gerry says you won't visit us because you are jealous because Mark married her, and they took over the house. She thinks that you are hoping to catch Max instead.''

"Gerry must have a mean, nasty, little mind,'' Anthea said, gripping her hands below the table. "She has got so much. Is she never satisfied? Tell her I have no designs on her stepbrother, but if I had I guess he is well able to take care of himself.''

"I must go,'' Mrs. Gordon said, getting up hastily and pulling her coat around her. "You are always impossible — just like your father. Good-bye.''

"Good-bye, Mother,'' Anthea said as her mother left. She closed the door and stood with her back pressed against it, trying to gain control. She was shaking from the effort to resist telling her mother just what she thought of her and Gerry. *Why does Mother bother to visit me when all she does is upset me? Is it because she is as discontented and dissatisfied as ever, and she has to have someone on whom to pour out her bitterness?*

Jean Thompson hobbled out and took one glance at Anthea's stricken face. "I couldn't help hearing her parting shot, dearie, but don't let it worry you. She is miserable herself and wants everyone to be the same. Just thank God that you haven't got to live with her. You need some food and a cup of strong tea.''

Anthea's eyes filled with tears. ''I have prayed so long for her, but nothing seems to crack that hard shell.''

''God can do it—just like He did for me. But perhaps she'll have to suffer and have her pride broken before He can deal with her. Probably in her heart she is mad because you are independent, and she can't order you about any more.''

On Monday morning Anthea dressed in her uniform and drove to the hospital. Sometimes she thought of selling the old car, but it would bring very little, and it made traveling much easier. Besides, it would be useful for Jean and Anthea to get away from town occasionally.

Those first few days were a kaleidoscope of mixed impressions. What impressed Anthea most was that there was never enough time. From the moment she went on duty she hurried to wash patients, give out trays, and help with beds. She was only a raw beginner, but it was taken for granted by the patients and staff nurses that she knew everything.

On Thursday morning Anthea was pushing a wheelchair down the corridor, taking a patient to X-ray, when Max Sinclair walked by with a fellow doctor. She saw him glance at her casually, look again, and say something to his companion.

''What are you doing here, Miss Gordon?'' he asked.

''I'm a first-year nurse,'' she replied, her eyes dancing.

''Why did you never mention it?''

''I only started on Monday, but if I don't get this patient

191

to X-ray at once I'll have a very short stay. Good morning, doctor.''

Anthea hurried away, knowing that Max would have a lot to say the next time he saw her. She chuckled inwardly as she remembered the expression on his face.

That evening Anthea was preparing to go to bed early because her legs ached and her head buzzed with all she was trying to learn from her textbooks. Max arrived without warning.

''Hope I'm not too late,'' he said calmly. ''I've just finished surgery.''

''Come in. I intended to go to bed early to rest my weary bones.''

''How are the boarders?''

''No trouble at all. I hardly see or hear them. It will have to be the kitchen as usual.''

''Good. Then we can have some coffee. Now tell me why you kept your flight into the maze of the medical world a secret.''

Anthea laughed. ''First, you might have tried to dissuade me. Second, I like to decide things for myself. And third, I did not want my family to think that I had been accepted on your recommendation.''

Max shook his head. ''Sometimes I'd love to spank you. You knew you were starting at the hospital where I would visit, yet you never gave me an inkling that this was in your mind. When I asked about a job you put me off by saying that you were too busy with the house alterations.''

''So I was, but they are finished now.''

''You have a devious mind, young woman. I am beginning to realize that I don't know what goes on in that head of yours.''

''Good,'' Anthea said, setting out cups and pouring water in the teakettle. ''I was afraid you did.''

"And what does that mean?"

"There are a great many thoughts I'd hate anyone to guess at. Max, will you pretend that you don't know me when we meet in the hospital? Just treat me as you do any other probationer."

"Why?"

"Because I certainly don't want any of my group to think I know one of the important doctors who petrify us with fright."

"Are you making fun of me by any chance?"

"Not really, but it would be better if no one guessed we are even remotely connected."

"Then I suppose I can't take you out to dinner again?"

"Well, perhaps, if we are not likely to meet anyone who knows us. We could go to one of those little out-of-the-way spots you know."

"Are you going to the 'shindig' at Tall Timbers next weekend?"

"No. My mother is annoyed because I said I was not free."

"Does she know about your nursing career?"

"I had to tell her when she called on Friday. She thinks I am mad and says that I am as impossible as my father." In spite of herself her voice shook, and she turned away quickly.

Max put his hand over hers as she put his cup on the table. "I would take that as a tremendous compliment. I believe that he was one of the sanest men I have ever met. I only wish I had known him better."

"Thank you," Anthea said huskily.

"What about Christmas? I believe that Gerry and Mark are having a big party. I suppose you know that they have plunged unexpectedly into parenthood? Did your mother tell you the great secret?"

"Mark did when I met him accidentally in town last week."

"I hope that he is more excited about it than my selfish sister. She is hopping mad, and the poor little baby won't get much of a welcome."

"Why on earth did she get married if she did not want a family?"

"Gerry was engaged, but the man went off with someone else just before the Towers moved to Bewdley. Mark fell hard. I guess his adoration soothed her ruffled feathers, and she wanted a house of her own with an easily managed husband like Mark. Gerry will always be the boss but starting a family was another thing she didn't plan."

"Poor Mark," Anthea said, her heart aching for the friend she had shared her life with for so long.

"He'll get by. My stepfather will make everything easy for his daughter and his future grandson. I'd better go and let you get your beauty sleep. I must say, you look very attractive in your uniform."

Anthea laughed. "I feel as if the cap will fly off at any minute, and the collar slips around my neck."

"You'll soon get used to it, but I guess it is going to be hard work with this place to look after as well as your hours on duty."

"Jean does a lot, and I have a woman who comes in one day a week, so I think we'll manage. My biggest problem is trying to understand all the little details. Flowers and shrubs were less vulnerable than patients."

"Well, if things get too tough you have my private phone number. I have told you before that I want to help all I can."

"Thank you, Max. It is good to know that I have one friend I can depend upon in an emergency."

14

The days flew past for Anthea. There was so much to learn—so much to do—that Christmas was upon her before she realized it. It seemed useless to buy her mother anything when she could afford whatever she wanted. Anthea ended up by buying a small bottle of very expensive perfume that she used to prefer, a warm cardigan for Jean, a few, small items for her fellow nurses, and box of candied fruit for each of her tenants. She decided that a book would be permissible for Max Sinclair as an expression of her thanks. That was the extent of her Christmas shopping.

She would not spend money on Alan Towers, Gerry, or Mark, as they never bothered about her. She was trying to live within her income and not touch the small amount of savings that remained from Aunt Ellen's estate. It had cost more than she had planned for the alterations and extra furnishings, but so far, things were working out well with Jean Thompson and the other tenants.

Her mother phoned to ask if she was planning to be with them, and Anthea had to agree. Knowing that Anthea would feel obligated to spend Christmas Day with her mother, Jean had accepted an invitation from a family from the church where Aunt Ellen had attended and where Anthea took Jean if she was free on Sunday. Jean had made sure that Anthea was not on duty those two days and insisted that she ought to spend that time with her mother, even if the prospect did not fill her with joy.

"She is your mother," Jean said when they argued over the matter. "She has invited you, so don't give her cause to say that you have turned against her. We keep praying for her, so don't let her feel you harbor any ill feelings."

"But I'll need new clothes," Anthea protested.

"Then get what will be useful afterward. No reason why you can't wear what you had for the weddings, but you need a new winter coat and dress anyway."

Anthea smiled. "You boss me around like Mother used to do."

"Only because I love you," Jean replied, her eyes on Anthea's face with its clear skin and lovely blue eyes. "You have the kind of looks which will last far longer than surface prettiness. Make your mother proud to show you off to her friends."

"More likely I'll feel like a drab barnyard fowl among a crowd of gorgeous peacocks. But you win. I'll phone Mother and inform her that her impossible daughter will be with them on Christmas Eve, but I'm glad it only will be two days."

Feeling utterly miserable, Anthea drove to Tall Timbers. It was the first time that she had been inside the house, and she might as well have been going to prison.

A maid opened the door and showed her to her room. "Mr. and Mrs. Towers are out but will be back for dinner. Would you like a drink?"

"No, thank you," Anthea replied. "I'll change and wait until my mother returns."

The maid looked startled. "Is your mother coming too?"

"Mrs. Towers is my mother. Did she not tell you?"

"I have only been engaged to help out over the holiday season. I did not realize Mrs. Towers had a daughter."

"Are there many guests coming?"

"About eight, I think. I suppose that is why you have such a small room. The larger ones are needed for couples. The bathroom is at the end of the corridor. This floor is usually only used by the cook and the maids."

"It looks very comfortable," Anthea said, looking around at the room with its single bed, chest of drawers, built-in closet, and a rather worn carpet on the floor.

She opened her suitcase, hung her few clothes in the closet, and looked out of the window. The gardens were almost devoid of color, but the lawns were still green. The edges of the flower beds were well trimmed.

There was nothing reminiscent of wilderness now. Her room was at the front of the house, and she wondered where the fruit trees and rock plants that had been brought from the nursery had been planted. It would be like seeing old friends to walk around and recognize some of the things which she and her father had grown.

It was too early to get ready for dinner, so she sat down in the well-worn armchair by the window, a book in her hand, but her thoughts were in the home she had shared with her father only a few miles away.

How much had happened since last Christmas. She had never imagined that in little over a year she could lose her father, her closest friend, her home, her aunt, and would have to stand completely alone and make a new life. How good it was that God did not let her see the future, but only the immediate present. What would her father think if he could see her now—visiting like a stranger in the house belonging to his wife and the man she had chosen simply because he could give her all she wanted.

Had she been silly to come and expose herself to unhappy memories and rude remarks that she knew would come her way? Did she really owe her mother anything after the way she had treated her father and herself?

"Stop being sorry for yourself," she said angrily. With a determined effort Anthea tried to concentrate on the anatomy textbook she had brought with her.

She heard a car drive up and watched from behind the filmy curtains. She saw Alan Towers get out and open the doors, while a man came down the steps to take the luggage. She recognized her mother wearing a beautiful fur coat and saw another woman wrapped in a mink stole and a man with snow-white hair, who limped badly.

They disappeared, and a few moments later another car arrived and two more people disappeared inside while the luggage was lifted out and the car driven away.

Anthea's heart sank even lower. She had told Jean that she would feel like a barnyard fowl among peacocks. Now she knew she also would be like a fish out of water. These sophisticated, wealthy people always made her tongue-tied and nervous.

A few moments later the maid she had first seen tapped at the door. "Mrs. Towers asks that you please come to the lounge."

Anthea glanced in the mirror. Seeing that her hair was tidy and the skirt of her pretty light blue wool suit was hanging properly, she followed the maid downstairs.

The men stood up as she entered the long, beautifully furnished room where the lights were already lit.

Her mother came forward, saying effusively, "Anthea, I am sorry we were out when you arrived, but now I want you to meet our dear friends, Jane and Andrew Blair, Julie and Leon Le Brun—my daughter, Anthea."

"My dear, where have you been hiding her?" someone exclaimed. "We had no idea that you had such a beautiful daughter."

Alan Towers came in at that moment. "Hello, Anthea," he boomed. "Glad you have consented to visit us at last. Anthea is one of the liberated young women who believe in being completely independent. She has her own home and is a nurse."

"Which hospital?" Andrew Blair asked, and the others laughed.

"Would you like her to soothe your fevered brow when you are sick?" Julie Le Brun giggled, and the others laughed as if she had made some tremendous joke.

"I am only a beginner," Anthea put in.

"Bet you look like a doll in your uniform," Leon said, and Anthea hated the way his eyes roved over her.

"Would anyone like a drink before you change?" Alan asked.

"A whiskey for me," Andrew Blair answered.

"Gin and tonic, please," the three women said together.

"Leon?"

"Small brandy and soda. Too early to start seriously yet."

"You Anthea?"

"Nothing, unless you have orange or tomato juice."

"Great Scot, girl, this is Christmas. You'll need something livelier than that to keep you going."

"My daughter always likes to be different," her mother said with a light laugh, but Anthea recognized that already she had started off on the wrong foot.

The dinner was well cooked and well served, but for Anthea, trying to keep a conversation going with strangers on either side of her, it seemed to go on forever. Afterward the men went off to play billiards, and the women settled down to play bridge. Several guests who were not staying in the house had joined them, and Anthea hoped that she would be able to slip away unnoticed.

An elderly woman sat down beside her and took some needlepoint out of her bag. "May I join you, my dear?" she asked. "I don't play bridge. It makes my head ache. I like to be able to leave when I am tired, but I cannot do that if I get tied up in a game. People take it so seriously and get so intense. Why have we never met you before?"

"My father's aunt was very ill, so I nursed her until she died. She left me her house. As Mother had remarried and sold our home I kept my aunt's house. I have been very busy having alterations done. Now I have started nurse's training so I have very little free time."

"You mean that you live on your own?"

"Not really. I have a crippled friend who shares the ground floor with me, and upstairs I have two rented apartments."

"Eleanor ought to be very proud of you. I wish I had been blessed with a daughter. We never had a family. Now that my husband has passed on, I realize more than ever what I have missed."

"Do you live near?" Anthea asked, drawn to this woman who seemed different from the others. "I did not catch your name in all the introductions."

"Impossible to sort out such a crowd at the first meeting. Actually I am Margaret Lester—Lady Lester—but don't let that throw you. My husband was given a knighthood for the work he did as an engineer. It really doesn't mean much, but some people think that a title is very important. I now live in a small house near Melworth, and I met your mother some time ago at a charity fashion show. She has invited me for

200

dinner several times. I really prefer my own fireside and television in the evenings, but one has to make an effort occasionally to be sociable. I hope that the party does not go on too late, as I need a lot of sleep these days and I am having my sister and her family with me tomorrow. In many ways I am always glad when Christmas is over.''

''I expect that it is fun when there is a big family of children. I always envied my friends who had brothers and sisters.''

''How long will you be here? I would love for you to visit me.''

''I only have two days. Tomorrow relatives are visiting. On Boxing Day Mr. Towers' daughter and her husband are having a housewarming, and I expect that will be a big party.''

''I've been invited, although I don't really know them. Did I hear that they bought your old home and had it completely modernized?''

''Yes.''

''Will this be your first visit since then? That will be hard for you, my dear.''

''My father loved it,'' Anthea said quietly. ''Without him the house does not mean much.''

Her companion nodded. ''People are far more important than places. A beautiful house can be an empty shell if the people who live there are not happy. I would have been content in a cottage as long as my husband was with me. Sometimes we did live in very primitive conditions when he was traveling on different assignments. Once we were in a tent for three weeks, and another time we were in a small cabin cruiser for a month.''

''What an interesting life you must have had,'' Anthea said.

Her new friend smiled. "Very interesting, although sometimes very exhausting. How glad I am now that I always went with my husband and shared his problems when I could. Now I have only memories, but they are happy ones. My dear, I have talked far too much. I think I will bow out graciously. Will you take me to the room to collect my belongings?"

Thankfully Anthea helped her on with her coat and went downstairs with her to her car.

"It has been a pleasure to meet you, Anthea. I will look forward to seeing you again soon. I hope your Christmas is as happy as possible under the circumstances."

"Thank you," Anthea said, bending down at the car window. She went up to her small bedroom, sure that no one would miss her. She was very tired, and she longed to get to the early service the next morning. She and her father had always attended. She imagined that he would be with her in spirit. It would help her for the day ahead.

It was late before she heard the cars driving off and later still when the maids went to bed. She felt lonelier in this house full of people than she had when she was alone after Great-Aunt Ellen died. How good God had been to give her a home of her own so that she need not be dependent in any way upon her mother or Alan Towers. "Oh God, help me to get through these next two days—especially the evening with Mark and Gerry," she prayed as she turned over in the narrow bed and tried to get to sleep.

The alarm clock that she had put under her pillow went off when she felt she had just dropped off to sleep. It was a temptation to snuggle down again, especially when she pulled the curtain aside and saw that the rain was pouring down and it was still dark. But she knew that the rest of the day would be involved with social activities and there would be very little thought of the real meaning of Christmas.

She dressed in her warmest clothes, pulled on a raincoat, and taking an umbrella she tiptoed downstairs, startling the maid who was setting the table for breakfast.

"Merry Christmas, Doris," Anthea said with a smile at her bewildered expression. "I will be back later for breakfast, but I have always loved the early service on Christmas Day."

"There is tea in the kitchen. I can bring you some if you would like it," Doris suggested.

Anthea glanced at her watch. "Thank you, but I haven't much time. I'll have breakfast when I get back."

Sarah, the cook, Robert, the chauffeur and gardener, and Millie, the other maid, were finishing their early breakfast.

"Mrs. Towers' daughter has just gone to church, even though it is pouring down," Doris announced, returning to the kitchen.

Robert nodded his head. "Miss Anthea and her father were very different from the present Mrs. Towers. No stuck-up airs about them."

"Seems a sensible girl, but from what I hear things have been tough for her. Maybe you don't know, Doris, being new, but Mr. Towers bought their home when her father died and had it all done up for his precious daughter who was marrying the boyfriend Anthea Gordon was almost engaged to."

"Well, I'm blessed," Doris replied. "Mr. Towers married her mother before then."

"Yes, just a few months after her first husband died, who was a real gentleman," Robert put in. "Miss Anthea, who had worked all the hours necessary to make their nursery business a success, was shown the door."

"Where does she live now?" Doris asked, who was enjoying this spicy bit of gossip.

"In Newbridge," Millie replied. "She went to look after her father's aunt until she died, leaving her the old house. Mrs. Towers told me that she had tried to get her daughter to live here, but she wanted to be independent. She has kept the house and has started training as a nurse."

"Poor girl. She's had all the hardships, while Gerry Towers, or Gerry Latham as she is now, got all the breaks. You keep your eyes open when we go over there to help tomorrow night, Doris. You'll learn a lot. The Lathams have a couple called Simpson living in, and Annie Simpson told me that Gerry is furious about having a baby. She sulked for days. Her husband, Mark, has to sweeten her up all the time or she flies into terrible tantrums. I bet he wishes that he had stayed with Anthea Gordon. She's worth four of that spoiled.madam. All she is good for is dressing up and showing off on a horse."

Anthea drove along the flooded road with her headlights on and the windshield wipers working overtime. The church would probably be almost empty, but in many ways she would be glad if she did not have to talk to a number of old friends and acquaintances.

There were only about a dozen people in the congregation and no choir, but as Anthea sat in the familiar building that had been part of their life for so long, a sense of quietness enveloped her.

As the vicar stood up to give his sermon she remembered how he had helped in the days after her father's death, and his words lifted her heart. As he read the age-old story of the coming of the Holy Child to Mary, the simple maid of Nazareth, and to Joseph, the most obedient character in the Bible, her eyes were moist. How hard the birth must have been for the young mother who longed for the very best for her precious baby. How anxious Joseph was for the welfare of the mother and the child entrusted to his care. God had allowed His Son to be born in a stable, with no one to help except the inexperienced Joseph. What puzzled thoughts must have filled their minds as they heard the report of the shepherds, then later watched in awe as the wise men, in their strange, ornate garments, knelt before the young child in all His helplessness, and offered Him gifts such as they had never seen before.

"Not one of you was born in such conditions," he went on. "Not one of you had to be taken by night to a strange country. Joseph had to find a home and start a new business. Think of how little they had with them, how poverty-stricken their condition. As far as we know, all they possessed were a few clothes and a donkey. Why do we put so much value on material possessions, when God can provide for us just as He did for this refugee family? God allowed His Son to live in such circumstances so that He would know every problem we have to face. He was the eldest of a large, poor family; He worked as a carpenter to provide for His brothers and sisters; He started his ministry with nothing, often had nowhere to sleep, and had no certainty of the next meal. He was honored, then rejected. He had ministered to hundreds of lame, deaf, and blind people. He brought the dead back to life and fed thousands from a boy's lunch. But finally He was taken away. He allowed His persecutors to scourge and degrade Him. They nailed Him naked to a cross which stood between the crosses of two violent criminals.

"As you enjoy your Christmas festivities, remember that you are celebrating the birth of the One who was willing to suffer for your sins and mine, so that we can claim forgiveness and be accepted by a holy God. We are only a very small congregation, but may each of us have the compelling sense of being one of those for whom God sent His own Son as a baby and allowed Him to suffer and die. He did not stay in the grave. He rose again. After being seen many times He returned to Heaven, but He still lives in our hearts by the power of His Holy Spirit. May the comforting sense of His presence be very close to you today and throughout the year ahead. Some of us may have to face many problems before next Christmas, but remember that we never have to face those problems in our own strength.''

Mr. Andrews took Anthea's hand in his and said smiling, ''What a pleasure it was to look down and see you with us again, Anthea. This is a very special Christmas present for me.''

''It was a beautiful service,'' Anthea replied huskily. ''If only more people had been able to attend.''

Mr. Andrews sighed. ''Our congregation gets smaller, I am afraid. Rain always makes a good excuse to stay at home. Can you join us for breakfast? My wife would be so glad to see you.''

For a moment Anthea hesitated before saying, ''Thank you so much for your invitation, but I am staying at mother's house. There are many guests, and I am supposed to help entertain them. I am only there for two days, and I don't want to upset her. I'd like to wish Mrs. Andrews a merry Christmas, but I cannot stay for breakfast.''

''Let me get my coat and umbrella, and we will walk over to the vicarage.''

Anthea spoke to one or two villagers who had lingered, then walked through the churchyard and a small gate into the vicarage, which had been designed in the days when vicars had large families and domestic help was cheap. Now she knew that most of the rooms were unused, as the Andrew's only son was a missionary in Africa, and Mrs. Andrews was crippled with arthritis.

They went in the front door and Mr. Andrews called, "Joanna, I have a surprise for you."

Mrs. Andrews limped out of the kitchen and exclaimed, "Anthea Gordon, what a lovely Christmas present! How are you, my dear? Will you have breakfast with us?

"Perhaps a cup of coffee," Anthea said, knowing that she would hurt Mrs. Andrews if she refused her hospitality. "I ought to go straight back, although I expect that most of the ladies will have trays in their rooms. However, as I am a guest, I don't want to appear too casual."

"Tell us how things are with you? Mr. Andrews inquired, pushing a chair for Anthea near the glowing fire. "We heard that your aunt died."

"I was glad that I could look after her—she had been so good to my father when his parents were killed. She left me her old house, and I have been very busy having it made into apartments. Now I am starting to train as a nurse."

"That is a change from horticulture," Mr. Andrews said as he handed Anthea a cup of coffee and took one himself.

"I am seeing if I can settle into that sort of work," Anthea said. "It is good on a cold, wet day to be in centrally heated wards, but when spring comes I know that I am going to miss being outside in the good country air."

"It is such a useful profession," Mrs. Andrews said, limping between the table and the stove. "I am so grateful for the help Nurse Somers is to me."

"Is the arthritis no better?" Anthea asked.

"Some days it is easier, but the winter is always the worst, so I am glad when Christmas is over and I can look forward to the brighter days. However, I have much to be thankful for. James is so good to me, and many of the church members help in all sorts of ways. We get so many pots of jam, fresh eggs, fruit, vegetables, and other gifts that we are often overwhelmed. My greatest grief is that I feel I am holding James back. He deserves a much bigger parish, but he stays here for my sake."

"Joanna, you know my days of hard parish work are over, and these people need us just as much as those in a big city."

"That is always the answer," his wife replied, shaking her head. "How is your mother, Anthea? We never see her or Mark Latham either."

"She is well but very involved with all their traveling and social activities. We are all invited to Mark's house tomorrow. It is to be a sort of housewarming as the place has taken so long to get finished. It is to be a big party, and I am not looking forward to it one bit. I shall be glad to return to my own modest place and to the hospital, even though I am such an ignorant beginner. I think that I ought to get back, but this has been a lovely start for Christmas Day."

"And for us too," Mr. Andrews said, walking with her to the door. "We miss you from the choir, and I have no other friend who can take your father's place.

15

Anthea found Alan Towers with a couple of other men in the dining room. The food was kept hot on an electric heating plate on the sideboard so that guests could help themselves, while Doris supplied fresh coffee or tea. The ladies were either skipping breakfast in preparation for the big meals during the day or having trays in their rooms.

"Merry Christmas, Anthea," Alan boomed when she went in. "Was that your car I heard? Have you been out already?"

"I went to the early service," Anthea replied quietly. "I'd like coffee, Doris, please. I will help myself to food."

"Great Scot, you mean that you have been to church on a morning like this? I thought that all the ladies were still warm in bed."

"Were there many hardy souls like you?" another asked.

"Not many, but I was so glad I went for the vicar's sake. He was so kind to me when my father died, and we attended his church for years."

"I hope you remembered to say a prayer for all the wicked sinners you left behind," Alan Towers said with a laugh.

Anthea flushed, but did not reply. "Do you think that Mother needs me for anything this morning?" she asked after a pause.

"Why not ask her when you have had your breakfast?"

Anthea took a small piece of bacon and some scrambled eggs, but the food tasted like ashes in her mouth. Why did this man her mother had married always make her feel so inadequate and uneasy?

"Please excuse me," she said as soon as she had eaten the small amount on her plate. "I hope you all have a very happy day."

She made for the door, but before she escaped she heard one man say, "Uncommonly pretty girl, your stepdaughter, Alan. You ought to be rounding up some eligible young men for her."

In spite of herself, Anthea hesitated.

"Too staid to attract any man with an ounce of spunk in him. I believe she fancied Mark, but one look at Gerry and he forgot all about Miss Prim and Pretty."

Anthea went upstairs, her mind seething. How dare Alan Towers speak like that about her! For a few moments her temper flared, and she felt that she hated him and could not stay a moment longer in his house. She hurried to her room and sat looking out of the window until she had gained control of herself. Then the message of the morning came back to her. What right had she to complain? Jesus Christ had been despised and mocked, and she had promised years ago to live by His standards.

Alan Towers was a pompous, small-minded man whose only asset was the money he had made—probably by foul means as well as fair. The more she saw of him the more she wondered how her mother could bear to share her life with him after being married to a man like her father with his gentle, kindly ways and well-educated intellect.

She prayed for a quiet mind herself. Lifting the small gift she had for her mother, she tapped on her door. Her mother was lying in bed in a beautiful nightdress which consisted mostly of expensive lace, her hair in an attractive ribbon cap. Without her makeup Anthea was struck by her pallor, the dark circles under her eyes, and her thin, almost claw-like hands.

"Merry Christmas, Mother," she said gaily, bending to kiss her on the forehead and putting the small parcel on the bed. "It is only a tiny gift, but I remembered that it used to be your favorite perfume. You have so much that I could not think of anything you might need."

"Thank you, dear," her mother replied. "Actually we will be exchanging gifts after lunch, so why not put it with the others by the tree in the lounge? Have you had breakfast already?"

"I went to early service, then I helped myself in the dining room."

"And probably you were the only lady present. Most of us need extra rest after the late nights we have. I noticed that you disappeared early."

"When Lady Lester left I thought that I would not be missed."

Her mother nodded. "You made a great impression on her. She is quite an asset to the neighborhood and often spends the evening with us. Have you bought a new dress for tonight's party, Anthea?"

"No. I intended to wear the one that I had for your wedding. It is so pretty, and I have not worn it since."

"Then I hope you will change your mind and wear what I have bought you for Christmas. I could not resist buying it for you when you consented to spend these two days with us. I hope that it will fit. I will give it to you now in case it needs a slight adjustment."

"But Mother, I did not need such a big present," Anthea protested.

"Maybe not, but I want you to look your best tonight."

Anthea opened the box and gave a little gasp as she lifted out a deep blue velvet dress and held it up before her.

"Try it on," her mother insisted. "By the way, Alan does not know I bought it. There is another smaller gift in the lounge. Let him think you brought the dress with you."

What an odd, complex personality she is, Anthea thought. *Sometimes she almost seems to despise me, yet here she is showering expensive gifts on me. Am I just another possession that she wants to show off?*

She slipped the dress over her head, her mother leaned over to fasten the zipper, then made her turn around several times.

"Yes, I was right," she said, nodding approval. "Look at yourself in the long mirror."

Anthea stared at her reflection. The dress had a tightly fitting bodice, wide sleeves with cream lace at the wrist, a very full skirt that swished around her feet, and a high neck of the same lace insert in the bodice and fitting around the neck.

"Wear your hair piled on top of your head. My small present is a pair of tiny diamond earrings and a brooch to match. You are not the frilly, baby doll type, but I have never seen you look so lovely."

A lump was in Anthea's throat. if only her mother were always like this—what a different relationship they could have.

"I have never had anything so beautiful, Mother. I am so grateful that you have planned this for me. Even if I cannot wear it often I shall always treasure it."

"I have something else that I want you to have now."

Reaching into the small bedside cabinet her mother took out an oblong box and handed it to Anthea. Inside was a picture of Anthea and her father taken from a small snapshot when they were on one of their brief visits to Switzerland. In the background were the towering mountains still covered with snow, and at their feet the beautiful Alpine meadow. Anthea, in a blue dirndl skirt and white blouse, had some bright red flowers in her hands, while her father stood with his arm around her shoulders.

Her eyes blurred as she looked at his face, and she said softly, "It is one of the best photographs that we ever had taken."

"Put it away," her mother said firmly. "Alan cannot bear me even to mention your father. He is jealous, and in his heart he knows that he cannot measure up, in spite of all his money. I made my own choice, so I must make the best of it."

Anthea observed the bitter note in her mother's voice, then turned away quickly. Probably in a few days her mother would regret the confidence. Perhaps something had upset her, or the fact of Christmas had made her look back to those she had shared with her first husband years ago.

"Can I do anything to help this morning?" she asked to break the tension.

"Just make yourself available to talk to anyone who is at loose ends. No one will go out in this weather. See that drinks are available. Now I must get up. We will have a very late night, so it will be wise if we can have some rest this afternoon."

"Again, thank you a thousand times for the photograph and the dress, Mother."

Her mother laughed. "The photograph comes before the dress, I notice."

"I would like to have one of you to hang beside it," Anthea replied. For a moment she felt sure that she saw a look of pleasure in her mother's usually cold eyes.

"I suppose the one taken at my marriage to Alan would not be appreciated. I will try to find one which does me justice."

Anthea took her presents to her small room, hung up the beautiful dress without a second look, and sat with the photograph in her hands, her mind back on those happy, carefree days with her father. How beautiful the weather had been, and how they had enjoyed climbing the lower slopes looking for unusual specimens. They had traveled by car and had wandered among the out-of-the-way villages that were not crowded with tourists. They had stayed in small chalets and had enjoyed every moment. This trip had been her father's present for her twenty-first birthday, and she had chosen this rather than have a party or any other sort of celebration. That was over three years ago now and had been the longest time that they had taken for vacation. Mark had promised to join them after his exams were over, but the arrangement had been canceled as Mrs. Latham had bought the house in Newbridge and insisted that she needed Mark's help with the move.

Looking back Anthea could see that that was the beginning of the break in their friendship, but at the time she had not been unduly disappointed as Mark had not the same enthusiasm for the simple pleasures that she and her father found so satisfying. She gave a deep sigh, then realized that the thought of Mark had ceased to hurt. She thought of her mother's revealing remarks and again felt a great relief that she was not involved with the situation. How awful it would have been if she had been younger and had been forced to live with her mother and Alan Towers.

The guests drifted downstairs and eventually gathered in the lounge before the gong sounded for lunch.

"We are having Christmas dinner now," her mother explained. "We will have a buffet supper at Gerry's this evening, because she has invited too many for a sit-down meal."

"Splendid idea, Eleanor," Julie Le Brun exclaimed. "I hate heavy meals late at night."

Doris and Millie served the grapefruit or soup, turkey with all the trimmings, cranberry sauce, then the Christmas pudding with rum sauce, followed by ice cream or trifle.

Robert kept the various glasses filled with wine or liqueurs, and Anthea was amazed at the amount of food and drink that even the slim, elegant ladies tucked away. She smiled at Robert's thoughtfulness as he kept her glass filled with orange juice and did not embarrass her with the offer of anything more potent. They moved into the lounge for coffee, by which time many of the guests were decidedly merry and talkative.

"Now we can be children and open our gifts," Mrs. Towers announced, clapping her hands. "Alan will play Father Christmas, but without the red cloak and white beard. Anthea, will you hand him the gifts from the tree?"

Obediently Anthea handed the various gift-wrapped packages to Alan, and stumbling over an occasional word he read out the names. A great deal of kissing, hugging, and exclamations such as "Oh, how darling," "How did you guess my favorite color?" and "Couldn't have made a better choice," were repeated.

Anthea found several small, unexpected gifts beside the earrings and brooch from her mother. These people must have added them at the last minute as she was quite sure that they had not known she was coming, but she appreciated the kind gesture.

"Now I propose that we retire to the billiard room to relax or play as we desire," Alan suggested. "I know the ladies will probably rest before the great effort of dressing for the evening."

"Could do with a nap myself," Andrew Blair exclaimed. "Wretched day, or we might have had a stroll to shake down that enormous meal. See you later, folks."

Gradually the group broke up and faded away to amuse themselves as they desired. Anthea wondered how to fill in the rest of the afternoon. Picking up some magazines she wandered up to her room. As her father's smiling face greeted her in the photograph, she felt less alone.

She took off her dress, lay down under the covers, and opened the top magazine idly. From its pages she saw a picture of Gerry looking regal and assured on the large black horse she had ridden that first Sunday when Anthea and her father had seen her on their way to church.

"Miss Geraldine Towers, now Mrs. Mark Latham, riding her horse, Captain, on which she won several events at the Badminton Horse Trials. We expect to hear a great deal of this twosome in the coming year," said the caption.

No wonder Gerry was annoyed that her plans for many victorious moments had been upset. Anthea looked closely at her face. She was certainly very striking in her beautifully tailored riding habit, but her lips were too thin and her eyes very hard. Mark would be no match for her, but then perhaps he was content to play second fiddle and be a mere figurehead. Certainly his mother would be satisfied that he had chosen such an outstanding personality for his wife.

"How I hate the thought of this evening," Anthea muttered. She closed her eyes and drifted off into sleep, in which she dreamed that Mark, riding Captain, was chasing her up a Swiss mountain, and Gerry was standing at the top waving a bottle of wine.

When she wakened she chuckled at the absurdity of her dream. She noticed that it was already dark outside. She switched on the bedside lamp and gasped as she saw that it was half past five. There was a knock at the door, and Doris came in with a tray of tea.

"Thought you might like this before you start to dress, Miss Gordon. Cook and the rest of us are leaving soon, as we are helping at the Lathams' party this evening."

"Thank you, Doris. I appreciate this, especially as you have had such a busy day. I guess we ate too much lunch, and it made me fall asleep."

"Do you good," Doris said. "You have plenty of time. The guests will not be leaving until about seven o'clock."

"When do you have your own Christmas celebrations?" Anthea inquired.

Doris laughed. "We had our turkey after you had finished, and tonight cook says Annie and Jack Simpson at the Lathams are planning a 'do' for us when we aren't required. After the buffet supper, as long as there are plenty of drinks available, we'll not be needed. I hope that you enjoy the evening, miss."

"Thank you," Anthea said, sipping her tea. How little Doris guessed the repugnance and dread she had at the mere thought of entering her former home and seeing Mark and Gerry in possession. This evening would be one of the greatest efforts she had ever made in her life.

Before she started to dress she pulled on her dressing gown, then knelt down by her bedside and prayed again for strength to keep her emotions in check, no matter what happened at the place that used to be the Rookery Nurseries, but which now possessed the more imposing name of Markdene Place.

As she finished dressing her mother appeared, carrying a fur stole. "Borrow this for the evening," she said putting it around Anthea's shoulders. "The rain has stopped and this looks more in keeping than a coat." She turned Anthea

217

around and nodded her head. "You may not look as eye-stopping as Gerry, but you have more charm, and many people seem to appreciate your quiet manner. Alan thinks that the sun shines only on his daughter, but I am quite as proud of mine tonight. I always knew you would be worth dressing. You never did make the best of yourself, as I told you often enough."

Anthea cringed with embarrassment. She was sure now that her mother was using her to score against her husband. She wished that she could tear off all her finery and get back into the simple clothes that she had worn when she worked with her father. She hated the thought of being on show and used to compete against Gerry Latham.

"We will be leaving in ten minutes," her mother said, going to the door. Anthea gulped and said, "You look beautiful, Mother, but you have lost a lot of weight."

Her mother shrugged. "I'm thankful for that. I hate to see plump women decked out in low-necked, sleeveless, and backless evening dresses. Clothes hang so much better when there are no bulges, but it is a struggle to keep slim with all the dinners and cocktail parties we have to attend. However, I find that smoking controls the appetite."

"Will I know many people this evening?" Anthea inquired, knowing that her mother expected her to express disapproval.

"All our present guests will be there—Lady Lester whom you met last night, Mark's family, including his mother looking like a proud hen who had bred the prize-winning swan, and that objectionable part of the family, Max Sinclair. Most will be Gerry's friends from the horse-loving type she runs around with. I think that I can hear Alan blowing his horn. He is always in such a hurry."

The guests piled into the waiting cars, using as few as

possible to help with the parking. Alan Towers had obviously already been taking something to fortify him for the evening, and Anthea, who was seated between him and her mother, turned her face away from the smell of the strong cigar that he had in his mouth.

"Alan, all our clothes will smell of smoke," her mother complained.

"Smell of more than that by the time the evening is over," he snapped and trod viciously on the accelerator.

Anthea gripped the seat, wondering if they would get to Markdene all in one piece. What sort of a state would he be in to drive back after an evening of unlimited drinking? How dearly her mother was paying for the type of life she had chosen!

There were fairy lights strung along the drive and among the trees, and lights blazed from every window, but Anthea was relieved that it was too dark to see the grounds where her father had spent so many years of dedicated labor.

A man in uniform, whom she guessed must be Jack Simpson, opened the door and showed the men to the downstairs cloakroom, while Doris took the ladies upstairs to the room that had been the bedrooms occupied by her parents. They were so completely altered that Anthea could hardly believe that they were in the same house.

"What a magnificent place," Julie Le Brun exclaimed. "Just look at this white and gold bathroom. Have you ever seen anything so glamorous?"

Glancing at her mother's face Anthea saw the bleak expression in her eyes before she forced herself to smile and join in the chorus of admiration.

"Can we peek in some of the other rooms, Eleanor?" one of the women asked.

"Of course. That is why Gerry invited you. She wants everybody to see her beautiful decor."

219

She pushed open the door across the corridor saying, "This is the guest room, all gorgeous blues and greens. This used to be Anthea's room, but it never looked like this. The attics upstairs are attics no longer; Gerry can invite crowds of her friends, especially since she has an excellent cook who is the wife of the man who opened the door to us. They have a self-contained flat over the garage. And at the outskirts of the grounds there are several stables for horses and another flat for a groom. Alan is very proud of his gift to his daughter."

"And so he should be," a woman exclaimed. "I hope that Mark and Gerry are suitably grateful. Not many young couples can start off in such luxury."

They went down the staircase, now painted white and with rich blue carpet, and on the wall facing them hung a full length painting of Gerry on horseback.

"What a beautiful portrait," Julie said admiringly.

"That was Alan's present to Gerry on her eighteenth birthday."

"My, but that girl surely was born with a silver spoon in her mouth. Did Alan never wish for a son?" Janet Blair inquired.

"He only had one daughter, but he has a stepson whom he heartily detests. Fortunately we don't see much of him. He is a doctor in Newbridge. Probably he will be here tonight to look down his nose at our wicked carousing."

Her mother spoke in a half-humorous voice as if she was amused by it all, and probably only Anthea, who knew her so well, detected the bitter sting behind her remarks. She had lived so long when that bitter sarcasm had been directed against her father, herself, and the kind of isolated life they lived, that her ears picked it up immediately.

Mark in full evening attire and Gerry in a superbly cut white and silver gown, which showed off her lovely shoulders and arms, greeted them as they entered the lounge.

"You have taken so long to decide to visit us," Gerry said gaily. "I do hope you approve of what we have done with the house and will enjoy your evening."

Mark took her hand, and his kind eyes, which Anthea thought looked tired, smiled at her. "Anthea, this makes our Christmas party complete. Please save some time for me tonight. We hope to manage some dancing later."

He turned to meet other guests, and Anthea moved on, looking at the mass of strange faces. How big the room looked even with so many people in it. Then as she sat down on a vacant chair she saw that what had been her father's den/office and part of the kitchen had been made into this one room. No wonder the house alterations had taken so long, but she admitted that it was a great improvement. The old, black marble fireplace where they had burned tons of logs in winter had disappeared, and the room was heated with slim radiators below the windows.

The walls were pale silver and white stripes; the settees and lounge chairs were covered in light gray velvet, with the carpet the same shade. Bright, variegated cushions provided splashes of color, and there were two large pictures done in a colorful, modernistic technique on the walls.

"My dear, may I sit beside you?" a voice inquired, and Anthea looked into the smiling face of Lady Lester. "I had no idea that there would be such a crowd," she said, looking around at the varied collection of guests. "It was a delight to recognize you. Have you had a happy day?"

Anthea hesitated. She hated telling untruths, even for the sake of politeness. "It has not been as bad as I feared," she answered. "But quite honestly I feel out of my element at this sort of party."

"I like someone who is not afraid to tell the truth. Now who is that handsome, dark man who has just kissed our

221

hostess? I hope her new husband will not object.''

Anthea laughed. ''That is Gerry's stepbrother, Max Sinclair. His mother married Alan Towers after her husband died, and Gerry was their daughter.''

''He looks very distinguished. Does he live near?''

''He is a doctor in Newbridge, but I am afraid that there is no love lost between him and his stepfather. They tread on each others' toes frequently.''

''And is he not married?'' she probed.

''He says that he has seen too many unhappy marriages to even contemplate taking the plunge.''

''Silly man! One swallow does not make a summer, and one unhappy marriage does not mean that there are not dozens of happy ones. Now I believe that he is making his way over here. I hope that you will introduce me. I am not so old that I cannot enjoy the attentions of a handsome young man.''

Anthea's eyes were sparkling as Max stopped in front of them. ''Good evening, Anthea. I am glad that I recognized one kindred spirit at least.''

''May I introduce Lady Lester. Dr. Max Sinclair,'' Anthea said, standing up.

''Margaret Lester, please. I hate the fuss that people make just because Lady is tacked on, and I will drop the doctor, unless I have to consult you professionally. That will be much more friendly.''

Max laughed and looked quizzically at Anthea. ''Sounds as if you have found another kindred spirit.''

''Now what do you mean by that, young man? I enjoy watching the human race making fools of themselves and wasting their money. I only come to a party if I think I will be interested, and I leave as soon as I am bored. At my age I can afford to be a law unto myself. I don't play bridge and I

222

don't drink or smoke. I am not very good company, and I don't really know why people invite me."

"Perhaps a title adds a little prestige," Max said teasingly.

"How unkind, but I have come to that conclusion myself and have derived a great deal of amusement from it."

"Are you a newcomer to the neighborhood?" Max inquired. "I haven't heard your name before."

"How deflating! I have lived near Bewdley for six months. I bought what used to be the dower house of Bewdley Manor. Very quaint and old-fashioned, with uneven walls and unexpected steps, but it is all that I need for myself and one faithful helper."

"Lady Lester, may I introduce you to my son Philip and his wife, Angela, who are spending Christmas with us?"

Max moved away. Obviously Mary Latham had no desire to include him, but Anthea had known Philip Latham when she was a child, and he greeted her as an old friend.

"So you are our host's brother," Lady Lester said, her bright eyes roving over Philip and his wife. "What do you think of his beautiful home?"

Philip looked at Anthea and made a grimace. "I can't see what he has done to deserve it," he said lightly. "Angie and I have been married ten years, but we still live in the humble house we started off with. You really think we slum it, don't you, Mother?"

Mary Latham flushed, then tapped him on the arm playfully. "Don't talk nonsense, Philip. You have three children to provide for and had to make your own way."

"Young Mark would have been better if he had done the same," Philip said emphatically. "What we have is our own, not provided by a rich father-in-law. What are you doing these days, Anthea?"

223

"I have an old house that my great-aunt left me in New-bridge, and I have started nurses' training in the hospital."

"We never see Anthea now even though she lives not far from us," Mrs. Latham said plaintively. "She has turned her back on her old friends."

"I am too busy to socialize," Anthea said calmly.

"She and Mark used to be great friends at school," Mrs. Latham gushed. "Once upon a time I thought I might have her as a daughter-in-law."

"What a pity that did not happen," Lady Lester said coldly. "She is all that I would have wanted a daughter of mine to be."

"Sit here, Lady Lester. I want to introduce you to several people I know," and Anthea moved away, knowing that Mary Latham wanted to show the other guests that Lady Lester was a special friend.

Anthea greeted various members of Mark's family and one or two acquaintances, but there were many strangers that she had never seen before. She stood in the window half-hidden by the curtain, when Max stepped beside her, and she jumped as he said, "So this is where you are hiding. I guess your friend Lady Lester will be lionized by people who adore a title of any sort. You and she seemed to be on very familiar terms."

Anthea laughed. "I first met her last night at Tall Timbers. She is sensible and outspoken, and the flattery won't go down well, I am sure."

"Nevertheless, I am sure that my stepfather and Gerry will see that everyone knows of the distinguished guest they have netted for their parties. How long are you staying at Tall Timbers?"

"I am leaving tomorrow morning. I am due back at the hospital the next day. See how important I am already!"

"Your dress is the prettiest in the room," Max said, his eyes taking in the picture she made with twinkling lights from the darkened garden as a background.

"It is a secret," Anthea said in a whisper. "My mother gave it to me for Christmas, but your stepfather must not know. The earring and brooch are supposed to be their gift."

"Well, well, so the worm is beginning to turn," Max said, his eyes looking across to where her mother and Alan Towers stood with glasses in their hands, talking to some strangers. "He looks as if he has imbibed quite freely already."

"It was scary driving with him."

Max looked at her sharply. "You mean that he was already drinking heavily?"

"Well, he hadn't been on the water wagon," Anthea replied lightly.

"I'd better see what sort of state he is in before you leave. It takes a lot to knock him out, but he certainly won't be fit to drive."

At that moment Gerry rang a little bell, and Mark announced, "A buffet is served in the dining room. If you will move in there we will be able to prepare this room for dancing."

"May I have the pleasure of your company, Nurse Gordon?" Max said putting his hand under her arm.

Anthea was laughing as she passed Gerry in the doorway and saw the surprised look on her face.

"Good girl," Max whispered. "I am sure Gerry thought that you would be like poor little Orphan Annie tonight. Hold your head high, and don't let her patronize you."

Max filled their plates, then maneuvered her into a corner while he collected two cups of coffee.

Again Anthea's eyes gazed around the room in amaze-

225

ment. Two large bay windows had been built in front, and the old kitchen premises had been added to the back.

"What happened to the kitchen?" Anthea asked when Max returned.

"A new block was built on. A kitchen with every modern convenience, a large store room with a walk-in freezer, a utility room for laundry, and I don't know what else."

"It has made a beautiful house," Anthea said sincerely.

"A house is only as beautiful as those who live in it," Max replied tersely. "No home where people like my step-father and Gerry live will be happy. They are too self-centered and dissatisfied. I know because I lived in their orbit for my mother's sake until she died."

"What caused her death?" Anthea asked gently.

Max stared in front of him and said harshly, "She died because she did not want to live. Her will power had been taken from her."

"How old were you then?"

"I was eight when she married Alan Towers because she thought that I needed a father. I was eighteen when she died. Gerry was only nine. I started my training a month after her death, and I made sure that I worked every vaca-tion and never spent more than an odd night under Alan Towers's roof. Gerry used to be a sweet kid, and I loved her, but after Mother died her father spoiled her completely. He had started from nothing and made money fast, so I suppose he felt that she was an extension of himself, and he wanted her to have everything that he had missed when he was young. My mother had an insurance to help me through college, and I earned whatever else I needed. I don't owe Alan Towers anything, and I think that is one of the things which irks him so much. He would have liked to feel that I was dependent upon him, so he could have cracked his whip. I've talked far too much, but you are a good listener. What about some more food or another cup of coffee?''

''No, thank you. We have done very little beyond eating today already.''

16

"Max, one of the guests is ill," Mark said, coming over to their corner. "Will you have a look at her?"

"No peace for the wicked," Max said, shrugging his shoulders and handing Anthea his empty plate.

"Sorry to break up your tête-à-tête," Mark said ruefully.

"Is the guest very ill?" Anthea inquired. "Perhaps I could help, although I have very little experience."

"She is complaining of severe chest pains. You can follow Max if you like, although you certainly don't look like a nurse tonight. That dress does all sorts of things to you."

"Fine feathers, you mean," Anthea said as she followed him out of the room.

Gerry and Mrs. Latham were in the bedroom that had once been Anthea's. Lady Lester, with her makeup standing out vividly on her pale cheeks, lay on the bed. Max was bending over her as they went in.

"Here are the keys to my car. Fetch my medical case, will you, Mark? I'll be back in a moment. I must wash my hands; they are sticky. Anthea, can you come outside for a minute? Gerry, you had better return to your guests. Best say nothing for the moment."

"Looks like a heart attack," Max said in a low voice

when they were outside the room. "We'll probably have to send for an ambulance. Will you be willing to accompany her to the hospital so that she has one familiar face with her?"

"Of course," Anthea said calmly.

"What a dreadful thing to happen to such an important guest," Mrs. Latham exclaimed. "Perhaps it is only the heat or something she ate that disagreed with her."

"Very probably, but I'd rather be on the safe side. Go back to the party before you are missed, Mrs. Latham. It will be better if as few people as possible know about her. Did she come alone, do you know?"

"She drives her own little car, so that she can leave whenever she is tired or bored," Anthea said, repeating what she had been told the night before.

Mary Latham looked indignant. "I am sure that no one is bored with this party. It is going splendidly."

"That is why we don't want it spoiled. Thanks, Mark. Where is the nearest phone if I need to call an ambulance?"

"In our bedroom," Mark replied. "Is she seriously ill?"

"Can't tell yet," Max said, unfastening his case. "Get back and look as if nothing has happened. The party must go on whatever happens."

"I suppose so, but I'm sure glad you and Anthea are here and can cope."

Mark disappeared, and Max went into action. After a few moments he said, "Get that ambulance, Anthea. Tell Emergency why we are bringing her in."

Lady Lester opened her eyes. "Why *are* you taking me in?"

"Because that ticker of yours is beating far too fast," Max said calmly. "You've had too much excitement today. A day or two in the hospital with someone like Anthea to look after you will soon put you right.''

Anthea called an ambulance and informed Emergency that an elderly lady was being brought in with a suspected cardiac condition.

''Bring me an extra pillow,'' Max said as she returned to the room. ''We'll prop her head up until the ambulance arrives. I hope that they have not had many calls tonight. Then go to the kitchen and ask the butler to be ready to bring the ambulance men upstairs without being seen.

''Swallow these,'' he said, handing the patient a couple of small white pills and holding her head up while she took a drink to wash them down. ''Anthea, could you unfasten her gown and possibly slip it off? I'll help you.''

Together they removed her dress and wrapped her in a blanket. In a very short time the ambulance men walked in and without any fuss lifted the patient onto the stretcher.

''Go down first and try to keep anyone from coming into the hall until the ambulance has driven off,'' he said to Robert and Doris, who had followed the ambulance men upstairs. ''And, men, don't sound the siren until you are well away from the house. Nurse Gordon will accompany you. I will follow in my car.''

The men gave Anthea a surprise glance but were too well-trained to express any opinion. As they carried the stretcher downstairs Robert kept his hand on the lounge door, from which came the sound of music, and Doris blocked the dining room.

''You are very kind to miss the party to accompany me,'' Lady Lester said, and Anthea was glad to see that her face looked less haggard.

''It made a good excuse,'' Anthea said, holding her hand so that her fingers were on her pulse. ''You told me last night that you always left when you got tired or bored.''

230

The patient tried to smile. "But this is too drastic an exit. Am I going to die, Anthea?"

"Not if Max Sinclair can help it; you can be sure of that."

She gave a deep sigh. "I don't mind very much. It has been lonely since I lost my husband."

"I don't want to lose you," Anthea said, pressing her hand. "We have only just become friends, and I was looking forward to visiting you. But you ought not to talk."

"You must tell Bertha, my maid."

"We will phone her as soon as we know what the verdict is. No need to frighten her if it is only indigestion."

"A likely story," she said and closed her eyes again. Soon they drew up outside the hospital doors, and she was lifted out and wheeled into the emergency unit.

"Please stay with me, Anthea," she said urgently.

Max Sinclair hurried in and had a word with the doctor on duty.

"Very well, Miss Gordon, you may stay if that will relax the patient. Dr. Sinclair says that you are a nurse, so you will know how to behave."

"Thank you," Anthea replied and sat down on a chair where she could be seen but was not in the way. She watched, fascinated, while all sorts of tests were made, a nurse wired the patient to an electrocardiograph machine and took off long strips of paper with patterns on them. A bottle of intravenous feeding was attached by tubes and tape to her arm, and when she had been wheeled into the cardiac unit she fell into a deep sleep.

"Nothing else you can do tonight, Dr. Sinclair and Miss Gordon. I guess that you want to get back to your party."

"We must phone Lady Lester's maid, who will be wondering why she hasn't returned," Anthea said as they left

231

the hospital. "I promised that I would do that as soon as we knew what was wrong."

"Why don't we stop at the house? That would be more reassuring than a phone call at this time of night. Do you know where the house is?"

"Yes, I can show you the way. It is at the entrance of Bewdley Manor. I used to pass it every day on my way to school. Do you think that we ought to go back to tell Mark and Gerry how she is?"

"I'd rather not, but I suppose that I ought to see what state my stepfather is in. I feel even less in the party spirit than I did earlier."

Anthea settled in the passenger seat and glanced at Max's clear-cut profile in the dim light and at his hands on the wheel. How strong and capable he was! What a contrast to Alan Towers. No wonder they had so little in common.

"What do you know about Lady Lester?" Max inquired after they had traveled a few miles in silence. "Has she any family?"

"She has no children, but I don't know if she has sisters or brothers. Her husband was an engineer, and she traveled with him to various places when he was involved in projects in primitive areas. Now she lives with an elderly maid named Bertha. Is her condition serious?"

"A heart attack is always serious but not necessarily fatal. We will be able to tell better after a few days' complete rest. Probably she will have to take life more easily in the future, with no more late-night parties, but she need not be helpless."

"Turn right here," Anthea said as they approached a crossroad. "The house is only a few yards further. It is on the left-hand side."

They drove up to the front door which flew open immediately. A woman in a long, gray dress stood in the light. She started to speak, but put her hand to her mouth as she saw the strange car and a man getting out.

Anthea slipped out of the passenger door and hurried up the steps. "You are Bertha, aren't you?"

"What has happened?" she demanded. "Where is the mistress?"

"She took a sick turn, so we thought it best to take her straight to the hospital. This is Dr. Max Sinclair who was at the party and attended to her immediately. She was very comfortable when we left her, but Dr. Sinclair thinks she should have a few days' complete rest and have some heart checks."

"You mean that she has had a heart attack?" Bertha demanded.

"Only a very slight one, but we want to make sure that she has complete rest. You can visit her tomorrow and see for yourself."

"Will you come in?" Bertha said, her voice trembling but suddenly remembering her manners.

Max and Anthea walked into the hall, and Bertha closed the door to shut out the cold wind.

"Sit down," Max said kindly. "You have had a bad shock. What about a cup of hot tea by the fire?"

Bertha looked bewildered. "There is a good fire in the kitchen."

"Then that is where we will go," Max said. "Show us the way."

Bertha pushed open the kitchen door and, still looking dazed, turned on the kettle.

"Can I help?" Anthea offered.

Bertha shook her head.

"Better let her keep busy," Max said in a low voice.

"Put lots of sugar in your cup," he ordered as Bertha pushed the cups towards them.

"I never take sugar," she demurred.

"But tonight you should," Max said gently. "Your mistress is going to need you when she comes home."

"You are sure that she will come home? You aren't just preparing me for the worst?"

"It wasn't a massive heart attack," Max replied, "but she will need to take life more quietly."

"I told her that she had been going out too much," Bertha said after a few moments. "She has had several parties lately. That Mr. Towers and Mrs. Latham are always inviting her somewhere."

"Has she ever had an attack before?" Max inquired.

"Lately I've noticed that she has tired quickly, and sometimes she looked gray and worn-out when she got back from a dinner party or an evening out. She hated me to fuss and said I had to remember that she wasn't as young as she used to be."

"How long have you been with her?" Anthea asked, seeing that talking was doing the older woman good.

"Since I was twenty-five. My husband worked for Sir William—he was just Mr. Lester then. My Tom was killed in an accident, and in those days folks didn't get pensions and help like they do now. I had a baby two years old and the mistress offered me a home where I could bring up my son and help in the house. Often she went with her husband all over the world when he was in charge of building a dam or some other sort of engineering work, and I was left in charge of the house until they came back."

"Where is your son now?" Max inquired.

"In Australia. He started in Sir William's firm when he left school and worked his way up. Then he transferred to

234

the Australian branch and has an important position. He is married and has three children. He wanted me to go there to live, but Lady Lester and I have been together a long time. This is my home, and I know that she needs me. I've prayed many times that she'll go before me, because no one else will know her little ways like I do, but I hope that she'll have many years yet."

"I am sure that she will with someone like you to take care of her. I want you to take these pills and go to bed. Don't start worrying and spend the night tossing and turning. The calmer and stronger you are, the better it will be for your mistress. Do you mind being alone in the house?"

"I'm never alone," she said quietly. "The Lord is always with me."

Max patted her bent shoulders. "That is one of the loveliest things I've heard anyone say this Christmas."

"I've prayed for a long time that the mistress will feel like that, but she's been too busy. Maybe if she has to go more quietly she'll have more time to think."

"Promise that you will go straight to bed," Anthea said as they made for the door. "You can phone the hospital tomorrow."

"Does Lady Lester have her own doctor?"

"Dr. James came when she had a bad dose of the flu."

"Right. I'll get in touch with him and inform him of what has happened. Good night, Mrs. . ."

"It is Robinson, but everybody calls me Bertha. Thank you for all your kindness. Did you say you were at the party?"

"Mr. Alan Towers is my stepfather," Max replied. "Mrs. Gerry Latham is my half sister."

Bertha nodded. "My lady said they were a mixed-up sort of family."

Max laughed. "She was right; we are mixed up all right."

Bertha put her hand to her head. "I beg your pardon. I did not mean that, but I am in such a dither I don't know what I'm saying or thinking."

"Never mind. All you have to do is rest, and everything will look better in the morning."

"Poor woman," Anthea said as they drove off. "Obviously Lady Lester is the most important person in her life—even more so than her son."

Max nodded. "Not many of that type of servant left, but I guess that she is more like a close friend after all these years."

As they approached Markdene, they could hear that the party was still in full swing.

"I feel as if it is hours since we left, but it is only eleven thirty," Anthea said, looking at her watch.

Simpson answered the door.

"How is her ladyship?" he inquired anxiously.

"Very comfortable now," Max answered. "I think that she will be much better in a few days."

"Thank God for that. Horrible if somebody had died during the party."

"Can you ask Mr. Latham or his wife to speak to us in the den?"

"Certainly."

"I'll leave you to give the report," Anthea said, slipping away. "I'll find my mother."

She tidied her hair and wandered into the crowded lounge. Couples were still dancing, but most of the older people were playing bridge or talking in little huddles in the dining room. The air was thick with smoke, and empty bottles and glasses stood on the sideboard. After a few

236

moments she caught her mother's attention and waved to her. Mary Latham saw her at the same time and both women came across the room. Obviously they had had several drinks but were still in command of their senses.

"How is dear Lady Lester?" Mrs. Latham demanded, grasping Anthea's arm.

"Much better. She had a heart attack, but Dr. Sinclair thinks it was only slight."

"You mean Max," her mother said. "Why be so stuffy when he is your stepbrother? Good thing that we had a doctor and a nurse in the family, don't you think, Mary? Margaret Lester will be very grateful. I must tell Gerry."

"And I must tell Mark," Mary Latham added. "Such an upset at their lovely party, especially when it was someone as important as Lady Lester."

"Dr. Sinclair has already told them," Anthea said firmly. "Are you nearly ready to go home, Mother?"

"The party's not over yet," her mother said, although she looked as if her eyes might close at any moment. "I'm tired, but Alan won't leave until the end. I am sure he won't be fit to drive," she said with a giggle. "Mark and Gerry are certainly not stingy with refreshments. You go and enjoy yourself, Anthea."

"Shame you missed the dancing," Mary Latham said coyly. "Might have found yourself a young man to take Mark's place."

Anthea felt herself getting tense and turned away hurriedly. She moved into the hall and almost bumped into Mark.

"Thea, I'm so sorry that you had all this trouble," he said, holding her hands. "I wanted you to enjoy yourself tonight."

"It is all right, Mark. I was glad to help, although really I did very little except to go in the ambulance."

237

"Mark, where have you gone? You are supposed to be dancing," Gerry said, hurrying out of the lounge.

Mark dropped Anthea's hands hurriedly. "I'm coming, darling. I was just thanking Anthea for her help."

"I expect pretending to be a trained nurse was much more in her line than any entertainment we could provide," Gerry snapped. "Quite a feather in her cap to attend someone with a title. That doesn't happen every day."

Mark laughed. "I guess one patient is the same as any other," he said, putting his arm around Gerry's shoulders, but she shrugged him off impatiently.

"Don't you believe it. Most women only take up nursing when they are desperate for a husband and think that the uniform will catch a rich patient or a doctor. Maybe Anthea was glad of the opportunity to show Max how clever she is."

"Silly girl," Mark said, leading her away. "You are tired and need another drink to cheer you up."

"No, I don't. I need my husband to remember that he married me, not the girl he went to school with."

Mark turned pale and pushed her forcibly in front of him. "Don't make such a fool of yourself," he said in a tone of voice Anthea had never heard him use before.

"Leave me alone," Gerry said, breaking away and dashing upstairs.

Anthea sat down hurriedly on the hall chair, her legs shaking beneath her. Mark hesitated and then followed his wife.

A moment later Max appeared. "What on earth is the matter?" he demanded.

"Nothing very much."

He gripped her hands and pulled her to her feet. "Get your coat and come out to my car. Then you can tell me the truth."

Obediently Anthea tiptoed to her old bedroom and grabbed her wrap. She could hear voices, one loud, the other low, and hurried downstairs.

Max put her in the car, slammed the doors, and turned on the interior light. "Now tell me what happened."

"There is nothing to make a fuss about," she insisted.

"Was it Gerry? She sounded angry over something."

"She was annoyed that Mark was speaking to me instead of dancing."

"What a spoiled brat she is. Do you want to go into the house again?"

"No. I'd rather go home. I wish that I had my own car here. I'd drive straight back to Newbridge."

"Haven't you got a suitcase at Tall Timbers?"

"Yes."

"Then I'll drive you there, and you can go to bed. I'll come back and tell your mother that you were tired. I'll probably drive my stepfather and his party back. It isn't far, but too far for him to drive in his drunken condition."

"That will only cause more trouble."

"Stick up for yourself, girl. You will have to be like me and go your own way. I'll see that you mother gets back safely, but bed is the best place for you."

He started the car, and Anthea had no choice but to relax and try to forget the spiteful things that Gerry had said. What a miserable jealous person she must be underneath all the fashionable veneer and in spite of all her material possessions and the husband she had chosen!

"Here we are," Max said as the car stopped. "Good thing I have a key so that you can get in if the servants are not back."

The lights were on, and music and voices were coming from the kitchen.

Max rang the bell and opened the door. Robert's surprised face appeared at the kitchen door.

"Miss Anthea came home first. See that she has a hot drink and goes to bed. I am going back to look after my stepfather and his guests."

"Very good," Robert replied, his face back to its usual deadpan expression.

"Good night, Anthea. Thank you for your help." In a low voice he added, "Stop worrying about Gerry and Mark. They have got to sort out their own problems."

Anthea tried to smile. "They can do what they like as long as I am not involved. I'm thankful I can leave here tomorrow."

Max grinned. "Hospital is a haven compared to this sort of set-up, isn't it?"

"Good night, Max."

"See you sometime," he grinned cheerfully and ran down the steps as Robert closed the door.

"Would you like a tray brought up?" he asked as Anthea started upstairs.

"A pot of weak tea, if cook doesn't mind," she said with a tired smile.

"Looks as if the party was a complete flop as far as she is concerned," Robert informed Doris and Millie, who were watching the late night television show.

"How is Lady Lester?" Millie asked, getting out a tray and teapot.

"I forgot to ask," Robert replied. "Miss Anthea looked very distressed. Maybe she'll talk to you when you take the tray to her."

Doris nodded. "Probably she was too upset to go back to the party. She doesn't fit in with folks like the Towers and Lathams."

"Neither does Max Sinclair," Millie agreed.

Doris carried the tray upstairs and found Anthea, still dressed, staring out into the darkened garden.

"Thank you, Doris," she said, keeping her face turned away. "You must be tired after such a long day."

"Can I come up again and prepare your bed?" Doris asked.

Anthea gave a shaky laugh. "I am not used to being waited on, but thank you for offering. I'll enjoy my tea and get to bed. I feel more tired tonight than when I have done a hard day's cleaning or been running around the wards in the hospital."

"Cook said I was to inquire how Lady Lester was when you left her."

"Much better. She was quite comfortable, and the doctor thinks it was only a slight attack."

"Probably because she had help so quickly. Millie says Dr. Sinclair is very clever and he knew just what to do. I used to want to be a nurse, but I was only seventeen when I got married, so I never started."

"I didn't realize you had a husband," Anthea said.

"I haven't. He walked out on me after two years, leaving me with a year-old baby. We had to go back to live with my mother, and I have done all sorts of jobs to keep us going—mostly helping folks when they need assistance in the house because they are ill or old or something. Angela, my daughter, is fourteen and used to staying with my mother. I hated missing Christmas with her, but this is good pay, and she and Mother have gone to my sister who has a family of kids, so they'll be having plenty of fun."

"So you are only thirty-two, Doris. You could still train as a nurse's aid or even a nurse."

"I never thought of that. Maybe I could make inquiries.

241

Of course it will depend upon the wages, but it won't be long before Angela can start work. Now I'll let you get your rest, Miss Anthea. I'll take the tray if you are finished. Don't you want anything to eat?"

"No, thank you, Doris. The tea was lovely."

"I hope you sleep well."

Doris took the tray back to the kitchen. "Didn't eat much," cook remarked.

Doris shook her head. "Poor girl—something had upset her. She had been crying when I went in."

"Lady Lester didn't die, did she?"

"No. Miss Anthea said it was only a slight attack, and she was very comfortable."

"Maybe she's still grieving for Mark Latham," Millie said thoughtfully. "Must have been hard for her seeing that stuck-up Gerry showing off in her old home with the man she had expected to marry."

"Poor kid! Some of us seem to be born unlucky, but at least she is free. Good thing that she found out what Mark Latham was before they got married, not afterward like I did."

It was a long time before Anthea heard a car drive up, doors slam, and loud talking. Finally the house quieted down, but still sleep would not come. Over and over the words that Gerry had spit at her were repeated in her mind. She prayed that she could forgive the hateful insinuations. Was she never going to be free of the selfish cruelty that had made her suffer so unnecessarily?

She was still awake when Doris brought in her morning tea.

"Good morning," Doris said, looking at Anthea's pale face and heavy eyes. "Would you like me to bring breakfast? Most of the guests are still sleeping. I guess that they are suffering from a hangover and don't feel like food.''

"How is my mother?"

"She left word that she did not want to be disturbed until she rang. Mr. Towers is up but has been sick and only wants another drink.''

Anthea smiled. "People have strange ways of enjoying themselves. I will be leaving as soon as I am dressed. I'll have breakfast when I get home.''

"It is a horrible morning," Doris said, pulling the curtain aside. "I will bring you a tray gladly.''

"No, thank you," Anthea replied. "I'd rather get home as soon as I can.''

She dressed, packed her small suitcase, and went downstairs. The Do Not Disturb sign was still on her mother's door, so she scribbled a note and left it on the hall table. Letting herself out with a sigh of relief, she drove off in her old car.

In the afternoon she drove to the hospital to visit Lady Lester.

"Anthea, how good of you to come. I wanted to thank you for all you did last night. I did not feel well yesterday and should have had more sense than to go to a party where I knew there would be a big crowd.''

"You look much better today.''

"The doctor says he believes that it was a slight attack, but he is keeping me here to do further tests. He says that this will be a good warning to me to teach me to live more quietly. Bertha has visited me, and although she didn't say so, I know she thinks that it was my own fault. She has been telling me for a long time that I ought to remember that I am not as young as I used to be. What a blessing it is that I have got someone like her to care for me.''

"She was very upset last night.''

243

"I was afraid that she would be. She and I have been through so much together. I just couldn't face life without her. Dr. Sinclair has been to see me too, so I feel very important. Look at the flowers which have come from Gerry and Mark and from Mark's mother. I suppose I'll have a throng of visitors after they have recovered from their Christmas excitement. What fools some people make of themselves at a party."

"I'll be back on duty tomorrow morning," Anthea said as she prepared to leave. "I'll be able to slip in to see you when you have no visitors. Is there anything I can bring you?"

"Thank you, dear. Bertha has gone back to collect what I need, but I hope that you'll pop in often. You don't put on an act like some people. I wish I could have you for my special nurse."

Anthea laughed. "I am only a raw beginner and not capable of an exalted position in the cardiac department. Now I must let you rest."

Lady Lester took her hand and pulled her down to kiss her. "I believe that you and I are going to be good friends, my dear. I'd like to pretend that you are my daughter."

"And I'd like you for a mother," Anthea said huskily, then walked out of the ward.

Gerry was speaking to a nurse as Anthea went into the corridor. The nurse said, "I am sorry, but my patient has had several visitors already, and visiting time is over. She must not have too much excitement."

Anthea tried to slip past, but Gerry turned and her face flushed.

"So you got in first," she said in a low voice as they walked out together.

"I did not expect she would have any visitors today. I

thought that you and my mother would be too tired."

"You were very rude to leave without thanking me for inviting you, and I hear from my father that you never even spoke to him or your mother this morning. I suppose that you were in too big a rush to stake your claim on Lady Lester. Perhaps you hope that she will remember you in her will if you play up to her."

"Good-bye," Anthea said coldly and hurried over to her car. From now on she would see that Gerry Latham had no opportunity to insult her again.

Jean Thompson returned just after Anthea got into the house, and she looked at Anthea's pale face.

"You certainly don't look as if you've had a merry Christmas," she said bluntly.

"I didn't," Anthea replied. "I'm thankful it is over. Now I can settle down and let my mother and her relations go their own way. I am determined not to get involved with them again if I can help it."

"What happened?"

"I don't want to go over it. They were just true to form. Lady Lester had a heart attack, and it upset them that I went to the hospital with her in the ambulance. They think that I am playing up to her because she has a title."

Jean gave a low laugh. "Just exactly what they are doing, obviously."

"Did you have a good time?" Anthea inquired.

"Quite good. People were kind, but I'm glad to be home. I think that you should get to bed early if you are working tomorrow."

Anthea nodded. "I'll be glad for an early night."

17

Most of the other nurses on probation moaned at having to return to work after the brief time of freedom, but Anthea breathed a sigh of relief to be back into a routine when she was so busy that she hadn't time to think about Gerry's unpleasantness. She managed to spend a few minutes with Lady Lester every day, and she offered to drive her home when she was discharged, but she was always careful to make sure that no other visitors were present. The ward was very busy; an epidemic of influenza had broken out in the district, and some of the nurses fell ill, so everyone had to do double duty. Anthea had not seen Max since the night of the party, but she knew that like every other doctor he was working almost around the clock.

After she had seen Lady Lester settled, with Bertha hovering over her like a fond mother hen over her best chick, she went home longing for extra sleep. It was becoming increasingly difficult to drag herself up in the mornings and to appear cheerful.

She had just made herself a pot of tea when the doorbell rang and she heard Jean stumbling to open the door. She went into the hall and was amazed to see Mark stepping inside.

"Hi, Thea, I'm glad to find you at home. I wasn't sure what time you finished."

"Come into the kitchen," Anthea said calmly. "I do my entertaining there, as we use the other rooms for our bedrooms. Have you met my friend Jean Thompson?"

"Happy to meet you, Mrs. Thompson. I think I remember coming into your shop for flowers occasionally, but you were in a wheelchair then."

"Yes, I am fortunate to be able to get about with the use of a walker. I feel like a different person. I'll leave you to chat."

Mark followed Anthea into the kitchen and looked around.

"You've done a lot to cheer this place up. Are you happy living here?"

"I am not unhappy. Like Jean, I am thankful for what I have, although I miss my father and the work that I loved doing with him. Why did you come tonight, Mark?"

"I wanted to apologize to you for what happened at the party. Gerry is unpredictable these days. I believe that women are often like this when a baby is on the way, so I wanted to ask you to forget what she said."

"We'll both forget it, but it will be better if we have nothing to do with each other. Gerry has got what she wanted. She has no reason to feel so bitter against me."

"But we have been friends for years. I don't want to lose you."

Anthea went even paler. "You did that when you got engaged. Gerry won't share you, and I certainly have no desire to cause trouble."

Mark shook his head. "I don't understand women. I love Gerry, but she is full of strange moods."

"I expect she will be better once you have your baby."

"Perhaps it would have been better if we could have waited for a year or two before we plunged into parenthood. I have wanted to tell you for some months how sorry I was

247

that you have had such a tough deal all around. I still feel guilty that we took your home and you were thrown out on your own.''

''You have no need to worry about me, Mark. We are grown up now and have to go our separate ways. I haven't really got time to be sorry for myself,'' she said as brightly as she could.

''Same old independent Thea,'' Mark replied, patting her shoulder. Anthea moved away and stood on the other side of the table.

''I was just going to make some tea. Will you have a cup?''

Mark looked at his watch. ''I guess I'd better not stay. I am meeting Gerry in town and going to a show after a meal. Try to think kindly of us, Thea. Very few girls would have stood up to the problems that you have had.''

''When there is only one way to go there is no choice. Thank you for coming, Mark, but please don't come again. The past is over and finished.''

''Very well, if you feel that is best,'' Mark said as they reached the front door. ''But I'll never forget the good times we used to have.''

''Good-bye, Mark.''

Anthea closed the door suddenly and went into her bedroom before Jean could get into the hall. She continued to shake. Throwing herself on the bed she bit the edge of the pillow, afraid that she would burst into sobs but determined that no one would guess how upset she was.

''Oh, God, help me to forget the hurts and not let the bitterness eat into me,'' she said desperately. ''Obviously Mark is unhappy and beginning to realize his mistake, but he means nothing to me now. Please make them stop tormenting me. I wish I had moved hundreds of miles away and made a completely new life for myself.''

A little later when she had calmed down she went to the kitchen, made fresh tea, buttered some toast, and went to Jean's door.

"I'm going to bed," she said, the tray in her hands. "I'm exhausted, so if you don't mind I'll stay in my room to-night."

Jean, who had been watching the news on television, nodded her head. "Do you good, dearie. Shall I get you a meal later?"

"No, thank you. If I can fall asleep I'd rather not be disturbed. You don't mind, do you?"

"Of course not. But if you can't sleep and need anything, just shout. It is so wonderful for me to be independent and able to move about and go to bed without waiting for some-one to help me. I know how you feel when you want to be alone. Good night, dearie. Don't let that family of yours upset you again."

Anthea managed to smile. "I don't suppose I'll see much more of them."

"I hope not," Jean replied doubtfully. "I don't know why you have been treated as you have, but I believe that someday God will make up for what you have suffered. I can be grateful now even for the accident that made me a cripple, and for my husband being killed, because now I am free, and I am happier than I've been for years. I thank God every day for bringing you into my life, Anthea, and helping me to find a living faith."

"Bless you, Jean. You are a real comfort," Anthea said, her eyes suddenly moist. How good God was to give her even a little encouragement when things seemed so dark.

That evening when she got home she saw her mother's car at the door and tried to summon up a cheerful smile. Anthea saw her mother seated in the kitchen talking to Jean.

"Hello, mother, have you been here long?"

"Only about ten minutes."

"I'll leave you to chat together," Jean said, hobbling out.

"I'll take off my coat and tidy my hair," Anthea said, going to her bedroom. Her face was very serious as she looked into the mirror. Something was wrong, she was sure. She knew that expression of her mother's.

"Would you like to share my meal, mother?" she asked, going back to the kitchen. "I am only having scrambled eggs on toast, and it won't take long."

"No, thank you. I don't snack between meals, and we are going out for dinner."

"What about a cup of tea or coffee, then?"

"Coffee—yes, I'd like that."

Anthea switched on the kettle and turned around suddenly as her mother asked bluntly, "Why did Mark Latham come here last night?"

"To apologize for the way Gerry behaved at the party."

"Alan is furious. Gerry came to tell us last night. She and Mark have had a row, and she says that she won't go back to live with him unless he stops seeing you. Gerry is a spoiled, immature creature, but Alan thinks that she is perfect, and he is crazy about the coming baby. He insisted that I tell you that he will make Mark suffer if he keeps on upsetting Gerry in her present condition. Somehow he has got it into his head that you are running after Mark."

Anthea reddened angrily. "Tell him for me that I have only spoken to Mark three times since he was married. We met accidentally in town, I saw him at the party, and he came yesterday to apologize for Gerry's behavior. I told him that he should never come here again, and I want to be left alone. Tell him also that I have already thought seriously about moving hundreds of miles away since Gerry is so vindictive. I have no idea why."

"Because she is a silly, jealous baby. I am sorry, Anthea, but if my life is to be bearable I have to fall in with Alan's wishes."

"Gerry has no need to be jealous. Mark means nothing to me now. But if she continues what she is doing, she'll lose him. He loves her now, but he isn't altogether stupid. Mark is easy to manage, but he has a stubborn streak if anyone goes too far."

"He knows on which side his bread is buttered," her mother said. "Alan and Gerry hold the upper hand, so Mark has got to toe the line. I want you to keep out of it."

"I intend to," Anthea said coldly. "I'll be here if you ever need me, Mother, but I'll never come to Tall Timbers again. Mark understands how I feel, so please make Mr. Towers understand that Gerry has nothing to fear from an ordinary person like me."

"But you aren't ordinary, Anthea. I can't describe it, but you have something about you which makes you different in a distinguished, unusual way."

Anthea blushed. "Thank you, Mother. I am glad you aren't ashamed of me, but I think that it will be better if you don't visit me too often either."

"Did you mean what you said about moving?"

"Yes, I've thought about it."

"But what about your training?"

"I could probably transfer to another hospital or get another job. Jean Thompson can look after the house in case I need to come back later on."

"But I don't want you to go far away."

"For the sake of peace in your new family it may be better, but I haven't quite decided yet."

"I must go," her mother said, and Anthea thought her eyes were suddenly sad. "Sometimes I wish that we could have a quiet evening like we used to have. I didn't appreciate

251

how easy life was in those days. Good-bye, Anthea. Don't do anything without telling me. I have got to calm Alan down as he has high blood pressure, and the doctors have warned me about letting him get upset.''

''I'm sorry, Mother, but I don't intend to be a bone of contention either at Tall Timbers or Markdene. I value my own peace of mind too much for that.''

Her mother sighed. ''Very well, Anthea, but please keep in touch.''

''Of course; I'll always leave an address. Take care of yourself.''

Her mother put her arm around her and gave her an unaccustomed hug.

''I'm sorry that I failed you, but I've got to make the best of things.''

Anthea's heart was heavy as she made her supper and ate it by the kitchen fire. Her mother and Mark were already finding that their exciting lives were not free from problems, and her heart ached for them. Whatever had happened, they were still dear to her, and she hated to think of their unhappiness.

As she finished, the door bell rang. This time it was Max who stood on the step.

''May I come in, Nurse Gordon?'' he said whimsically.

''I seem to be swamped with guests today,'' Anthea replied, opening the door wide. ''My mother has just left.''

''Has Mark Latham been here?''

Anthea stared at him blankly. ''Why should I answer that question?''

''Because I had to drive out to see Gerry this afternoon. Evidently she walked out on Mark last night after a flaming row. My stepfather says that she believes Mark is meeting you, and Gerry refuses to go back until Mark promises that he will never speak to you again.''

"She must be mad," Anthea said.

"Not mad, but in a highly emotional state. Is it true that you and Mark were engaged, and that you expected to marry him?"

"I have told you before that we were only school friends."

"Nevertheless, he was here last night. I was going to call, but I saw his car outside the house."

Anthea's face flamed. "This is my house, Dr. Sinclair. I do not have to account for who visits me."

"But can't you see that you cannot have the same relationship with Mark now that he is married to a jealous woman like Gerry?"

"I don't see anything, except that I am sick of all the insinuations and unpleasant remarks. I think that you had better go. I have already decided that I never want to see anyone connected with the Towers family again. Now I'll say good night."

"I'm sorry that you feel like that," Max replied. "But when you simmer down you'll realize that you have got to make a complete break with Mark Latham."

"If you have such a low opinion of me, I refuse to bother to argue. Now please go. Gerry has been thoroughly spoiled, but that is Mark's problem—no one else's."

"Nevertheless, if Gerry loses her baby both you and I would be sorry."

"In her present state she isn't fit to be a mother," Anthea said sharply. "It is a pity that she hadn't stuck to breeding horses, not children."

"I agree, but it is too late to alter what has happened."

"Good night," Anthea repeated stonily. As Max took a step back she closed the door firmly and went to her room, glad that Jean was visiting a friend and she could be alone.

253

She hadn't felt well all day and had a nagging pain in her side. Now her head was throbbing, and her heart full of misery. Was everything and everybody being taken from her? Her father, her home, the man she had loved, her mother, and now Max Sinclair, who had recently become important in her life. Surely it would be better to move away from all the old associations and painful memories.

She had a bath and was in bed when Jean's friends drove her back and helped her into the house. After they had left Anthea put on her dressing gown and went into Jean's room.

"Had a good time, Jean?" she asked, trying to speak brightly.

"Thank you, yes. Another couple from the church joined us for dinner, and we watched a good TV documentary. People are very kind to include someone like me."

"They enjoy having you because you are so appreciative. Anything you want? I switched on your blanket."

"No, thank you, dearie. You look washed out, so get back to bed."

Anthea tossed and turned, dropping asleep occasionally, then being awakened by the pain. Twice she got up to refill her hot water bottle, which gave her a measure of relief. She felt nauseated and decided that something she had eaten must have upset her or she had caught the twenty-four hour gastric flu bug, which was going around.

In the morning all she could take was strong tea, and she wondered if she ought to phone to say she was unwell, but the ward was short-staffed, and she felt that to keep busy and forget the unhappy thoughts was preferable to a day on her own. She felt better out in the fresh air, and for the first hour she managed to carry on the routine jobs. Suddenly another fit of nausea struck her, and she gripped the sink in the ward kitchen.

Sister Rouse, hurrying in with a tray of empty medicine glasses, stared and made Anthea sit down.

"What on earth is the matter?" she said, reaching for a thermometer, glancing at it, and pushing it under Anthea's tongue. She put her fingers on her pulse saying, "Have you any pain?"

Anthea nodded, and when she could speak said, "In my side."

"Go into the small side ward, put on a hospital gown, and lie on the bed."

"I'm sorry, sister," Anthea said humbly.

"Strange how nurses never learn that pain is the body's way of showing that something is wrong. Sure you can manage?"

A few minutes later Sister Rouse, accompanied by the doctor on duty, walked into the side ward.

"Tired of being a nurse and decided you'd rather be a patient?" Doctor Anderson asked with a grin. "Now where is that pain?" He prodded gently. "Mighty tender around there, isn't it?"

"Better take her along to X-ray, sister. I guess that appendix needs looking at."

When Anthea surfaced a few hours later she looked around the room, unable to grasp where she was or what had happened.

A nurse popped her head in. "Good, you are awake. How do you feel?"

"Strange. What happened?" Anthea asked dazedly.

"You had an appendix which was about to rupture, so it had to be removed immediately. Now try to sleep again, and you'll feel more lively when you wake up. Take a sip of this, but don't try to sit up."

During the next week she learned a great deal about being a patient. It was the first time that she had been in the hospital, and she realized the little details that added to, or detracted from, the comfort of those who were ill and dependent on others for everything, especially when she was transferred to the large ward because the side ward was needed for a woman who had been seriously injured and needed special nursing. She learned how trying was the lack of privacy, the way sleep was often disturbed at night, and how much more obliging and thoughtful some nurses were than others.

Before the operation Anthea had called Jean Thompson, insisting that Jean not inform Mrs. Tower unless there were serious complications. So Jean was her only visitor. One morning she saw Max Sinclair come into the ward to visit one of his patients. Sliding down in the bed she hid her face with the sheet, pretending to be asleep.

The operation had been quite straightforward, but the surgeon was puzzled that she had made such a slow recovery.

"You ought to be feeling much more energetic by now, young lady. Is anything worrying you?"

"No. I am tired, that is all."

She saw him and the sister talking quietly as they walked from the ward and thought she heard her own name.

Next day the supervisor herself stopped by the chair where she was sitting near her bed.

"Well, Nurse Gordon, how have you enjoyed being at the receiving end of nursing?"

"I have learned a lot," Anthea said with a smile.

Her superior nodded. "Actually it is the best way to find out what a sick person needs. Now we can't do anything more for you here, but you need a time of convalescence. I believe that you have no family at home, as your mother has remarried. Can you go to her?"

"No, that would not be possible."

"Doctor Anderson insists that you go away for a change as soon as you are strong enough. You will have a month before you report for duty again. You can leave here on Friday if you can have complete rest afterward."

"I can rest in my own house," Anthea said.

"No, you need a change of location. I know that you have had a lot of problems in the last year, but there is nothing like a complete change to help us put things in their proper perspective. Let me know before you leave where you intend to go."

"Very well. Thank you for all everyone has done for me."

"A promising probationer is worth looking after," she said firmly. "I have had excellent reports regarding your work. You have the makings of a good nurse."

A few moments later Anthea took out the small writing case Jean Thompson had brought in and began a letter to Lorna Hadley, who as Lorna Wilson had been her closest girl friend at school. Lorna had gone to a teachers' college while Anthea took her horticultural training. They had written regularly and visited during vacations. Then Lorna had met and fallen in love with James Hadley, five years older than herself, who was the curate of the church she attended. James was offered a church in Birmingham. Lorna and he were married, and she found her life full to overflowing. It was a downtown church that served a mixed community of all sorts of nationalities with many needs and problems, especially among young people growing up with a lack of parental control or parents who were too busy to bother about their children. Broken marriages, working mothers, and alcoholic fathers gave little stability to many families.

Lorna had written many times asking Anthea to visit her. "We have a big old house, and you'd love some of our problem kids," she had written. "I want you to get to know

257

James properly. After all, you were my bridesmaid, so you ought to see what you were partly responsible for. Now that I have the twins, I have to stay at home much more. I long for someone like you to talk to. Mother has kept me informed about all that has happened since you lost your father, and we have prayed so much for you. I am not sorry that you broke your relationship with Mark. He was never good enough for you. Someday you will meet a man whom you can admire as I do my James. I have decided that respect and admiration is as important as love, certainly more so if it is only infatuation which soon wears off when the glamor disappears. Just let me know if you can spare a week or a month any time, and I'll put out the red carpet.''

Anthea had kept that letter; it was so like Lorna. It had comforted her to think that at least one old friend had not changed.

If it was convenient she would pay Lorna that long-promised visit. Birmingham wasn't exactly a health spa, but it would be a complete change of scene. She certainly wouldn't have time to dwell on her own problems.

Two days later she returned home, and that night she had a phone call from Lorna telling her that she and James were thrilled that she was coming to them. ''James will meet you at the train in our old bone-shaker, and you are to have breakfast in bed every day. I'll try to keep the twins from bothering you, but I am sure that you will love them—they are such lovable bundles of mischief. Which day will you come?''

''Would Monday be suitable? There is a train which arrives in Birmingham at one thirty.''

''Lovely. Monday is James's day off. Usually he is as busy as ever, but he will be able to meet you. I am so excited at having you to myself that I could dance a jig.''

258

Anthea laughed. "Doesn't sound as if you have changed. I thought you would be a mature, organized vicar's lady by now."

"Not me. James has so many dreary people to deal with that I am determined to make him laugh when he is at home. I know many of the folks think that I haven't grown up yet. You won't mind the house being old and inconvenient, will you, Thea? I'll see that your room is warm. A big house is a blessing when people are always calling or there are sewing meetings or parish meetings. Besides, we often have people staying here who need beds for a few nights, but I won't let any of this bother you."

Anthea was feeling stronger but still tired quickly. When she arrived at Birmingham station she saw Lorna waving from the gate. James took her case, and Lorna hugged her.

"What a sight for sore eyes," she said gaily. "We had to park a few streets away, so we'll wait while James brings the chariot."

"Where are the twins?" Anthea asked as James hurried away.

"A missionary couple who are staying with us until Friday offered to keep them. They have two children, and the twins have great fun with them. I do hope our house won't be too much activity for you."

Anthea smiled. "It will do me good to have a bit of excitement."

"You'll get it, I promise. We never know what will happen next. There is one thing we are sure of—that we'll never die of boredom."

From the moment they entered the big shabby hall, Anthea felt a quiet peace that she had not sensed since her father's death. The paint was scuffed, the carpets worn, but it was a home.

Lorna took her up to a room overlooking a back garden having a patch of worn lawn and some dusty shrubs, with a line of washing down the middle.

"Not a beautiful view, I am afraid," she said ruefully, "but it is quieter than in the front. We have always meant to make a flower garden, but have never got around to it. I do hope that you will be comfortable."

"It is a lovely room," Anthea said, looking at the fresh curtains and bedspread.

Lorna laughed. "James and Ralph, the missionary who is staying with us, papered and painted it after we got your letter, and Lilian, his wife, helped me make the covers. I was afraid that the smell of paint might be very strong."

"What a lot of trouble you have taken," Anthea said.

"You made a lovely excuse. We plan to do so much in the house, just like the garden, but so many other things hinder us unless something or somebody gives us the reason for making a superhuman effort. That is why the house gets done so slowly. The church decorated the kitchen, dining room, and our bedroom, but that was all. We managed the huge lounge ourselves and later on the nursery for the baby that turned out to be two instead of one. Now I will bring you a tray of tea and leave you to rest. We will eat about six when the babes are in bed, so come down when you are ready. I want you to feel absolutely free to do whatever you wish."

"Can't I see the twins before they go to bed?"

"How did you guess that I am bursting to show them off? I'll bring them in when they have had their bath. They always look so angelic then, but don't be deceived. They are a pair of little rascals at times."

For the next two weeks Anthea saw a type of home life that she had never experienced before. Lorna was so happy although she had to economize wherever possible and share her home with missionaries, young people who had left home, and groups of workers who used the lounge for their gatherings. In spite of the long hours James worked, and the calls that were made on him, often through the night, he always had a joke to share with his visitors, managed to play with the twins, and had time to show his love for Lorna. As Anthea saw them together her heart often ached with loneliness.

What a contrast Lorna and James made to Gerry and Mark or to her mother and Alan Towers in their beautiful houses with unlimited money to spend.

Sometimes the thought of Max Sinclair disturbed her. She had felt that there was a real affection developing between them, and they had many things in common, but Max was too involved with the Towers for their friendship to go further. She longed to see him again, but at the same time she dreaded to go back to the bleak, lonely life she had experienced in the past months.

During her second week Lorna startled her by saying, "Anthea, do you need to go back to Newbridge? You aren't happy there, are you? I wish that you would stay here with us. It has been wonderful having you with me these past ten days. I long so often for someone young to share things with when James is so busy. Now with the twins I can't get out in the evenings. You are wonderful with the young people and the lonely, unhappy souls who need friendship."

"But I have my job at the hospital waiting for me."

"Why don't you see if you could transfer? There is always a shortage of staff in our hospitals."

Anthea hesitated. "I'd love to stay with you; these have been the happiest days I have had since my father died, but there is my house, Jean Thompson, and the other people in the apartments to consider."

Lorna nodded. "I know that it is a lot to ask. Would your mother mind?"

"I don't think so. She has made her own new life, and I don't fit in with her new family. I'll pray about it and perhaps call at the hospital to see if a transfer is possible. You are sure that James wants me under your feet all the time?"

"It was his idea that I should ask you, but I don't want to pressure you. We'll understand if you feel that you have got to go back."

That night Anthea's mind was in a turmoil. She had wished so often that she could get away from Newbridge and put a distance between herself and Gerry and Alan Towers. Was this the way the Lord was providing a way out? Next day she rang to make an appointment at the nearest hospital and decided that if she could transfer and continue with her training she would accept this as God's way for her.

Jean Thompson could look after the house with the help of a woman to do the heavy cleaning a couple of days a week, and she could spend her vacations with her. It would be wonderful to be free of the complicatons with Gerry and Mark.

The hospital was very different from the one in New-bridge. The outside was shabby, and the building looked like an enormous prison. As she went inside there was the usual smell of disinfectant, polish, and humanity. Anthea felt a thrill as she saw nurses scurrying around with wheel-chairs and ambulance attendants pushing stretchers to Emergency.

An orderly directed her to the supervisor's office, and there was the familiar beating of her heart as she knocked at the door.

"Miss Gordon, you rang for an appointment? You indicated you would like to train here."

"I have already done six months in Newbridge hospital."

"Why did you discontinue?"

"I had to have an operation for appendicitis, and I have been spending my convalescent leave with my old school friend. She is married to the Reverend James Hadley who is the vicar at St. Marks. They would like me to stay on with them if I could continue my training here."

"Have you no family to consider?"

"My father died, our business and home were sold, and my mother remarried, so I am on my own."

"I am afraid that the Newbridge supervisor will not be at all pleased, but we would be glad to have you if you feel that you will be happier living here with your friends. Of course you would have to send in notice of your resignation, and we would require a report on your work before we make a definite decision. When do you return?"

"I still have two weeks before I start work."

"Then suppose you write and explain your decision to your supervisor, and I will contact her if you give me her name and address. I will get in touch with you, and we will arrange when you will join us if everything is satisfactory. Good morning, Miss Gordon."

"What happened?" Lorna asked as soon as Anthea entered the house.

"I have to send in my resignation to see if I will be released, and the supervisor here will send for a report on my work. We'll see what happens."

"It will be all right. I know it will," Lorna said, hugging Anthea and dancing around the kitchen with her. "Auntie Anthea is going to stay with you, darlings," she said, laughing at the expressions on the faces of Kirsty and Kenny who had been playing in their outsized playpen.

Anthea wrote to the supervisor in Newbridge asking her to accept her resignation and thanking her for the help that she had given her. She wrote to Jean Thompson explaining that she would like to stay on with Lorna in Birmingham. Could Jean manage to look after the house if she lived rent free and Anthea engaged a woman to look after the heavy cleaning? She would come home to make the arrangements before starting her new work in Birmingham. But she asked her not to give her address to her mother or anyone else who inquired about her. She wanted to break with her family, but she would give Jean the phone number so that she could always contact her, and if her mother wished to write, Jean could forward her letters.

A month later Anthea started at the new hospital. She had spent a short time at home, and arranged for a young widow to come in for a few hours each day to do the cleaning and help Jean with the shopping and laundry.

She wrote to her mother saying that she was moving to another hospital, and if she wished to write, would she address the letter to Jean Thompson, and she would forward it.

As Anthea drove to Birmingham in her old car she felt that gradually all her links were being severed one by one. Surely now Gerry would be satisfied that Anthea had no hankerings after Mark. She would have liked to have told Max Sinclair where she was going, but it was better that no one connected with Alan Towers knew her whereabouts. If she settled in Birmingham, or Jean found it impossible to continue, Anthea would sell the house. The final link with her old life would be broken. For the time being she was glad to feel that her home was always available if she wanted to return.

18

Life in a huge city hospital that served a rather poor, almost slum area, was very different from Newbridge, which had been more rural. But people in pain all had the same needs of encouragement and patient understanding, whatever their background, and some of these women were making less fuss about their suffering than those who had lived more pampered lives.

Anthea was so busy that she had little time to dwell on what had happened. Lorna's house was what James called "organized chaos," so that she found few spare moments even when she was off-duty, and sometimes it was hard to get quiet time for extra study.

Nevertheless, at the back of her mind there was always the ache of loneliness. She longed for her father's understanding love, wondered if her mother appreciated why she had cut herself off, and often thought of Max Sinclair. No other man that she met had attracted her, although some of James's visitors and some of the younger doctors made it obvious that they would like to be more than casual acquaintances.

Seeing James and Lorna together made her realize that marriage was much more than just physical attraction. In spite of the constant calls upon their time and the need to economize, there was always a feeling of unity that had been so missing between her own father and mother. In James's and Lorna's lives there was a continual give and take; with her parents it had been all take on her mother's part and all give on her father's.

Anthea had no desire to enter into light flirtations and often wondered at the shallow infatuations of many of the nurses, some even older than herself. Perhaps the kind of life she had lived and the unhappiness of the last year had made her more mature and unable to join in the light, sometimes even sordid, conversation that was usual in the nurses' dining room or lounge.

Maybe she was old-fashioned and "not with it," as one young nurse snapped one day when Anthea did not laugh at a crude, off-color story, but she was willing to go her own way. She loved her work on the wards and was happy with Lorna and James, so she maintained a quiet dignity and conscientiousness, which annoyed some of the younger, more irresponsible nurses, but was quickly recognized by sisters and doctors. The younger ones might sniff at her "uppishness," as they termed it behind her back, but if they needed extra help, needed a mistake covered up, or wanted to change duties, it was to Anthea they always turned.

She had arranged for Jean Thompson to forward the *Newbridge Gazette* each week so that she could keep up with local events. She wrote to her mother regularly but only had one reply in which her mother told her that she was going to America with her husband and would probably be away for two months. Alan wanted to be back in time for the birth of his grand-child. She expressed no interest in Anthea's new life, except to say that she was amazed that Anthea would leave a woman like Jean Thompson, who was virtually a stranger, in charge of her house. She would let her know when she returned. As an afterthought she added that Max Sinclair was taking a further course in surgery in

London and would in all probability stay there, as Gerry believed that he was interested in one of the lady doctors who was taking the course with him. He had brought her to visit one weekend.

Anthea had put down the letter and stared ahead without seeing anything. Had Gerry guessed that Anthea and Max were becoming friendly and was this her way of telling Anthea to leave him alone? Was this report true or just another of Gerry's warning tactics? She got up hurriedly and blinked the moisture from her eyes. What right had she to even wonder what Max was doing? She had severed their acquaintanceship of her own accord. He needed a wife. So why be a dog in the manger?

From the announcement in the *Newbridge Gazette* she saw that Gerry and Mark had produced a son, Alan Towers Latham, so even that had gone right for them. Probably this would be the end of their family, as Alan Towers had got the grandson he wanted, and Mark had a son to carry on his name. No word came from her mother, but Anthea could imagine the celebrations and fuss that would be made.

A few weeks later there were pictures of Gerry riding in the local point-to-point, so obviously being a mother was not going to interfere with her activities.

Often in the following issues Gerry's name was mentioned as taking part in local events. There were pictures of her riding in the horse trials, of Alan Towers presenting the cup to the junior champion, and of Mark and Gerry at the hunt ball.

Anthea wrote several times to her mother, but there was no reply. One evening she was called to the phone to hear Jean's voice saying, "Anthea, I have someone who is determined to speak to you. He has news for you."

"Max Sinclair here. Anthea, your mother is ill, and she is asking for you. I think you should come."

267

"What is the matter?" Anthea said with a little gasp.

"I'd rather not discuss it over the phone. Will you let me know when you can come home? I'll meet you at the station."

"Is it an emergency?" Anthea demanded.

"She isn't likely to die tonight, if that is what you mean, but I believe that it is vital for you to come back at once."

"I must phone the hospital. I'll get a train as soon as possible."

"There is one leaving Birmingham at ten thirty, arriving in Newbridge at four thirty tomorrow morning. Can you get that?"

"I think so."

"Very well. I'll see you then."

Anthea put down the phone, feeling cold with shock, and went in search of Lorna.

"What has happened?" she asked, catching sight of Anthea's white face.

"I have just had a phone call to say that my mother is very ill and I must go home at once, but I don't really know what is wrong. I am to get the ten thirty train. I must call the hospital and pack my bag."

"I'll phone, but you must have a hot drink first. I'll help you throw a few things into your suitcase. James should be home in plenty of time to take you to the station. Come into the kitchen while I put the kettle on," Lorna said, putting her arm around Anthea and leading her down the hall, then pushing her into the old basket chair by the stove.

"If only I knew what was wrong," Anthea said in a low voice.

"Who phoned?"

"Jean Thompson," Anthea replied. This was only half the truth, but for some reason she hated to mention Max Sinclair's name.

268

"Then probably she did not know herself. Perhaps it isn't as serious as she suggested. There is a doctor in the family, isn't there?"

Anthea nodded. "The last that I heard he was in London and intended to stay there."

"Well, it's no use guessing," Lorna said. "Drink that up, and I'll phone the hospital while you pack your suitcase. There isn't a lot of time to waste. Don't spend all that time worrying. I guess being a nurse almost makes it worse, but remember that we'll be praying for you and your mother. Maybe this was the only way that the Lord could reach her. You know, there are some things that all the money in the world can't buy—those are peace with God and peace of mind."

Anthea tried to doze during the journey, but her mind was too busy. Had she done right in cutting herself off from her mother? Ought she to have stayed nearby in spite of Gerry's stupid behavior? Why had Max Sinclair been called in, and why had he been so reticent over the phone? Would this mean that her time in Birmingham was at an end? She dreaded the thought of being entangled with the Towers family again, but there was a warm glow at the thought that she would have Max Sinclair to support her. Obviously he was not settled in London, so maybe the story of his imminent engagement was a figment of Gerry's imagination also.

She stared at her face in the speckled mirror in the lavatory as she tidied up before reaching her destination. She was pale, and there were dark circles under her eyes.

"Nothing very much about me for anybody to look at twice," she muttered. "Max Sinclair must meet many glamorous, capable women. I guess he was sorry for me, and I read into his kindness more than he intended. I must

269

be careful not to let him guess that I would like him as more than a casual friend.''

Her heart was beating fast as she walked down the dim platform, handed her ticket in at the gate, and felt her suitcase being taken from her hand.

''Glad you could make it,'' Max said, moving to the entrance. ''My car is just outside, so you'll be home soon.''

''You mean Tall Timbers?''

''No, your mother is at your house.''

''What exactly is wrong with her?'' Anthea asked as the car moved off.

''She has had a complete breakdown, mentally and physically. We may have to take her back into the hospital, but she begged to go to your house and kept asking for you.''

''You say that she is mentally ill? You mean that her mind is affected?''

''I'm sorry, Anthea, but you have got to prepare yourself for a shock. She is in a very strange, unstable state. I could not tell you over the phone as other people could have heard what I said. Even Mrs. Thompson does not know that your mother has been in the hospital because she tried to end her life by taking a massive dose of sleeping tablets.''

''But why?''

''My guess is that the life she had to live with my stepfather was too much for her. She couldn't keep up the pace, and she has just cracked up.''

''Is Alan Towers with her?''

''She refuses to see him. Sometimes she weeps for hours, sometimes just sits and stares. Nothing interests her.''

''Did she ask for me specifically?''

''Several times she has asked Mrs. Thompson why you haven't come home yet. I don't think she remembers that you went to Birmingham. In fact, I believe that very often she imagines your father is still alive.''

"What can be done?"

"Very little at present except be patient, show her that you care about her, and get some nourishing food into her. She is pitifully thin."

"Do her husband or Gerry come to the house?"

"I have told them not to until she is stronger and asks for them. She is on a drug to quiet her mind, and she has to have sleeping pills. That is why I am glad that you came so that you can take control of them. She'll be asleep now, so perhaps you'll manage a couple of hours in bed before you see her. Remember she has been very sick."

Jean Thompson, in her dressing gown, hobbled out of her room, and Anthea hugged her.

"Will you come in for some hot soup, Dr. Sinclair?" she whispered as Max closed the door gently.

Max nodded, put down Anthea's suitcase, and slipped off his coat.

"The front apartment is vacant," Jean said, leading the way to the kitchen. "I have made up the bed for you. Your mother is in your room, so that I could listen to her, although she seldom wakes in the night."

"Shall I peek in before I go upstairs?" Anthea asked after she had swallowed her soup and eaten some crackers.

She saw Max and Jean Thompson exchange a quick glance.

"Better not in case you disturb her," Max replied. "Time enough to go on duty tomorrow. I'll put my head around the door to make sure that she is asleep, and I'll put my head down for an hour also. I'll see you sometime in the morning, but if you need me, phone anytime, day or night."

"Thank you for all your kindness," Anthea said with a gulp, conscious of how inadequate the words were. Her mother was nothing to him, yet he was concerned for her and had missed badly needed sleep to meet Anthea at such an unearthly hour of the morning.

"You and I have a lot of talking to do, but at a more convenient time," he said and lightly ran down the steps.

Anthea closed the door and tiptoed into her mother's room. She bent down to look at her in the dim light that was left burning on the bedside table. Her breathing was heavy, and now and then she gave a low moan; her face was thin and colorless, her eyes seemed sunken into her head. If she had not been told that this was her mother, she would have been unable to recognize her. The last time that they had met she had been so smart, alert, and self-sufficient. Now she looked years older and could have been any one of the elderly patients Anthea had nursed in the last months.

"Oh, Lord, don't let her die until she has accepted You as her Savior," she prayed. "Please help me to forget her past coldness and to be able to love her and help her to see her need of Someone greater than herself."

Wearily Anthea climbed the stairs, pulled off her clothes, and after hastily washing slipped into bed where an electric blanket was on at a low heat.

"Who put it on?" Anthea wondered. She knew Jean could not climb the stairs. Had she asked Max to do it?

Her head throbbed when she laid it on the pillow, and she was sure that she could not sleep, but the next thing she heard was a knock on her door, and Mrs. Baxter, the woman who helped in the house, came in with breakfast on a tray.

Anthea started up guiltily. "What time is it?" she gasped.

"Only half past seven. I have been coming early to help Mrs. Towers to wash and to tidy her room before the doctor calls."

"I am sorry that I slept in."

"Mrs. Thompson says that it was after five o'clock this

morning when you got here, so you hardly have got to sleep. Eat your breakfast. We have not told your mother that you have arrived. She always does very poorly in the mornings. I am sure that having you with her will make all the difference."

"I'll be down as soon as I can. I am so grateful to you for all the extra work you have taken on. Mrs. Thompson says that you have helped her tremendously."

"We've helped each other. I used to feel sorry for myself, but when I see how cheerful Jean is with her limitations I have to stop grumbling. It was a blessing that the folks moved out of this apartment last week. They managed to get a house as they are expecting a baby. There is another couple anxious for it, but Jean phoned them last night and told them that it wasn't vacant yet as you were coming home. Now I must get on."

Anthea hurriedly swallowed her tea and toast, but left the bacon and egg. She dressed, tidied her room, and carried her tray downstairs.

Jean was sitting beside her mother but got up and left as soon as Anthea went in.

In daylight her mother looked even worse than she had in the early morning. "Mother, did Jean tell you that I had come home?"

"You oughtn't to have left me, Anthea," her mother gulped, tears pouring down her cheeks as she opened her eyes and stared at Anthea.

Anthea put her arm under her thin shoulders, raised her up, and made her pillows more comfortable.

"I am sorry that I did," she said gently. "But now I'll do everything that I can to make you get better."

"I don't want to get better."

"That is because you are so sick. When you feel stronger you will feel different."

273

Suddenly her mother gripped her hand. "Promise me that you will never leave me again. I won't go back to Alan Towers. I hate him and Gerry and their silly baby. Alan was always getting in furious tempers and never cared if I didn't feel well. All he cares about is money and making a big fuss."

"Don't upset yourself, Mother. You'll only make your head ache."

Suddenly her mother threw herself back in the bed, beat the covers with her hands, and burst into terrible sobs. Anthea put her arms around her, holding her close until she quieted and lay back exhausted on the pillows.

"Let me wash you and do your hair. Perhaps you will be able to sleep again."

She had just finished making her comfortable when Max Sinclair knocked and walked into the room.

"How do you feel this morning?" he asked quietly. "Did you manage to sleep?"

Mrs. Towers cowered down in bed and stared at him without speaking.

"Are you pleased to have your daughter home with you?"

Again there was no reply, and Max looked baffled.

"Has she eaten any breakfast?"

"Only half a cup of tea."

"Try to eat something nourishing, Eleanor," Max said, taking her hand to feel her pulse, but she pulled it away.

"I'd like to talk to you outside, Anthea."

"Leave my daughter alone," Mrs. Towers said loudly. "She doesn't want anything to do with you. You'll make her as miserable as your stepfather made me. You are all rotten."

"I will be back in a few moments, Mother," Anthea said

274

firmly. "Remember that I am a nurse, and I have to obey a doctor."

They moved down the hall away from the bedroom door, and Max said grimly, "I will have to ask one of my partners to take over this case. Obviously my connection with the family upsets her. I feel that she ought to be in the hospital. She is in a highly emotional state and will need constant supervision. Keep all pills out of her reach, and at the first sign of violence call the police or hospital. I will talk over her condition with Dr. Walker, and my stepfather will have to arrange for another nurse to share the load with you. Either that or she must return to the hospital. We must try to get her onto protein food or start intravenous feeding. Can you give injections?"

"Yes."

"I want you to give her one I am prescribing every four hours. This will quiet her, and she will probably sleep most of the time. I will try to arrange to call again with Dr. Walker. In the meantime don't leave her alone, even when she is asleep. I don't want to alarm you, but she is still irrational in her behavior. Can you arrange for the woman who helps to stay until a nurse arrives? Mrs. Thompson would be no use in an emergency."

"I am sorry that you will not be in charge," Anthea said sincerely.

"So am I," Max replied, "But for both our sakes it is better if I am out of it. I'll call when possible, and you can phone me if there is any difficulty. I'll help all I can from the background."

"What if Mr. Towers or Gerry calls?"

"I have ordered them not to, much to their relief. My stepfather is the last person on earth to understand illness of any kind, and Gerry is too busy with her equestrian achievements to bother about anyone but herself.''

"What about the baby?"

"He has an excellent nursemaid and only appears when Gerry wishes to show him off," he replied bitterly. "I guess that he is just one more medal to hang with the rest."

"Does Mark agree with the arrangement?"

"Mark has no say in the matter. He is merely a figurehead, poor sap. He is too busy trying to make money and keep up with all their social commitments to have time to breathe. Try to get some milk or an eggnog into your mother, give her this injection, and keep her as quiet as possible. Tell her that I won't be coming back."

"Very well, doctor," Anthea said in a subdued voice, and Max suddenly gave her a very unprofessional hug. "I'll be back, but not in a medical capacity, so forget the doctor and nurse relationship." He bent, kissed her quickly on the lips, and before Anthea could get her breath he was out of the house. She hoped that neither Jean nor Mrs. Baxter had peeped around the kitchen door during the last few moments.

Her mother looked so ill when she went back that she bent down and stroked the hair from her forehead.

"Mummy, will you try to drink some milk if I bring it for you?"

Her mother opened her eyes suddenly. "It's a long time since you called me that. Has Max Sinclair gone? Bossy like all of them."

"He won't be coming back to visit you again. Dr. Walker will come instead."

"Why has he dropped me?" her voice rose again. "Alan has never visited me, nor Gerry. Now Max Sinclair thinks that I am not worth bothering with either. Gerry said that you were in love with him. It isn't true, is it?" she asked, grabbing Anthea's arm.

276

"I haven't seen him for six months, Mother. He is handing your case to one of his partners because he knows that you don't like him. I'll get you a drink; then you can rest."

Her mother took two sips of milk and turned her head away. "No more. It makes me feel sick."

"Then I am going to give you an injection to make you sleep again. The more rest that you can get, the quicker you will grow stronger."

"Why should I let you stick a needle into me?"

"I won't hurt you. I give injections every day. You haven't forgotten that I am a nurse, have you?"

"No, I haven't forgotten. You went to be a nurse to get away from me."

Anthea made no reply and almost before her mother realized she was ready she was wiping her arm with alcohol.

"There. That didn't hurt, did it? Shall I read to you until you go to sleep?"

Anthea went to her own bookcase and pulled out a book of poems that she and her father used to enjoy together. In a soft but clear voice she read on until her mother's eyes closed and her breathing was steady. She sat still, the book in her hands and her eyes on her mother's face. How worn and fragile she looked. She had never been plump, but now she looked like nothing but skin and bones. What a price she had paid for her short time of excitement.

Anthea tiptoed out and went to look for Jean and Mrs. Baxter. She found them in the kitchen having coffee.

"Just in time for your cup," Jean said, filling the empty cup that stood on the tray.

"Will you go into my mother's room, Mrs. Baxter, while I drink this? Dr. Sinclair says that she must not be left alone. He is arranging for a nurse to help us as she will need someone with her day and night at present. She is asleep now as I have given her an injection, but call immediately if she shows signs of waking. Later will you make up the other bed in the apartment that I am in?''

Mrs. Baxter nodded, put down her cup, and hurried out.

"I am glad that you two get on so well together," Anthea said, sipping her coffee.

"She is a good worker and doesn't mind doing a bit extra. She's glad for the job because she can be home by the time her two children get home from school. Her mother lives with them, but she's not very strong."

"Has Aunt Kathleen been to see my mother?"

"Did you not know that she has moved to London? After your mother started traveling so much, her sister sold her house and got an apartment in London. I guess that she wanted to have some excitement too. You certainly didn't get many letters from them. That Lady Lester was your best correspondent."

Anthea smiled. "It was strange that I had known her for such a short time, yet we have become so close simply by correspondence."

"Has she quite recovered from the heart attack?"

"I think so, but she says Bertha makes her live like an old woman and watches her like a hawk—won't let her go out at night and only allows a certain number of visitors. I must phone her and call as soon as I have the opportunity. By the way, Dr. Sinclair is handing my mother's case over to his partner, Dr. Walker. My mother gets too upset when she sees him because he is connected with her husband."

"She didn't do so well for herself after all. Just like your Aunt Ellen used to say, 'The mills of God grind slowly, but people have to pay for their stupidity.' Unfortunately often innocent people have to suffer as well. I hope that when your mother gets better she'll appreciate the fact that you came to her as soon as you knew that she needed you, and that is more than she deserved.''

"She is still my mother," Anthea said with a sigh. "If he can find peace and faith in God, I don't mind what I have to do for her. Now I must get back."

Later in the morning Dr. Walker called just as Anthea and Mrs. Baxter had finished changing the patient's bed and tidying her room.

"Good morning," he said cheerfully. "Dr. Sinclair says that you don't like the look of his face, and he wants me to take care of you, so let me check up on you."

"What has she eaten today, Miss Gordon?"

"Nothing solid—a few sips of tea and milk, that is all."

"Hm, that won't do. We've got to put some color into those cheeks. Try and tempt her with anything she fancies. I'll give you a prescription for a food drink, but if she won't take that we'll have to put her on intravenous feeding tomorrow. A nurse will be coming this afternoon to share the load with you, as you can't do day as well as night. Have you any pain anywhere, Mrs. Towers?"

"I feel as if I ache everywhere."

"I expect that that is mostly weakness. If you could force yourself to eat you'd feel like a different woman. Your daughter will give you some soup or a soft-boiled egg and another injection. I'll look in again this evening to see how you are."

Anthea followed him into the hall. "She seems a little more relaxed, but one never knows what to expect with a case like this. For the time being we'll keep her partially sedated."

Anthea went back and found her mother with tears pouring down her face and her hands clenched in front of her.

"What is it, Mummy?" she asked gently.

"I am sure that I have cancer and that you are just pretending."

"No, darling, the doctors say that there is nothing like that. You are just tired out with all the rushing around, and you need a long rest to get strong."

"It is all Alan's fault. He had no patience with me. If I said I was too tired to go anywhere he flew into a temper and asked what I had married him for. He expected me to be able to be up until all hours of the night and rush off the next morning. He drank far too much and was beastly when he was drunk. How often I wished that I had never set eyes on him. Gerry and Mark didn't care either. She said horrible things to me and turned her father against me. She said that I had only married him for his money, but that when he died I wouldn't get any of it."

"Mummy, try to forget them. I want you to get better, and you will only do that if you can stop worrying."

"It's all right for you. You are free. Even Kathleen went away and has married a man twenty years older than herself. I've got no one to care about me."

"I care, and I'll do everything I can to make you happy. Here is Mrs. Baxter with a light lunch," Anthea said with relief. "Let me help you up and feed you. It smells delicious."

She wiped her mother's face, put the napkin under her chin, and fed her like a baby, coaxing her to swallow a few spoonfuls. She would not take the egg or the bread and butter.

"Try a tiny mouthful," Anthea persuaded, but her mother closed her lips firmly and suddenly pushed the spoon away so violently that the contents spilled on the sheet.

"Take it away. I won't eat it," she screamed. "Why can't you leave me alone?"

Anthea calmly removed the tray, covered the sheet with a clean towel. After a few minutes when her mother was a little quieter she gave her another injection.

"Now I am going to sit in the armchair and have a nap," she said. "I didn't get much rest last night." Keeping her eyes open just a slit, she waited until her mother was asleep again and began to doze herself.

Later she heard the bell and roused when Mrs. Baxter tiptoed in. "The new nurse is here, Miss Anthea. Shall I stay with your mother while you introduce yourself to her and show her to her room?"

Anthea gave an inward sigh of relief when the nurse turned out to be a plump, motherly looking woman about fifty.

"Mrs. Loxham," she said, holding out her hand. "Dr. Sinclair called me this morning. I only do occasional nursing now, but I like to keep my hand in. My family are grown, and my husband doesn't mind me doing a few weeks at a time as my daughter looks after him. It is your mother who is ill, I believe, and you are a nurse yourself?"

"Not fully trained by any means." Anthea smiled. "I only got back from Birmingham early this morning, and I'll be so glad to have someone with your experience with me. I don't really understand what is wrong with my mother, except that she has had a complete breakdown. Now let me take you up to your room. We'll have to arrange a sort of rotation schedule between us, as the doctor said we must never leave my mother alone. Have you ever nursed anyone like this before?"

"Yes, I've had several, and I must admit that they are very trying. It is easier with a specific complaint, but we can only be patient and do our best."

"The biggest trouble is that she won't eat."

Nurse Loxham nodded. "Dr. Sinclair and Dr. Walker have decided that she will have to have intravenous feeding if there is no change by tomorrow, and she probably won't like that. I'll do duty tonight as you had so little sleep last night. Then we'll decide the off-duty hours. Do we have to cook as well?"

"Mrs. Thompson who lives in a bed/sitting room downstairs does quite a lot, and we have Mrs. Baxter who comes in every day to do the cleaning and laundry. With the four of us it should not be too bad."

It was three weeks of constant nursing before Mrs. Towers showed any sign of improvement and began to take ordinary food. Gradually the amount of sedation needed was lessened, and she became more normal. There were still times of depression and weeping, but the fits of uncontrolled temper disappeared, and she was quieter and more amenable.

"I think we should get her out of bed for a few minutes tomorrow," Dr. Walker suggested. "Go slowly at first, but make it longer each day. Try to get her interested in someone or something; this apathetic attitude is not good. What about a little TV or radio?"

"She can't bear the noise. I read to her sometimes, but even that tires her after a short time. What about visitors? Her sister has suggested coming from London for the day, and some other friends have asked if they can call for a short while."

"Yes, just as long as she doesn't get too much excitement. If she goes on like this she should be able to do without Nurse Loxham soon. Now it is only a matter of getting her strength back and making her feel that life is worth living."

Max Sinclair phoned several times to inquire about Mrs.

Towers, and that evening he called again, inviting Anthea to go out for dinner.

"It is time that you had a break," he said calmly. "Nurse Loxham will be with your mother, so you need not worry about leaving her. Dr. Walker says that she is improving rapidly. I'll pick you up at six thirty tomorrow evening."

"Could you meet me at the end of the road?"

"Why?"

"I'd rather no one knew where I was going, and I hope it will be somewhere quiet and where we are not likely to meet anyone we know."

"Ashamed of being seen with me?" he teased.

"No, afraid of hateful gossip."

"All right then, six thirty tomorrow evening."

19

The next day however all thought of the evening engagement was forgotten when Mary Latham phoned to say that Gerry had been seriously injured when she was thrown from her horse that had then rolled on top of her. Alan Towers had suffered a stroke from the shock.

"It is so terrible for Mark and the baby," Mrs. Latham babbled, "Mark is shattered; Gerry is unconscious. Her pelvis and both arms are broken, besides head and other injuries. I don't understand why your mother has refused to see any of the family, but surely at a time like this she will forget her grievances."

"My mother has been very ill," Anthea replied coldly. "I dare not pass this news on to her without Dr. Walker's permission."

"I thought that Max Sinclair was attending her."

"No, Dr. Walker is her physician. Where are Gerry and her father?"

"Gerry has been taken to Frensham as her injuries are so serious. Alan Towers is in Newbridge General. You might have been his nurse if you hadn't gone to Birmingham. Fortunately baby Alan has a splendid nurse so at least he will not be neglected. I will go to stay with Mark for the time being to keep the house in order. Even good servants need a mistress."

284

"I do hope the news is better tomorrow, Mrs. Latham, but you understand that my mother is quite unfit even to be told about it."

"Well, as far as I am concerned, I feel that a wife's place is with her husband when he is ill. Eleanor wanted all the good things Alan could give her, but always wanted her own way as usual, and Alan was made of different stuff from your father who had always spoiled you both."

"Good-bye," Anthea said briefly and replaced the receiver. Even in a time of trouble Mary Latham's tongue was just as bitter as ever, and obviously the double tragedy only boosted her feeling of importance.

It was almost nine o'clock when the phone rang again and she heard Max say, "Anthea, can you forgive me? I forgot all about our dinner date."

"I didn't expect you," she said quietly. "Mrs. Latham rang to tell me the news and to ask me to pass it on to my mother."

"I hope you did nothing of the kind."

"No, I told her that my mother was still too ill to be upset, but she did not like it and was very rude."

"Pompous, interfering creature," Max exclaimed.

"How are Gerry and her father?"

"Gerry is badly injured, but she'll mend with time. At first we thought that she would not recover consciousness. However, her head and face injuries are not too serious. Maybe it is too early to tell yet, but I don't imagine that she'll ever ride again. My stepfather is paralyzed down one side and cannot speak. Again, it is too early to forecast the full extent of the damage."

"I am so sorry," Anthea said sincerely.

"Bless you. I know you mean that."

"Will you keep me informed of how they are, and if later you think my mother should be told? Meanwhile we can pray that this will give them time to think."

"Anthea, if I drive to your house now, could you spare me an hour? I want to talk to you, and so much is always happening to keep us apart. Will you meet me outside in fifteen minutes?"

"Very well," Anthea replied calmly, although her heart was beating so loudly that she wondered if Max could hear it.

Nurse Loxham had taken over at nine, so Anthea put her head around her mother's door and called her out into the hall. "I am going out to visit a friend for an hour. I have been in all day and feel in need of a change. I have my key so that I can let myself in if I am late."

"Do you good," Nurse Loxham said with a good-natured smile. "Your mother has just settled down, so I am looking forward to reading a good book."

"I guess that we'll be able to give up the night duty soon, and there is no reason why you can't nap on the settee. It is seldom that she wakens before five o'clock, and I'll be ready to take over at six."

Anthea ran upstairs, changed her dress, and pulled on her best coat and smart little fur hat. She made a face in the mirror. "Getting all excited because someone is taking you out for a drive for an hour to talk about all our sick relations," she muttered. "Pull yourself together, girl, and don't act like some moonstruck teenager."

The car was waiting when she opened the front door, and Max exclaimed, "One young woman who doesn't keep a man waiting while she puts on a fresh face!"

"Not worth the effort in my case."

"Now who is fishing for compliments? Would you be surprised if I told you that your face is lovely and that it can't be improved upon?"

286

Anthea turned in her seat and stared at him in the dim light.

Max gave a low laugh. "Yes, I know that you think I'm speaking out of character, but somehow I don't think that you really know me very well. I guess both of us got off to a bad start, and we've kept up a kind of facade with each other ever since. Anthea, I've waited a long time. I love you, and I want you to marry me."

"But there's my mother and your family," Anthea stammered.

Max pulled the car into a side lane and switched on the interior light so that he could see her face.

"It came to me today that we have let our family connections become a nemesis, and they don't count one scrap. What does matter is what is just between ourselves. I love you, and I want you to share my life with me. All I want to know is if you feel that you can care for me and forget about everybody else."

"I've loved you for a long time, Max, but I was frightened to admit it even to myself, because I felt that it was an impossible situation. I couldn't live near Gerry or your step-father."

Max suddenly switched off the light and pulled her into his arms, and for a few moments everybody and everything else was forgotten.

He held her close, after he had kissed her with an intensity Anthea had never experienced before. Max said softly, "Darling, God planned that we should come together from that first day I saw your adorable, serious face bending over those rock plants as if every one was something very special. Why did you have to run away to Birmingham and pretend that you were finished with me, beloved?"

"I had to, Max. Gerry had said such horrible things, and

287

your stepfather was making Mother miserable because of me. I decided that a complete break was the only answer."

"And you managed to forget me—or did someone else try to fill my place?"

"No. I couldn't put you out of my heart. I was happy enough with Lorna and James, but they made me realize what a real marriage could mean."

"And you think we could have a real marriage?"

"Like you, I believe that God has brought us together— two rather lonely people who both belong to Him."

"My precious darling," Max said, and again Anthea was awestruck at the wonder of his love.

"Are we being selfish to feel so happy when Gerry and Mr. Towers are so ill and my mother and Mark are so unhappy?"

"They have done enough damage between us in the past," Max reminded her.

"But, darling, I can't leave my mother as she is at present."

"I know, and I wouldn't love you half as much if you didn't feel like that, but things are changing. She is getting better and will be able to take care of herself in time, even if she doesn't go back to live with my stepfather. I don't think that Gerry will dare to insult you once I have made it clear that you are to be my wife. Also, there is another matter that we have to consider together. Last year I volunteered to go to a hospital in Nigeria for a two-year period as a short-term medical missionary. My five-year contract with my present partners expires at the end of this year, and I will be free to move wherever I wish. Will you marry me and come to some unknown mission hospital with me, or would you rather I applied for another post in this country?"

"I will go wherever you feel that you will be happiest,

Max. I haven't done much training, so I wouldn't be much use to you as a nurse.''

''Bless you, my darling. I don't want a nurse; I want a wife. I don't want someone always on duty; I want a wife to make a home where I can relax—where we can have our children and enjoy them. I hope you want a good-sized family.''

''Half a dozen if you like,'' Anthea said with a happy laugh. ''I was an only child, and I always envied other children with brothers and sisters, even if they did squabble and had to share everything.''

''Three boys and three girls, then,'' Max said, chuckling. ''Just what the doctor ordered!''

''Darling, could we keep this a secret a little longer?'' Anthea asked.

''But why? I want to announce it to everyone I meet. And I want to make sure of you by putting a ring on your finger tomorrow.''

Anthea laughed. ''I never thought that the sedate Dr. Sinclair could be so impulsive and impetuous.''

''You have a lot to learn yet about the staid Dr. Sinclair,'' Max replied, ruffling her hair. ''But you haven't told me why you want to keep it a secret.''

''First, because I don't want it spoiled by a lot of gossip. Second, it isn't the ideal time to announce an engagement with all the upset over Gerry and her father. Last, I'd like to feel more certain about what is going to happen to my mother.''

''She didn't worry about you when your father died,'' Max demurred.

''No, but she is still my mother, and I keep praying that somehow she will realize her need for faith in God, and I have seen glimpses lately which have made me more hopeful. She has let me read articles and my *Daily Light* portions without turning me off. I'd hate for her to get the idea that I was going to leave her very soon. For the first time in my life I believe that she wants my affection. Stop at the end of the road," she said as they drove near her home.

Max stopped the car and pulled her to him. "You won't keep me waiting too long, will you, beloved?"

"I wish that we could get married tomorrow," Anthea said seriously. "It will be so wonderful to know that I belong to someone. I've been so lonely these past months."

"I know, and I promise that I'll do all in my power to see that you are never lonely or feel unwanted again. Now I suppose we have to say good night, but will you phone me to tell me when I can see you again? I have a half day free on Thursday. Could you manage to spend it with me?"

"I'll try. Nurse Loxham will be finishing this week as my mother does not need night nursing now. I'd better take some hours off before she leaves."

"Good. I'll be at the end of the road at one thirty on Thursday. We'll drive into the country and have tea at one of my favorite places. Good-bye for a few hours, sweetheart. I hope that you are happy as I am tonight."

"I never imagined that I could feel so happy. It has been worth the loneliness to come into this safe harbor."

"Bless you; that is a wonderful thought," Max said, as he went around to open the car door. "Mrs. Max Sinclair sounds good to me, and our first little son will be Andrew Gordon."

Anthea gave a low laugh. "We've come a long way since I left the house. I feel like a completely different person."

"And so you are. You belong to me, and you hold my life's happiness in your hands."

"It's a big responsibility," Anthea said soberly.

"But not too big for someone with the capacity for the loving unselfishness that you possess. I want to say like Solomon, 'Thou art all fair, my love; there is no spot in thee.' "*

Anthea ran along the street and up the steps to the door as if she had suddenly acquired wings and turned to wave at the dark shadow that stood by the car. She put her key in the lock and tried to fix a serious expression on her face. She hoped that Jean would be in bed. Her eyes were too sharp, and Anthea did not want to share her happiness with anyone at present. She wanted to meditate over the wonder of it in secret. Later on she knew that there would be complications, and maybe gossip, but for these few hours she wanted to feel that she and Max had this wonderful secret all to themselves.

She peeked into her mother's room and saw that Nurse Loxham was dozing on the settee and her mother was fast asleep. Anthea tiptoed upstairs and quickly took a bath. As she brushed her hair she looked at herself in the mirror and saw how her eyes sparkled and her lips smiled in spite of her effort to be dignified. In two short hours her whole world had changed. She had been afraid to admit even to herself how much Max Sinclair had come to mean to her. Now the thoughts of how he had broken down the barrier of reserve and had poured out his love on her filled her heart with a deep sense of wonder and gratitude. Whatever the future held, if she could be sure of Max's love and support, nothing ever would be as black as those times after the loss of her father and Mark and the sense that no one needed her.

*Song of Solomon 4:7, King James Version.

20

When Dr. Walker called the next day, he suggested that Nurse Loxham's services could be dispensed with; he had another patient who was seriously ill. Would Anthea mind if he stole the nurse from her?

Anthea hesitated. If Nurse Loxham left immediately, how could she have the afternoon with Max as she had hoped?

At that moment the phone rang. Excusing herself, Anthea went to answer it.

"Is this Miss Anthea Gordon?" came Max's voice.

"Anthea here."

"Sweetheart, I've got more bad news for you. We'll have to cancel our afternoon together. My stepfather had another stroke early this morning and is dead."

"Oh, Max, how awful!"

"The big problem is your mother. She'll have to be told, but is she fit to cope with all the complications?"

"Dr. Walker is here. I'll let him decide."

"Call me back as soon as you can, darling. There are all sorts of arrangements to make, since Gerry and your mother are both out of action. I'll wait here at my flat until you call me."

"Dr. Walker, there is a message for you," Anthea said, going back into the room and indicating that he should follow her into the kitchen where Jean was peeling some vegetables.

"I'll leave you," she suggested.

"It's all right, Jean. You might as well hear what has happened. Alan Towers had another stroke early this morning and did not recover. Max Sinclair has just called with the news. The problem is telling my mother. Is she fit to be told about her husband and about Gerry's accident?"

Dr. Walker looked at Anthea's white face and said slowly, "We haven't much choice. She will have to know about her husband, if not about Mrs. Latham. Perhaps I am the best one to break it to her. I can see how she reacts."

"I'll be so glad if you will," Anthea said fervently.

"Mrs. Towers, are you strong enough to hear some unpleasant news?" Dr. Walker said, taking her hand and keeping his finger on her pulse.

"Is someone dead?" she demanded.

"Yes, I am sorry that we have to tell you that your husband had a second stroke this morning and did not recover."

Mrs. Towers stared at him unblinkingly.

"A second stroke! I did not know that he had a first. When was it, and what caused it?"

"Some days ago, but we hoped that we need not tell you until he was better and you were stronger."

"Did he have one of his terrible rages? His doctor had warned him that his blood pressure was too high, and he would have to control himself."

"His daughter had a serious accident when riding, and the shock caused the stroke."

"Is she dead also?"

"No, she is not as seriously injured as was thought at first, but it will be a long time before she can ride again."

"Who will make all the arrangements?"

"Max and Mark, I expect," Anthea put in. "They will try to spare you as much as possible, Mother."

Mrs. Towers nodded and lay back on the pillow. "I'd like a little time to think about this," she said steadily.

"Shall I give you something to help you over the shock?" Dr. Walker inquired.

"No, thank you, I have had enough pills and been an invalid too long. It is time I stopped being a coward. Anthea, bring me my clothes. I am getting up. Call Max Sinclair and Mark Latham and tell them I want to see them."

Anthea looked at the doctor in perplexity. He nodded and walking into the hall said, "Better humor her. Maybe this shock is just what she needed to make her take hold of life again. Call me immediately if you need me. Perhaps Nurse Loxham should stay with you until tomorrow in case your mother has a relapse."

When Max and Mark arrived about an hour later Mrs. Towers was fully dressed and looked like a very different woman from the one Anthea and Mrs. Loxham had nursed during the last weeks.

"I am delighted to see that you are so much better," Max greeted her.

Mark bent down to kiss her cheek. "I wanted to visit you, but Alan and Gerry insisted that you had refused to see any of us. I am sorry that you have been so ill."

"And I am sorry to hear about Gerry," Mrs. Towers said calmly. "Sit down where I can see you. Anthea will bring some coffee."

"Gerry's life is out of danger," Mark said, his voice trembling. "But she has sustained so many injuries that she has had a great deal of pain. She is so unhappy and frightened that she will be a cripple, or that her face will be

294

permanently scarred, that she has to be kept sedated most of the time.''

''And the baby?''

''He is well,'' Mark replied flatly.

''Excuse me,'' Anthea said. She stood outside the door a moment, clenching her hands. She could have wept for the unhappiness in Mark's face. The boy she had known had disappeared, and in his place was a man who could have been twenty years older. His shoulders were bowed, his eyes sunken and lifeless. Gerry had the physical injuries, but it was Mark who was suffering mentally.

Jean Thompson had the coffee percolating, so Anthea carried it in, just in time to hear her mother say, ''Alan insisted that he should be cremated, so there will be no need for a church service. Will you arrange for the cremation, Max? We will make a list of people who should be invited—no need for a big crowd or flowers. And we must get in touch with his lawyer, Mr. Barnes, of the London firm who had charge of Alan's legal affairs. I had suggested that Alan employ you, Mark, when he made a new will, but he refused to have anyone in the family involved.''

''Did he make a recent will?'' Max inquired.

''Yes, but I have no idea what it contained. Before we married the money for the house and nurseries was put in my name, so that if anything happened to Alan, that would not be included in his estate. He said that he had put the property in Gerry's name and spent so much on the alterations for the same reason.''

Mark suddenly looked up, his face even more stricken. ''But it is less than seven years since he gave that to Gerry, so it will have to be added to his estate.''

Mrs. Towers did not reply at once, and there was an awkward silence. Finally Max said, ''Surely you don't have to worry, Mark. I guess that my stepfather has left plenty to cover all that.''

''I'm not sure,'' Mark said slowly. ''I have heard rumors that things were not good with him.''

''You may as well know that that is why I left him,'' Mrs. Towers said quietly, sitting up very straight. ''He had been gambling heavily, and I believe that many of his wild speculations had gone wrong. He told me that unless I gave him the money I had received, Tall Timbers would have to be sold to avoid bankruptcy. I refused because I said that the property had been bought with my first husband's money, and rightfully belonged to Anthea. He flew into an insane rage and told me that I had only married him for his money. He said that unless I helped him I could get out. So I did.''

''What a ghastly mess,'' Mark exclaimed. ''Probably Gerry won't even have a home to come back to. Somehow we can't let her hear about this. She knows that her father had a stroke, but I am afraid to tell her that he is dead.''

''Mother, I think that you have talked enough,'' Anthea said, watching her mother's drawn expression. ''I think that you should rest now.''

Her mother shook her head. ''We haven't finished yet. Max, you must go to Tall Timbers and give Millie and Robert their notice. As soon as I can I will return to help them get the place ready for sale. I suppose that the furniture will have to go too. Now, about that list of announcements and invitations. Will you get a sheet of paper, Anthea?''

Finally it was agreed that the announcement of the death would be put in the *Newbridge Gazette* and *Times* for the sake of Alan's business associates, and a list of names was drawn up of those to be invited to the short service at the crematorium chapel as soon as Max had determined the time and place. Gerry would have to be told, because visitors would be sure to mention it; then it would be a bigger shock. Nothing need be said about the financial problems.

There would be no reception afterward, but those who wished could return to Anthea's house where Mr. Barnes could read the will to those concerned.

"I am going to visit Gerry now," Mark said heavily.

"Let me come with you," Max suggested. "She is tougher than you think; maybe I'll be able to break it to her better than you. In the meantime, Mark, remember that God often uses what we think of as tragedies to bring something good into our lives."

Mark stared at him. "Easy for you to talk," he said moodily. "How would you feel if your wife was smashed up and you faced the threat of your house being taken from you?"

"Gerry will recover," Max said consolingly. "You have a good job, a lovely son, and you'll get another home— even if it isn't so ostentatious. My stepfather and Gerry were both living in a fairy-tale world."

"A number of us have been fools, Mark," Mrs. Towers said gently. "I've done a lot of thinking while I've been lying here, and I agree with Max that the pretense of the party life that we put up was an empty sham. I failed Andrew and Anthea, but you still have Gerry and baby Alan and can make a life that could be much more worthwhile."

Max and Anthea exchanged glances. What did houses or money matter if Mrs. Towers and Mark could find their way to faith in God and believe that He had a purpose for their lives?

"I'll come back later after I have seen Gerry and made the necessary arrangements. You should get back to bed and

297

rest now, Eleanor,'' Max said.

"Probably I will. There is nothing more that I can do tonight."

Anthea walked to the door with them, but beyond Max's giving her hand an extra squeeze, there was no sign that they were more than casual acquaintances. This was not the time to announce their happiness to Mark.

"Good-bye, Mark,'' Anthea said, taking his hand. " will be praying for you and Gerry."

"Thank you, Thea. I need those prayers. I guess I' forgotten God existed these last months; now when I am in trouble I expect Him to help me."

"He will, Mark. He'll help you face your problems if you ask Him. I've proved that a hundred times since my father died."

Mark nodded. "I know you have. You have often made me ashamed."

"Don't feel like that. My father died without pain, and have found a new sort of life which satisfies me. I have much to be thankful for."

"We'll talk again longer. Max is waiting, and I know he has evening surgery."

Anthea returned to find her mother staring straight in front of her. "Let me help you undress and get back to bed,'' she suggested, putting her arm around her shoulders

"Yes, perhaps I should rest now, but tomorrow I must stop being an invalid. I want you to drive me to Tall Timbers. There are some things I wish to collect, and I must give orders to the servants. They must have a month's notice so at least they can do most of the heavy work. Surely when the house, the furniture, the cars, and the other expensive things that Alan was always buying for himself are sold there will be enough to let Mark and Gerry keep the house."

298

"Perhaps it would be better for Mark if they had to live in a more normal way."

"You may be right. Mark was only a figurehead in that household. Gerry, with her father behind her, ruled the roost because they held the purse strings. Mark had to toe the line, but at times he looked henpecked and miserable."

"Shall I run a bath for you, Mother? It might help you rest."

"You are like your father, Anthea; you have unlimited patience with me."

After her mother was in bed again and had a light snack, Anthea said, "Would you like me to read to you?"

"Later, perhaps. I'd like to talk for a little while."

"Aren't you too tired?"

"I'll feel better if I can put things right. I soon realized after I married Alan Towers what a fool I'd been. I was miserable, but I went on pretending life was exciting. I tried drinking because I couldn't bear to remember how I had treated Andrew and you. Alcohol made me feel so ill in the morning; I was disgusted at the way Alan and others behaved when they had taken too much. The doctor I consulted without telling Alan warned me that I'd have a serious breakdown if I did not cut down on smoking and drinking and try to relax more, but what chance of relaxing was there with a man like Alan Towers? He was as hard as iron and had no sympathy with what he termed a woman's 'vapors.' Then the rows over money started. I was frightened of him when he became violent. I thought so often of the long quiet evenings with you and Andrew—how much I had then that should have made me happy. I knew even in those days that Andrew's faith was what made him different, but I wouldn't give in. I knew I had left God out of my life. I kept persuading myself, and Kathleen encouraged me, that I had been cheated, that my husband ought to have been someone far more important than what I termed a gardener. How often I slighted him and hurt him, but I know he and you kept on praying for me, and I want you to know that those prayers have been answered. I have prayed myself many nights when I couldn't sleep, and I know that God has forgiven me. It is too late to tell Andrew that I am sorry for all the years of coldness, but I am asking you to forgive me, Anthea.''

''Mummy, I am so happy for you, and I am sure that Dad will be rejoicing too. Someday you'll meet him again, and there will be no sadness between you then. This means more than if someone had given me a million pounds.''

She bent down and kissed her mother, who said with her eyes full of tears, ''I believe that you really mean that, darling. I have learned these past months that people and peace mean far more than big houses and a lot of excitement.''

''But you need to sleep now,'' Anthea said softly. ''You have already had too much excitement today. Let me read tonight's verses; then I'll give you your sleeping tablet and turn down the lights.''

Her mother was fast asleep, and Anthea was longing for bed herself by the time Max returned.

''Sorry I'm so late, beloved,'' he whispered. ''I had an emergency at the hospital.''

''Come into the kitchen,'' Anthea said in a low voice. When the door was closed Max took her in his arms, and for a little while the shocks and surprises of the day were forgotten.

''I'll make a hot drink,'' she said at last. ''Are all the arrangements made? How did Gerry take the news?''

''Everything is fixed for Thursday at eleven o'clock.

Gerry was upset, but I guess the full impact hasn't hit her yet. Anyway, she has too much discomfort to bother much about anyone else. She is on so many pain killers that her mind is not functioning very clearly. Mark is the one that I feel sorry for. With that awful mother of his and a wife who will be an invalid for months he has a miserable time ahead, and somehow Mark has never struck me as being tough.''

"Not tough enough for the Towerses' sort of world; his nature is too kindly, and he is easily hurt. I suppose that that is why he gave in to his mother and to Gerry. Now he may have to face up to a new set of problems. But, Max, something wonderful has happened.''

"Something more wonderful than discovering that we love each other?'' Max teased.

Anthea hesitated. "No, quite different. My mother has asked me to forgive her because she has realized her failure and has got right with God.''

"Darling, no wonder your eyes are sparkling. I'm so happy for you both. So something good has come out of this mess after all.''

"How I wish my father could have shared this with me. We prayed so long for her.''

"We'll go on believing that somehow Gerry and Mark will find what really matters when the things which meant so much to them have been taken away. My mother taught Gerry many Bible stories before she died. Alan Towers did his best to make her forget what Mother implanted, but I can't believe that the seed which was sown will not bring fruit, just as it did in my case.''

"Mark too used to join in church activities, but his mother did her best to turn him away. After he went to live in Newbridge he lost interest, and then when he met Gerry I suppose nothing else mattered.''

"God sometimes has to jerk people very hard to make them remember His existence."

"I feel like a millionaire," Anthea said with a low laugh. "First there is the wonder of your love, and now I feel that I have a mother who cares for me for the first time in my life."

"And the loneliness and heartache have made it all the more wonderful, my darling."

The funeral of Alan Towers was noticeably small for a man who had thought himself so important. He had had many acquaintances but few close friends, and in the last months there had been a big change in the attitude of those with whom he had tried to do business. News of his tottering financial empire had leaked out somehow and made people wary.

Mark and his mother, Max Sinclair, Lady Lester, Aunt Kathleen, and Mr. Barnes, the attorney, returned to the house for the refreshments Jean had prepared. Lady Lester excused herself as she said she tired very quickly these days, and Bertha worried about her, so only Mrs. Latham and Aunt Kathleen were left when Mr. Barnes suggested that he read the will.

He shuffled some papers, coughed, and said, "The will itself is quite straightforward. Everything which Mr. Alan Towers possessed at the time of his death is left to his daughter, Mrs. Geraldine Latham, and her son, Alan Towers Latham. This includes bonds, investments, and the house Tall Timbers, with its contents. Unfortunately I must warn you that Mr. Towers recently made some very unwise speculations and against our advice removed large sums and mortgaged his house. I will read the will as it stands, but am afraid that there is very little actual substance in what it contains."

Mrs. Towers looked pale but composed, while Mark sat with his head bowed so that no one could see his face.

"I am sorry that I had to bring such unpleasant news," Mr. Barnes said, as he finished reading the lengthy legal wording which in essence meant very little. "You realize that it will be some time before the estate is settled as there are a great many outstanding debts, and there will be death duties to pay on the money and possessions that Mr. Towers possessed during the last seven years. Will you call at my office at your convenience, Mrs. Towers, as legally you are his next of kin? I am sorry that Mrs. Geraldine Latham cannot be present today, but Mr. Mark Latham can act as her representative if I need information. I will leave you to inform your wife how affairs stand when you feel that she is well enough, Mr. Latham. At present there is little any of us can do."

"I have already arranged for Tall Timbers and its contents to be put on the market," Mrs. Towers said calmly. "And the servants have been given a month's notice."

Mr. Barnes nodded slowly. "There is no immediate hurry, but if you have a good offer, maybe it will be well to accept it. People always think that they can acquire property cheaply if there is a hint of bankruptcy. I hope that what I have told you this morning will not be made common knowledge before it is necessary. There is no need for you to leave your home immediately, Mrs. Towers. A few more months will make no difference. Now I will wish you good afternoon and trust that we can get everything straightened out as soon as possible."

Max accompanied him to the door and walked with him to his car. "Thank you for being so frank," Max said, shaking his hand. "I am sure that you did the best that you could do for my stepfather, but he was a stubborn, pig-headed man who always thought that he knew best. Nobody will really suffer desperately, but there will be less luxuries and lavish entertainment."

"An unfortunate waste, nevertheless," Mr. Barnes replied. "Now I must go, as I have another client to visit on my way back."

Max walked inside, his face grave. He was glad that Alan Towers had run true to form and not even recognized him, but he had been vindictive to his wife, and it was she, along with Gerry and Mark, who would suffer for his stupidity.

"Why are you in such a rush to sell that lovely house, Eleanor?" Aunt Kathleen was asking in her loud autocratic voice. "Will you come to London and buy an apartment near me?"

"No, I don't think so, Kathleen. I will live very quietly from now on. I want to stay near Anthea if she will have me."

"You will feel differently when you are stronger. You have been ill, but as soon as possible I want you to come and stay with me and forget what you have been through. Now I must go as I am going to Brighton tomorrow for a long weekend. Good-bye, Eleanor. You will be free to go where you wish now."

"Your mother needs cheering up, Anthea," Aunt Kathleen said emphatically as she prepared to leave. "Alan Towers wasn't all that she had hoped for, but he is gone now, and she will be well off."

"This must be kept in the family, Aunt Kathleen. Everything was left to Gerry and the baby. My mother will have the money she received for the house and nurseries. Please do not tell anyone else, but it is better if you understand that Mother is not a wealthy woman."

"You mean that Alan Towers cut her out of his will?"

Aunt Kathleen gasped. "Of all the spiteful, mean things to do after all that she had to put up with from him. I'd contest it if I were Eleanor. She is entitled to half of all he had."

"Please, Aunt Kathleen. Keep your voice down. I don't want Mother upset again. She will not be destitute, and the lawyer will attend to all that is necessary. You will find Mother greatly changed by her illness."

"Well, I don't understand it. I will come back next week to talk things over with her. Gerry Towers has no right to come into everything. It's preposterous. I know that you and your father turned up your noses at money, but Eleanor has earned every penny that she can get for what she put up with from Alan Towers with his temper and his drunken bouts. Sometimes he was like a pig, and as for his precious daughter, she was a selfish, stuck-up, spoiled brat."

"It's better not to get worked up, Aunt Kathleen. You have a long drive back on busy roads. I'll take care of Mother and see that she has all she needs."

"But your ideas of what a woman needs aren't the same as ours, Anthea. I'll see you again about the middle of next week. I am sorry that I was abroad and could not help you with the nursing when Eleanor was so ill, but I guess your training came in useful. Good-bye for now." Giving Anthea a peck on the cheek she got into her car and drove off.

"I hope that Alan left Gerry well provided for," Mary Latham burst out, obviously unable to contain her curiosity any longer. "The poor girl will need constant treatment, and your salary won't pay for the upkeep of the house and the extra domestic help."

"Mother, this is neither the time nor place to discuss private affairs," Mark said sternly. "Mr. Barnes wants nothing talked about by anyone until the estate has been settled. There must be no talk about the will to Gerry, but I

305

may as well inform you that our circumstances as well as Mrs. Towers's will be greatly reduced.''

"But I don't understand," she spluttered. "Alan Towers was a wealthy man.''

"Mrs. Latham, Mark has had a difficult time," Max intervened. "Please allow him to decide what is best for himself and his family.''

Mary Latham flushed angrily. "But I am his family. I am looking after his house, so I have a right to know how things stand.''

"I am going home, Mother, and I wish you to come with me," Mark said, standing up. "And I forbid you to speak to Gerry or anyone else about Alan Towers's affairs.''

Without a word Mrs. Latham collected her coat. With her head high and back straight she walked out of the door with Mark following.

"Good for Mark," Max said as the front door slammed. "I am glad to see that the tables are beginning to turn. What a shock Mrs. Latham has coming to her.''

21

A great deal happened during the month following Alan Towers's funeral. Tall Timbers and the contents had been sold for a great deal more than he had paid for them, Mrs. Towers was settled in one of the upstairs apartments in Anthea's house, and Max had hinted to Gerry at the problems the lawyer was having with the estate. Mary Latham had gone back to her own home fuming at the way Mark had been duped, and even Markdene was advertised for sale.

Gerry's face was unmarked, but she would probably always walk with a slight limp. During the week she returned home she arranged for Mr. Barnes to call with a copy of the will and a rough draft of the financial position as far as he knew it. She also asked Max, Anthea, and Mrs. Towers to be present. There was a hard implacability about her and a stubborn lack of thought for anyone else, which made her very like her father.

"This is all my idea," Gerry said coldly when they were all assembled. "My husband does not agree with me, but I want the position made perfectly clear to us all. Then I will know what steps to take. Without my consent, my home has been put on the market. I really do not understand why. I wish to hear the text of my father's will for myself. Then I wish Mr. Barnes to explain why he suggested that my father was on the verge of bankruptcy."

Mr. Barnes read again the legal terms, then proceeded to repeat what he had told the family on the day of the funeral, and gave a brief account of what had happened to the assets Alan Towers had possessed some years ago.

"He spent a great deal on buying your home and having it completely modernized. Although it was a gift, you understand that since it was given to you within the last seven years, it has to be included in his estate. The money he settled on his grandson must also be taken into account. His own home had a very heavy mortgage on it, so even though it brought a good price, the profit is very small. He had speculated with many of his bonds, sold shares, and bought others which have proved poor investments."

"So the settlement I was to have each month will cease."

"I am afraid so."

"And we cannot even claim our own home?"

"There may be some small assets left, but certainly not enough to keep up such an establishment."

"But Eleanor is allowed to keep her money."

"That belonged to her before she married your father and is in her own name and cannot be touched."

"So this means that I have to live in some ordinary little house and do all the housework and look after the child myself," she said, her voice rising.

"Gerry, please don't make a scene and upset yourself. We won't be penniless," Mark pleaded.

Gerry laughed mirthlessly. "You mean your pittance of a salary will keep us in comfort? Well, if the rest of you are satisfied, I am not. I shall want a detailed account of every transaction. I don't believe that my father was such a fool. Perhaps I ought to take further legal advice."

"Just as you wish, Mrs. Latham," Mr. Barnes said coldly. "You will only be wasting what money you have."

"According to you we have *no* money left," Gerry snapped back. "Max, you knew how much money that my father made."

"*Had* made, yes," Max replied. "But I also knew that he was spending it far too freely. He wasn't a millionaire, but he tried to live like one."

"You are delighted to blacken his name. You did well by him. Now that he is dead you haven't a good word for him."

"I refuse to wash dirty linen in public. I owed Alan Towers nothing, and he knew it. Now I insist that nothing will be gained by continuing this very distasteful conversation. Mr. Barnes has explained what has happened, and there is nothing any of us can do about it."

"I will leave now," Mr. Barnes said, putting his papers in his briefcase. "Good afternoon, Mrs. Latham."

"So you have come out best, Eleanor. You have the exorbitant price Dad paid you for your old place, and Anthea has a house of her own. Mark didn't do so well for himself after all!"

"Gerry, be quiet," Mark said in a voice she had never heard before. "You are insulting people whom you invited to your home."

"I thought you had grown up," Max added. "I hoped that you would be grateful that God had spared your life."

"I can do without your preaching," Gerry snapped. "Save that for Anthea. She will say amen."

"You have gone far enough," Max replied. "Anthea is to be my wife, and I refuse to allow you to speak of her like that. Come here, darling."

With her legs shaking Anthea moved to stand beside him, and he put his arm around her shoulders.

"Anthea was left with nothing when her father died. She

lost her home, her mother, her job, and had no money to live on. What have you to moan about? You have your husband to work for you and a lovely son to bring up.''

"I said that I did not need your lectures," Gerry shouted. "You and Anthea deserve each other." With an angry flounce she limped out of the room.

"Is it really true?" Mrs. Towers asked, a bewildered expression on her face. "Anthea, I'm so happy for you. Max, I will be delighted to have you for a son-in-law."

"Congratulations," Mark managed to gasp. Shaking Max's hand and giving Anthea a brief hug, he said, "Please excuse me. I must try to calm Gerry down. Max, do you think that her mind is affected by the accident or the drugs that she had?"

"I don't think so. Her trouble is her temper, because for once in her life everything isn't going as she wants it. It will be up to you to make her see straight. Don't give her her own way, or she'll trample on you. Let her see that you are the head of the house, and she must fit in with you. She always did have tantrums, but she'll get over it. You must exert yourself for the sake of your baby. And Mark, I don't want to preach, as Gerry calls it, but God will help you if you ask Him."

Mark nodded but made no reply. Quickly he went out of the room.

"We'd better go," Max said, his arm still around Anthea. Putting his other arm around her mother, he said, "I am sorry that my sister made such an exhibition of herself. She and Mark will have to fight their battles on their own."

Mrs. Towers sat down wearily when they got home.

"I'll make some tea," Anthea said, switching on the kettle.

"Can we call Jean and tell her your wonderful news?" her mother asked.

Max patted her shoulder. "Call Jean and everybody else you know," he said gaily. "I've had to nearly choke myself not to tell everyone I met."

"Andrew would have been delighted. He never felt that Mark was right for Anthea, but he was attracted to you from that first day you came to the nursery. I believe that he would have thought you good enough for his very wonderful daughter—she was his most precious possession. I used to be jealous of my own daughter because she meant so much to him. I know that it was my own fault, but I was too small-minded to share their happiness."

"Jean, what do you think of our great news?" she said as Jean hobbled into the room. "Did you know that Max and Anthea are engaged?"

"I didn't know, but I had my suspicions and my hopes," Jean said, hugging Anthea and pumping Max's hand up and down. "I've prayed for this for months."

Max laughed. "And we thought nobody guessed! Well, no more secrets. We are engaged, and we will be married as soon as possible."

"Where will you live?"

"We are not quite sure yet," Max replied, "but Anthea says she is willing to go with me to Nigeria. I am going to a mission hospital for two years at least."

"But not for a little while yet, Mummy," Anthea said, seeing the stricken look on her mother's face.

"I am being selfish as usual. I feel as if I have just found my daughter, and now she will be far away. At least I've changed enough to be able to say, 'God bless you both, wherever you go.' "

"Then you will want to sell this house, Anthea. Don't

feel that you have to hold on to it just for me," Jean put in.

"Or for me," Mrs. Towers added. "I will look out for a small bungalow or apartment."

"But I'd like you both to live here if you will. It would mean that we have a place of our own to come back to, or to come home to when on furlough. That is, if you could be happy here, Mummy."

Her mother nodded. "Yes, perfectly happy. Jean and I will be company for each other, but we can keep our own independence. Maybe we could use the other rooms we don't need for girls who are away from home. I have thought recently of how terribly lonely you must have been after your father died, Anthea. Max will make up to you for that, but there must be many who would appreciate someone to care about them. Of course we must be sensible and put it all on a proper financial basis."

"If you could pay for the heating, taxes, and repairs, I'd be delighted for you to live here. I know Jean only has her disability pension, and you will need your capital to live on, Mummy."

Max nodded. "Now that that's settled, what about plans for our wedding? I want it as soon as possible. My contract with my partners terminates in two months. Can we plan for a honeymoon then, before we leave for Africa?"

Anthea laughed. "I am sure I can. I don't want a big, expensive society wedding. I'd like to be married by Mr. Andrews in Bewdley Church. I could have my old village friends present then. I'd want Lorna and James, who were so good to me in Birmingham, with me. You will give me away, Mother, and Lorna can be my bridesmaid."

"But she is already married, darling," her mother put in.

"It doesn't really matter, does it? This won't be a conventional wedding."

"Then I'd better have James for my best man."

In less than a month, however, Max had an urgent request from the mission board. The only doctor in the hospital to which Max had been assigned had been killed while driving to an outpatient clinic. Could Dr. Sinclair take over immediately?

The other partners agreed to release him at once. At first Anthea suggested that he go there alone, and she would follow after he was settled. They could be married on the mission station, but her mother quickly squashed that idea. "Your dress is ready. Max can get a special license and arrange with Mr. Andrews to marry you at once. Book your flights, Max; there is no sense in going through the misery of separation. Jean and I are perfectly able to take care of ourselves. You need Anthea with you."

"Mother Gordon, you are a woman after my own heart," Max said, hugging her. "Come with me now, darling, and we will set the wheels spinning so that you will be Mrs. Sinclair even sooner than we dared to hope. We have our visas, innoculations, and all the other paraphernalia already, so get busy on the phone to Lorna and James and anyone else concerned. I'll call Mr. Andrews and ask him to announce our sudden marriage and departure in church on Sunday. I guess Ron and Mollie will see to it that the news spreads."

A week later Anthea stood beside Max in the little church where she and her father had worshiped for so long. The decorations were not very professional, and many of those present were only simple village people from Bewdley and Melworth, but no couple ever received more sincere good wishes for their future. Everyone knew how Miss Anthea had suffered. They had respected and loved her father and considered her to be one of them. This was a fairy-tale ending to what had once been a tragedy. Even Anthea's mother was surprisingly friendly.

For once Geraldine Latham had to take a back seat. No one was actually sorry that she and Mark and Mary Latham had been taken down a peg or two. It was only right that they should suffer after the way Miss Anthea had been treated. These villagers believed simply but sincerely that God had a way of righting what was wrong. Maybe they did not go to church regularly and were not perfect themselves, but they had a very pronounced sense of rough justice.

Anthea's mother, Aunt Kathleen, Mark, Gerry, Lady Lester, Jean, Lorna, and James all drove to the airport to see them leave. Looking at their faces as they waited for departure, Anthea thought how much most of these people had changed during the last two years. Gerry had come to some sort of terms with Mark and had settled down to a quieter life in a very adequate house with a maid to help look after baby Alan. There was a droop at her lips when she was not smiling, and Mark had lost his youthful exuberance, but it was obvious that he had the situation under control. Gerry was not the spoiled darling that she used to be.

Departures were hard, but as her mother hugged Anthea she whispered, "I am so proud of you, my darling. I can almost feel your father with me wishing you Godspeed. Jean and I will have many prayer sessions for you."

"Good-bye, little sister," Max said, holding Gerry close. "Make a happy home for Mark and the baby, and God bless you."

"And you," Gerry whispered back, her face suddenly crumpling and her eyes full of tears. "I have a long way to go yet, Max, but I have been remembering so much that our mother used to teach me, and I had forgotten. Take care of yourself; you have always been a very special brother to me."

314

As Anthea sat down in the seat that the stewardess had indicated, her eyes were moist. She saw that Max also had to wipe his eyes.

They fastened their seat belts, and Max took her hand in his. "You are leaving behind some precious trophies you have won, my beloved. Even Gerry is like a butterfly struggling from the chrysalis. God has brought much fruit out of your tribulation. We can go into the future with a great certainty of blessing."

Anthea nodded, too moved to speak for some minutes. Max said with a low laugh, "I never thought that I'd spend my honeymoon in Africa, but what does the place matter as long as you are with me? Actually I don't imagine that there will be a honeymoon. I suppose that I'll have to plunge into work immediately. Will you mind, sweetheart, that we won't have long days of leisurely sunbathing?"

"God has been so good to me; how could I mind anything? We are privileged to go together into His service. I know that there will be plenty of problems, and life won't be easy, but I'll never doubt again that the Lord has a purpose even in trials and tribulations."

Moody Press, a ministry of the Moody Bible Institute, is designed for education, evangelization, and edification. If we may assist you in knowing more about Christ and the Christian life, please write us without obligation: Moody Press, c/o MLM, Chicago, Illinois 60610.